THE LIST

An absolutely gripping crime mystery with a massive twist

MICHAEL LEESE

Martha Munro Crime Mysteries Book 1

Joffe Books, London
www.joffebooks.com

First published in Great Britain in 2022

Cover art by Nick Castle

ISBN: 978-1-80405-015-6

For Martha and Tom

PROLOGUE

Nasty things happen when prison routine breaks down: things like your cell door popping open at 5 a.m. It told Martha that whoever had deactivated the remote locking system was coming for her — and they meant her harm.

She pushed her self-pity aside. She needed to be ready, not whining that her life was unfair. Rolling off her hard cot, she balled her hands into fists and took deep, steadying breaths. The familiar movements gave her courage. She'd long known this moment would come: she was a cop in prison, and people were out to get her. Now that her fear was under control, she used it to fuel her aggression. She was about to need it.

Martha kept her eyes on the door. She could step outside, meet the challenge head on, but she was better able to defend herself in the tiny space of her cell. In here, it was her turf and they'd have to come at her one at a time.

A chilling scream pierced the heavy silence somewhere down the hall. As abruptly as it came, it was cut off. Martha didn't dwell on how the victim had been silenced, because now somebody was approaching her cell, feet slapping along the polished corridor outside.

Now they were at her door.

The door opened wide.

Standing there was the biggest woman she had ever seen. Athletic and tall, Martha was no lightweight, but this woman dwarfed her. She was well over six feet and must weigh all of 220 pounds of muscle and bone.

The giant was covered in tattoos and piercings. She boasted bright orange hair and had thick black liner around her eyes. It was an intimidating look, but there was even more reason to be terrified.

The woman was holding a knife that was covered in bloody gore.

Martha gritted her teeth and narrowed her green eyes. It was now or never. With a guttural roar, she launched herself forward.

CHAPTER 1

Six months earlier

The conversation that changed Detective Constable Martha Munro's life took place on a Wednesday just after midday. It was brief, intense and terrifying. She watched the sergeant's mouth form the words, doling out details that crawled into the dark places of her mind.

"Martha, there's a problem at home." Ice was forming on her spine. "It's Betty — she's been abducted. And your mother . . ." Sergeant Durrant paused, his face drawn.

Nausea and panic grappled with agitation and confusion.

"Martha?" she heard him say again, as if from a long way away. "I'm so sorry, your mother's been killed."

The shock crushed her. The result was inertia.

It reduced her to the role of a helpless onlooker, watching her own life turn into a disaster. She sat rigid, her hand fluttering towards her mouth, as if this was her only defence against a flood of misery. She tried to speak, but the words wouldn't form.

". . . two armed men," Sergeant Durrant was saying. "They smashed their way into your home, shot your mother and took your daughter before the neighbours could react."

Beyond the glass walls of the little meeting room, phones rang and reports were written up. All part of the busy working life for a detective based at Croydon police station, on the fringes of South London. She'd been part of it not ten minutes ago — now everything had changed.

The concern in her boss's face broke through to Martha. It gave her the strength to find a way back. "I need to get home . . . now."

Sergeant Durrant already had his keys in his hand.

"I'll drive you. No resource is being spared," he added. "They're going door to door right now and checking CCTV. By the time we get there, they may have some more news."

Martha followed the sergeant almost mindlessly. It was hard to walk in a straight line.

The dark-blue unmarked Audi pulled out of the police station. She pressed her face against the cool of the glass, feeling her sergeant's concerned gaze on her.

"There are a couple of bottles of water on the back seat."

Martha didn't respond.

"Would you pass me one?"

She twisted around, grabbed a bottle, cracked the seal and drained the contents. Still without speaking, she scooped up the second bottle, opened it and handed it to Sergeant Durrant. He drank thirstily.

They drove on in silence, quickly leaving central Croydon behind and running into an endless high street of small shops and takeaway outlets.

"There's something you're not telling me. Tell me everything you were told." Her voice was different from normal. Where there had been warmth, there was now an undercurrent of barely controlled anger and loss. Her feelings were so raw and deep they were rolling off her. "Tell me now."

Sergeant Durrant took a deep breath, but it was more delay than she could tolerate. She started beating the dashboard with both hands, spittle flying from her mouth. "Tell me. Give me the details, I need to hear it. Then maybe I can fix things."

"It's not pertinent – not really," said the sergeant in a tight voice. "They're checking to see if it's anything to do with your dad."

Martha stopped hitting the dashboard. She went very still.

"But surely . . ." went on the sergeant. "I mean, he left the police years ago, didn't he?"

"Yeah. He died two years ago."

"I'm sorry."

As they passed the looming Crystal Palace transmission tower and the shops of Crystal Palace Triangle, the high-rises and houses to their right hid and then revealed the heady dip to the park, rolling fields running below South London suburbia.

"Martha." The sergeant's tone was professional. "You're divorced, aren't you? Everything OK between you two?"

Of course he had to ask — she'd have done the same in his place. She knew the statistics on child abduction. "We're fine. We're not together, but my ex is a great father and he's happy with the custody arrangements as they are. He got on incredibly well with my mother. He called her 'mum', which was cheeky of him, but she loved it and treated him like the son she'd never had. So, no. There's no way he's behind something like this."

"OK. I had to check." They were nearing her house now. "I hate to state the obvious, but your home is now a crime scene. We have to go by the book when we get there."

She threw him an incredulous look. "I want to see it. I want to see exactly what happened."

"And you shall. We'll clear it with the officer in charge. An area commander, no less."

After a long pause, she nodded. "OK, sir. But don't take long. I'm not in the mood to wait."

CHAPTER 2

An ambulance, blue lights flashing, was right outside Martha's house. It was blocking the road, so they diverted a short distance to where they could park, then Sergeant Durrant guided her gently towards the crime scene — her home.

Martha had lived in the bay-fronted Victorian cottage in Idmiston Road for as long as she could remember, ever since her parents' divorce. She'd moved briefly away after school, but returned when her own marriage collapsed. Her head was playing a showreel of memories of her mum and daughter laughing together. The little girl adored — *had* adored — her grandma, and that feeling was returned in spades. They were separated by sixty years but they shared a sense of humour.

As they got closer to the house, the reel flickered out.

Martha and Durrant ducked under the police tape that cordoned off the front of the house and the pavement from the rest of the street. The area commander was already on the scene, conferring an aura of authority. Martha stopped when she saw who it was: Peter Shaw. Of course it would be him. Her father's work buddy. The old man cast a long shadow, even in death.

Commander Peter Shaw noticed Martha approaching, and his face creased in concern. He headed towards her, trailing a supporting cast of aides and bag carriers.

"Martha." He'd known her since her school days, distantly. "We're throwing everything at this. I'm taking personal charge. We'll leave no stone unturned."

"Any clues? Did anyone see who did it?" She wanted answers, not soundbites.

He shook his head. "Not yet. Neighbours saw two masked men. They arrived in a white van, parked two doors down, approached your house and smashed their way in. It happened quickly. Shots were fired, and the men ran out with your daughter, jumped in the van and took off. CCTV shows them arriving at 11.40 a.m. and leaving three minutes later. They didn't hang around."

Martha stood rigid as he talked. Betty must be terrified. "I need to go inside and see for myself."

He raised his hands. "That's not a good idea. Your mum's still in there. You don't want to see her as she is right now."

"You misheard me. I said I *need* to see her. I have to say goodbye and it has to be in the house. Not in some cold morgue. She needs to know I love her. That I'm there for her and she can stop worrying now. It's time for her to rest." Her reasonable tone did nothing to hide the underlying rage.

"Your mum suffered terrible injuries, Martha. At least let me make sure she's as presentable as we can manage."

Martha opened her mouth to object but then shook herself. "Yes, thank you. She'd want that. She was always very proud."

She waited outside while the commander went to make the arrangements. It was a warm day, but she felt cold. The front door was hanging open with the lock smashed off. They must have brought something with them, a lump hammer perhaps.

Off to her left stood a group of neighbours — quite a few worked from home. The women were holding each other and crying. She spotted Lucy from next door — they would share a glass of wine over the garden fence whenever they got the chance. Lucy's face twisted in grief as their eyes met, but Martha had no time for her now. She had to focus, collect information — prepare for what was coming.

Commander Shaw reappeared, made one more effort to dissuade her from going in and then watched her don protective gear before he led her into her home.

As Martha stepped through the door, her legs felt like they were going in slightly different directions. She prayed she didn't fall — he would have her out of the house if she did.

She stopped in the entranceway and closed her eyes, standing there for a moment as she made a promise to her mum and daughter that the people behind this would pay. The speed of the attack told her something, at least: it was impossible to dismiss this as a robbery gone wrong. Someone high up had ordered this. Someone who had crossed swords with her father when he'd led the anti-corruption squad at Scotland Yard.

A wave of dismay swept through her. Was her daughter already dead? She felt a sense of betrayal to Betty as she realised some part of her was already surrendering in a bid to make any loss easier. She couldn't stop thinking about how vulnerable Betty was, even if her daughter, at the grand age of four years old, was thoroughly independent.

She wouldn't allow it. She was going to fight.

Opening her eyes, she saw the commander looking at her compassionately. He indicated with a nod the door to the living room.

This was the family haven. Their special place where all three huddled together on the settee for TV shows like *Strictly Come Dancing* or *Britain's Got Talent*. Betty loved miming the songs and copying the dance routines, her grandmother clapping along with her.

Those moments were gone for ever. Martha's mother, covered by a blue plastic sheet, was lying on the ground, her head towards the front bay window. Martha stared at the shrouded figure. Her mother's feet were peeping out from under the sheet, and she was struck by the unwanted image of the Wicked Witch in *The Wizard of Oz*.

"I need to see her face."

"Please don't do that," said the commander. "Your mum was walking towards the living-room door when the shooter appeared. I hate to say this, but that's not a sight you want to remember."

The words made sense but she hardened herself. "I know you mean well, but I have to see."

Once again, the senior officer gave in. He nodded at one of the crime-scene techs, who gently pulled back the plastic.

It was shocking. Her mother had taken the blast on one side of her face.

"Thank you," she said, then stepped outside. She was hoping to see one neighbour in particular.

He wasn't there — at least, he wasn't in sight — but she would find him shortly.

CHAPTER 3

Sergeant Durrant approached her with a steaming mug of tea, which he'd scrounged up from one of the locals — but Martha turned it down. Anything going into her stomach would likely return faster than it went in. She was already regretting drinking the water.

Her boss shrugged and took a grateful sip himself.

"Poor Betty. How will she be coping?"

She snarled at him. "How do you fucking think? She'll be terrified."

She saw his stricken face and instantly regretted tearing into him. He'd met Betty and had got on with her.

She patted his shoulder. "I'm sorry, I didn't mean to go crazy on you."

"No, no. It was insensitive of me."

"I get what you were trying to say. Did she see them shoot her grandmother? How do you explain that to a sweet little girl who loves everyone?" Martha paused. "How can she make sense of something as awful as this?"

Her control evaporated and she broke down. Before the sergeant could react, he was swept aside. Lucy. They held each other, rocking gently backwards and forwards. Martha barely heard Sergeant Durrant's embarrassed farewell. Soon she was being ushered away from the prying eyes of the neighbours.

It was difficult to walk into Lucy's house and not make an entrance. Anyone with heels invariably clip-clopped in as they walked along the polished floorboards towards the kitchen. Normally this made Martha smile, especially when she was in her work shoes, but not today.

Lucy and Martha were almost the same age. Lucy was an artist, and her house was filled with half-finished canvases. It meant she was often at home at the same time as Martha, even when Martha's shift patterns were at unsociable hours, and they got on very well. She had brown curly hair with warm eyes and could normally make Martha laugh at anything. Not today. She sat Martha at the kitchen table and poured her a glass of water. Martha was bouncing between emotions — grief for her mother and fear for her daughter. Lucy instinctively gave her the emotional space she needed.

Nothing felt real. Just a few weeks ago she had been celebrating her promotion to detective; she'd even had her sights set on moving from Croydon to Scotland Yard. Now she was wondering if this had happened as some sort of cosmic punishment, a cruel rebalancing. She ran a hand through her short blonde hair, which was standing on end. She caught a glimpse of herself in the kitchen mirror: fists clenched, haggard. Her cheeks were tipped with red blotches.

"Martha," Lucy said urgently, "has anyone told Justin?"

Her heart sank. In her grief, she'd forgotten about Betty's father. "I don't . . . He's . . ."

Lucy held up a hand. "I'll call him. I've still got his number from when I did the nursery pickup last year." She got out her phone. "The kidnappers might try to contact you. And you're in no state."

The doorbell rang as she was dialling. Lucy went to answer it. Moments later, she was back.

"Harry's here, asking to see you. He says he can come back later, if that's better. I can't get through to Justin, but I'll keep trying."

Adrenalin surged through her. Harry the Hat was exactly who she wanted to see.

"If it's all right with you, please show him in."

Harry appeared, dapper as ever in a smart two-piece suit, shirt and tie, his creased face filled with concern.

One of the things Martha loved about Lucy was her generous nature. She didn't feel the need to keep her friend to herself. Lucy grabbed her purse, sensing that Martha and Harry needed some time. "If you're going to be here a while, Martha, then I need to get a few bits in . . . Actually, I need the essentials — wine and crisps."

She was quickly on her way.

Harry took Martha's hands in his. Harry Martin had mellowed over the years, to the point where it was pretty much impossible to see him as the frightening figure of his younger days. With his white hair and twinkling blue eyes, he looked like your favourite grandpa, someone who was kind to children and puppies.

Thirty years ago, at the peak of his infamy, he had been known as "Harry the Hat" because he was never seen without one. In this incarnation, he had been one of the most feared enforcers in South London. He had been very, very good at his work.

Wanted to give a rival a gentle warning? Harry was the man. Needed someone beaten within an inch of their life? Harry never went too far. He was especially famed for an almost magical ability to make people disappear — permanently.

In short, he was a man to be taken seriously. Even now, in his mid-seventies, he was still capable of looking after business. The local muggers and petty thieves knew to stay away. He operated by a simple credo: "I never break my word."

Now, as they stood in Lucy's kitchen, there was no trace of the infamous hardman. He couldn't keep the distress off his face.

"I'm so sorry, Martha. I promised your dad I'd keep an eye on your mum and you, and little Betty. I've let you down."

"Keeping a friendly eye on us for old time's sake is one thing, and you've always been a friend to me — but he didn't mean something like this." For the first time in hours, a touch of warmth reached her heart as she saw how upset he was. "You've never let me down, Harry. How could you have known this was going to happen?"

"It's my business to know these things." He took a deep breath. "I heard the gun go off. Nearly got the bastards. I ran down here as soon as I heard it — but they were jumping in the van with Betty. In the old days, I'd have had a gun on me and been able to shoot their tyres out. Then shoot them. I was that close."

"I'm guessing you didn't recognise them?"

He shook his head. "But they got in a flap when they saw me and started shouting at each other. They were speaking Bulgarian."

She didn't bother asking how he recognised Bulgarian. His brain was selective, but when it came to knowing his criminals he was Mensa level.

"Have you told the police any of this?"

At another time, his expression of disgust would have made her laugh.

"With apologies to you and your dad, I can't think of any reason why I would want to talk to the filth. I am, however, pursuing my own lines of inquiry and should have something for you very soon. I'm assuming you're in?"

She nodded, but only after a slight pause, which he must have noticed. She was a police officer who did things by the book, and that was exercising a strong pull on her. But she was beginning to think she stood a better chance of getting her daughter back by working with Harry, not sitting on the sidelines while the cops waited for the go-ahead.

The former minder spoke, intruding on her thoughts. "Good. I've got plenty of kit, so don't worry about that. Have you got any theories? Seen anyone hanging about? Been threatened? Maybe something to do with your dad?"

Martha shook her head. "I've got nothing at all."

He shrugged. "Well, I have every faith your little girl is coming home. My deepest condolences for your mum. She didn't like me — but she was always polite."

Despite her sorrow, Martha had to hide a smile. Her mum had been less than polite in private — but none of that mattered now.

Harry was about to leave when her mobile pinged to announce an inbound email with an attachment marked "FOR YOUR EYES ONLY".

It had to be about her daughter. She picked up the phone to open the message, but her hands were shaking so much she couldn't operate it.

Alerted by her distress, Harry stepped closer, deep worry lines emerging on his forehead. In a gentle voice he asked, "Do you want me to do that?"

Martha didn't respond; she just kept stabbing at the phone. It took a moment before the practical side of her won out and she gave the phone to Harry.

Harry clicked the link. A video. They watched together silently as Betty appeared. The girl looked tiny and scared, her big eyes dominating her face, but she showed her mother's determination as she kept still. The image wobbled, then a man's voice could be heard. "Speak." Concentrating hard, Betty kept her gaze on the camera, just like she always did for Martha. Her voice was surprisingly strong. "Come and get me soon, Mummy."

For just a moment Martha couldn't breathe. Her senses threatened to shut down. She was glued to the screen, trying to absorb every scrap, to see if she could spot some clue, anything at all. But her hands were steady. Taking the phone back from Harry, she ran the footage again, drinking in every detail. She noted that Betty licked her lips before speaking and was sitting on a wooden chair that was too high for her, her hands holding on to the sides for balance, her feet some way from the ground. Her hair hung down, framing her oval face. Martha searched harder. She noted Betty glanced up at her captors and that they had put her in front of a plain, painted wall.

Maybe this would be the last image of her daughter. Her grip tightened on the phone and sweat beaded her forehead.

Someone was going to suffer for this.

CHAPTER 4

Front-line police response teams had been scrambled to the scene after the initial panicked 999 call. These included officers from the highly trained Territorial Support Group, men and women deployed to the most serious incidents, from terror-related events to riots or anything deemed a threat to public order. The TSG team had been sent to what was at first described as an "officer down".

A key benefit of the TSG involvement was that the unit deployed highly specialised command vehicles — about the size of a medium mobile home, metallic grey, with blacked-out windows. These were kitted out with state-of-the-art communications overseen by two technicians, and offered a small area where command officers could operate free from surveillance.

It was in one of these that Martha found Commander Shaw, alongside a couple of serious-faced forensics technicians, radios chattering away. She told him about the email and forwarded it on to one of the techs. They all watched together as the video played on a large screen inside the vehicle.

"Bastards," a technician muttered under his breath as the little girl finished her plea.

Martha blinked away her tears.

"No ransom demands yet." Shaw was looking at her intently. "When did you receive this?"

"Five minutes ago." She showed him the timestamp on the phone. It was actually eight minutes.

The commander had an unreadable expression on his face. "You've had no other contact?"

She shook her head.

"Has anything else occurred to you about what's behind this, now that there's been contact? Events are moving fast."

Martha shook her head again. "Well, there was never any proof, but Mum said something that maybe I should have paid more attention to. She wasn't sure, but she said once or twice when she got home from being out, it felt like every drawer in the house had been searched through. Nothing was taken, and in fact there wasn't any sign of a break-in. I just put it down to paranoia."

Shaw leaned in close. "Nothing about your dad that might have triggered this? Something he gave you, maybe, that the shooters might have been after? There's no way this is just a robbery gone wrong."

"My dad and I didn't really have that kind of a relationship, sir."

He considered her closely. "A lot of the people who supervised your training say you're a chip off the old block."

She kept silent, eyes narrowed.

"Well, let's set that aside. You say Betty's father — Justin Bhagwat — is away?"

"Yes, he's on holiday in Cornwall."

"Convenient, that."

"Excuse me?"

"Statistics, detective constable. If a child is abducted, nine times out of ten the parent who does not have custody is the perpetr—"

"But not an armed abduction, sir! Not like this!" Martha couldn't keep the annoyance out of her voice. "Justin has no reason or wish to abduct Betty. And he *loved* my mother. Even after we divorced he remained on good terms with her."

"By the book. That's the way this investigation will proceed. And I'll remind you, since you seem to have forgotten your training, that anyone operating beyond the remit or control of this investigation will be charged with obstruction . . . or worse. Your father was a man willing to go where lions fear to walk. If you're cut from the same cloth, you might come up with your own plans."

Martha had had enough. Standing up, she said politely, "If you need me, you know where I am. By the way, it's 'where angels fear to tread'."

"I'm sorry?"

"It's a poem by Alexander Pope. It goes, 'Fools rush in where angels fear to tread.' It means don't jump to conclusions, among other things."

As she walked out, she could feel the commander's eyes burning into her back. Damn. She'd made an enemy when there was no need. Something her dad would not have been impressed with.

CHAPTER 5

Hristo Dragov was fretting. The job had gone badly, and he had no one to take it out on apart from the little girl — a course of action which would be the death of him. Literally.

He and his brother Ivan had been told — again and again — not to harm the child or the old lady — just get in there, get out and get to the safe house. Break any of these rules, they were told, and there would be a price. Hurt the little girl and that price would be measured in blood.

A seriously big man with enormous hands had delivered the instructions. Hristo was a shade under six feet tall, and he'd needed to crane his neck to see his eyes.

"Why don't we bring the grandmother too?" Ivan had said lazily. "You'll get more cash for two."

Suddenly, a very large knife was against Ivan's throat, pressing hard enough against the skin to draw a thin line of blood. Hristo had met men like this before and knew that being afraid was the only sensible approach.

His older brother's eyes had bulged out of their sockets as he tried not to tremble too violently for fear of cutting his own throat. Suddenly, the man drew the knife back and roared. Ivan screamed. Hristo watched in mute terror as the knife slashed down. At the last second, the big man had flicked his wrist so it was the handle end of the knife — not its point — which slammed into Ivan's forehead, briefly knocking him out.

The big man had put the knife away, before turning his merciless gaze on Hristo.

"I'm told you're the clever one, at least by your family's standards. Now, repeat your instructions back to me."

"We smash the door down, grab the little girl. Go to the flat in Peckham. Wait for someone to come and collect the kid and give us the money. No one gets hurt. If the kid gets injured, in any way, then you'll make us pay."

With unexpected speed, the huge man had gripped Hristo's head between his hands. He had applied so much pressure that Hristo worried he might crush his skull.

"If you fuck this up, I will skin you both alive. Your brother first, then you," the big man added.

Now sitting in the so-called safe house, Hristo Dragov was a cauldron of emotion, with fear and regret the most prominent. Every time he closed his eyes, the threat flashed through his mind. He didn't know who the man was. He didn't want to know. He wished he'd never clapped eyes on him, nor the suitcase of cash they'd been lured in with.

Almost four hours had elapsed, and they'd had no contact with either the huge man or whoever was coming to pick up the kid. They'd locked her in one of the bedrooms, together with a large supply of chocolate and soft drinks, and threats about what would happen if she made a noise. He'd felt a flicker of emotion as the little girl's eyes widened in terror, but he was relieved she'd stopped her crying for her grandmother, at least.

"What do you think's going on?" asked Ivan, adjusting his baggy trousers.

"I don't know. I wish you hadn't shot the old lady."

Ivan reddened. "It was an accident. She was trying to get the gun. I pulled the trigger by mistake. Nine times in ten, the bullet would have missed."

Sometimes Hristo despaired of his brother. There would be consequences, of that he was sure. His heart was going into palpitations. It could have been the little girl who had got hit. "Just be ready and make sure you apologise. And why are they late? They should have been here by now."

"We could just leg it. Take the money they've given us so far and drop out of sight. Go to the old country for a bit."

"Are you mad? You want to run from a psychopath? No way. We have to see this out. He's gonna make us pay for the grandmother — but at least the girl's safe."

Even as he finished speaking, there was a tremendous crash: the sound of a flimsy front door being smashed open.

The huge man burst in, demented with rage. His cold eyes were reptilian, latching on to the pair in a way that suggested he wouldn't need a knife to keep his promise to hurt them.

"You stupid fuckers. The only thing that'll save you is if the girl is all right. Where is she?"

"In the bedroom. She—"

The big guy turned to a woman who had followed him in. Most of her face was hidden by her overlong scarf. "Go see if she's in one piece."

"What happened with the old lady?"

"She—" Ivan choked as a large finger was jabbed painfully into his chest.

"You're lucky that was just my finger."

The woman reappeared, carrying Betty. She nodded at the man, and vanished out of the door.

He pulled some plastic handcuffs out of his back pocket. "Give me your hands."

"Why should we? Why are you tying us up? You should be paying us." Ivan Dragov was nothing if not persistent.

"When I suggested you were stupid, I should have said *very* stupid. Now stop talking and hold your hands out."

When Ivan refused to cooperate, the huge man moved with blinding speed. In moments, he had his hands around

Ivan's throat, squeezing hard, smiling in a way that promised a world of pain.

He released the pressure enough to allow Ivan to speak.

"OK, OK. I get it!" Ivan held his hands out and was cuffed tightly.

The huge man gestured at Hristo. "Now it's your turn. First the muscle — then what passes for a brain."

Both brothers were tied to a radiator.

"What about us?" asked Hristo.

"What about you? Now we find out if you can take your punishment. Let's start with your brother."

The huge man stepped forward and took a moment to set himself. He pulled Ivan so that he was sitting straight and then held him in place with his left hand. With his right hand he slammed a pile-driver punch straight into his victim's solar plexus. The effect was immediate. Ivan went bright red and made a loud gasping sound as the air was expelled from his body. His eyes bulged and he slumped back against the radiator, overwhelmed by the pain.

In other circumstances Hristo might have admired the surgical precision and brute strength. Now he was just terrified for himself and his brother. There was a chance one or both of them might not come out of this alive.

The huge man looked down at Ivan and spat on his face. Then he turned to Hristo.

"He was just a dumb animal. You knew better, so you get worse."

From somewhere inside himself Hristo found a sliver of courage. He managed to look directly at the huge man, even though he could do nothing about the shakes wracking his body.

"Do your worst, you bastard." If that proved his epitaph it would have to do. He wasn't in the right frame of mind for fancy words.

For just a moment a look of what might have been approval flickered across the big man's face. Then it was gone, chased away by an expression of gleeful malevolence.

"Big words for a small man."

He disappeared for a couple of minutes. When he reappeared, he was wearing a pair of mustard-yellow, heavy-duty work gloves.

He positioned himself with some care, making sure he was nicely balanced. Then he began slapping Hristo's face. They were brutal, concussive blows, delivered with alternate hands in a steady tempo, like the big man was counting it out in his head.

One . . . two . . . three . . . four . . . five . . . six . . . seven . . . eight . . . nine . . . ten. The brutal rhythm never varied. First one hand then the other. Towards the end, blood was flowing from Hristo's ears, his face was red raw and a crunching sensation in his head heralded the right side of his jaw breaking. The punishment was pitiless.

The slapping stopped, leaving Hristo trapped in a world of misery, just waiting for the next blow. The pain was intense, and he must have blacked out. When he came round his brother was sobbing.

"I thought you might not wake up. It would have been my fault."

Minutes passed and Hristo finally managed to get the pain under some sort of control.

"Where is he?" Those few words hurt.

"He's gone. But he left us a message. We tell the police that the little girl's mother did this to us. We're to say she attacked us after finding us chained up. She just went for us.

"He said if any word gets out about what really happened, he will find us and chop us, slowly, into pieces."

* * *

Earlier the big man had deftly skipped down the stairs, jumping into the front of a waiting black SUV. Ordering the driver to move, he twisted round to eye the woman and child sitting behind him. "Our passenger OK?"

"No problem."

23

The big man turned back. He was on a tight schedule and needed no more interruptions. He knew he was
on Harry's patch. Even without the trail he was leaving it
wouldn't be long before he and Martha were closing in.

He made sure not to glance behind as a cyclist wearing
a dark-blue hoodie started to follow the car.

CHAPTER 6

Martha's frame of mind while waiting for more news from Harry wasn't improved by receiving an angry phone call from Justin. Betty's father was close to breaking down as he shouted down the line.

"How many times have I said that you need to be more careful? Not only are you in the force, but your dad was a senior officer. Between you, you two must have made a load of enemies.

"Now, to really rub it in, you're telling me that you, and all your police pals, have come up with nothing. Our daughter is kidnapped, her grandmother shot dead, and you lot are chasing your tails."

"Justin, be reasonable. She's only just—"

Martha was cut off by a fresh round of shouting.

"Be reasonable? How am I supposed to be reasonable about this? How many times have I warned that your job was a risk? You know you could have done something different, you even turned down an offer — a potentially lucrative offer — to be trained by one of the biggest consultancy firms in the world. You'd have been safe and made for life.

"But oh no, you had to do it your way. Follow in the family tradition and be a bloody hero."

He had her in a difficult place when it came to her father. Through most of her life John Munro had been an absent dad, constantly blaming the pressure of work for not being around. But as she'd grown older, she had, reluctantly at first, seen a different side to him — one that, possibly, explained his behaviour. While she was still married to Justin, Martha had once admitted that some of her motivation for joining the police was to follow in his footsteps. That keeping people safe was a calling. It was a badly thought-out remark and she regretted saying it the moment the words left her mouth, but Justin had appeared to let it go. It resurfaced as their marriage broke down for what he felt was her overly "police" attitude to his dabbling in marijuana use.

Now that he had thrown this at her again she knew there was nothing she could say until she got Betty back. To her relief, Harry finally returned. Assuring Justin that she would get their daughter back, she ended the call before he could continue the one-sided argument.

In response to Harry's quizzical look, she explained, "Justin is super angry at me and super worried about Betty. He's not listening to reason. To be fair, I don't feel that reasonable myself. I need to do something."

Harry had changed outfits. This time he wasn't wearing a suit, but was in dark, nondescript clothes. "I've got an address. You ready?"

"You've found Betty?" A surge of nervous energy saw her inhale sharply. "An hour ago, I'd have rushed over to Commander Shaw, asked him to send a police hostage rescue team — but now? He's lecturing me about my responsibility as a police officer and seems to have forgotten there's a frightened little girl out there who needs her mummy. I can't bear the thought of her being held captive a moment longer than she needs to."

Harry grinned. "I know you didn't always see eye to eye with your dad, but you do sometimes sound like him. He never forgot the human element."

Martha had made her mind up. She was going with Harry. She convinced herself it was the best way to save her little girl. An unexpected memory surfaced, helping to seal the deal: her mother, a woman not given to singing Harry's praises had once explained why she could call on him in an emergency. "Harry's the best man to have at your side. He doesn't get bogged down with protocol, he just does things." She couldn't recall how they'd got onto the subject, but the words remained vivid. They firmed her resolve. If she had to pay a subsequent price for going against a direct order, holding Betty close again would more than compensate.

Lucy, who'd given them space till now, appeared in the kitchen. "What's going on?"

Martha gave her friend an enormous bear hug. "Might be best if you don't know — then I won't have to ask you to lie to the police."

As soon as they were outside, Harry said, "We got lucky. I still keep up with some of the main faces around here, and there's been some activity that was picked up in Peckham. The people I spoke to said there were some out-of-the-area types hanging around. They paid cash up front for some tatty flat off Peckham Rye, and they've been seen scoping out the area in these parts, asking the wrong kind of questions. The only people who behave like that have something to hide. My contact was concerned that maybe a new gang was moving in to the territory. You don't survive long in that trade if you don't listen to your instincts."

Martha knew now she was doing the right thing. This wasn't the type of information you could take to a man like Shaw; he'd have dismissed it out of hand, even if he had listened.

As they approached a dark grey Ford Focus, Harry used a fob to release the locking mechanism. She glanced at his outfit as they got in.

"I don't think I've ever seen you dressed down before, Harry."

"In case of bloodstains." He waggled his foot. "My finest steel toe-capped shoes. If you get kicked with these, you stay kicked. They're nicely balanced. Good for running, but not so heavy that you can't swing your foot when you need to."

It made her shins ache just thinking about it. "I like a man who knows how to dress." The police officer's voice inside her berated her for the joke. She ignored it. There were more important things at stake than her career. "Will Betty be there?" It had taken every scrap of control not to blurt it out sooner.

"We're on her trail," said Harry. "It's a bit more than just a hunch. We need to get to this flat in Peckham fast, and make them talk. They're probably hired hands, though. In my day, these people would have been brought in for one job, and the blokes in charge would be happy for them to take the rap."

"Who hired them? Who's behind this?"

"I haven't been able to get anything on that yet." Harry's face was grim. "This is my manor, has been for a very long time. I'm a bit out of touch nowadays, but I'm not so far removed that people won't do me a favour. "

Traffic was light and they were quickly in Peckham.

Harry tapped her leg. "Check the bag on the back seat."

Martha turned around and grabbed it, placing it on her knees. She reached inside. The first thing she felt was the familiar shape of a Taser.

Harry inclined his head her way. "That's an upgrade on what you lot use. Hundred thousand volts. It'll stop most people."

The police part of her wondered how he got it; the non-police part couldn't have cared less. More rummaging revealed a gun. Even though she had large hands and strong wrists, the weapon was enormous.

"What have you got in here? A small cannon?"

"It's a Colt .45. I was taught that, if you must use a gun, use one that fires big bullets. Get shot with that and you stay shot. I've had it for a long time. Back in the day, I only had

28

to show it to people to get them on my wavelength. If I ram this up someone's nostril, they always seem keen to help."

The last thing in the bag was a police-issue baton. She smiled. The flexible, extendable tool was a wonderful aid in a fight. Especially if you'd practised as hard as she had.

Harry pulled up by a mansion block. "Black front door, cracked glass pane on the left at the bottom, missing altogether on the right at the top. That's the place. According to my information, they're in the first-floor flat, right at the top of the stairs. Are you ready?"

A minute later, they were edging up the stairs. The door to the flat was hanging drunkenly off its hinges. There was no time to investigate. The answers they needed had to be inside.

Harry used his fingers to count them in — *one, two, three*. Then, with a chopping motion, he was racing inside, Martha hard on his heels.

He stopped so abruptly, Martha almost fell over him. She gasped at the scene. Two men were sitting on the floor of the living room, bound to a radiator. One of them was in considerably worse shape than the other, his face caked in blood. His whole face was badly swollen and he looked barely conscious. The other man was in better physical shape but squeaked in terror when he saw Harry was brandishing a gun. Harry, seeing the men posed no imminent risk, scanned the small room and then went stealthily into the back room of the flat. He returned with a shake of his head: no Betty.

Martha knelt down so she was face to face with the conscious man. "Who are you?"

Harry answered for him. "I think these are the two who got into your house, killed your mum and took Betty. Something weird seems to have happened, though. I wasn't expecting to see this."

Martha raised her police baton.

"Martha," Harry said urgently. "MARTHA!"

His shout caught her attention.

"Martha, don't do it. Betty's not here and these two are no threat, at least not in this state. We just need them to tell us what they know. I think Betty was here; there's drinks and snacks in the other room."

Martha stepped back and looked carefully at the brothers. The activity had even made the unconscious one stir. Harry was right, there was no need to hurt them. Frighten them, though? That was OK.

"Where's my daughter?" she shouted right into the man's face. "If you scumbags have damaged a single hair on her head, you'll regret it."

She raised her baton again.

"Wait, wait! I can help. Your daughter's OK. At least she was when she left here."

"What do you mean she left? When did she leave? Who did she leave with?" Her tone became lower and lower, making him strain to hear the words.

"It wasn't long ago, maybe ten minutes. The people who hired us took her. I don't know who they are. They had money and approached me and my brother. We were just paid to do a job. Our contact is a madman. He's the one who left us tied up here."

"You're telling me my baby is with a madman?"

"Yes, but look, it was only us he was aggressive with. Your daughter will be OK. He kept saying, over and over, that she had to be kept safe. Her and the old lady."

"The 'old lady' you murdered was my mother."

The man was talking again, pleading. He spoke fast, despite his injuries. "Listen to me. I can help. We have an ace in the hole."

"Tell me," she hissed.

"My brother thought we might end up being double-crossed, so we have someone following him, the one with your daughter."

She stiffened and leaned closer.

"There's a denim jacket behind you. In the pocket — my mobile. Ring Doug."

He started whimpering as the barrel of the Colt was pressed into the sweet spot right between his eyes. Threat applied, Harry left the talking to Martha.

"You're not trying to make fools of us, are you? What happens if that call to Doug is a warning to your team?"

Sweat was pouring off him as he desperately blurted out, "I swear on my brother's life. Call the number. If he answers, they're still nearby. If not, they're on the move. But let me speak to him first so he doesn't get spooked."

Martha paged through the contacts and called the number, then held the handset to his ear.

"Doug? You followed them, yeah? Where are you now? Good. Stay there. Keep out of sight until a young blonde woman and an old geezer turn up. Do what they ask. Don't mess with either of them." Call over, he looked at Martha. "He was able to follow them without being spotted. He says they're only a few miles away, in Herne Hill." He gasped for breath. "He'll be waiting for you outside the railway station. He's wearing a black top and a pair of aviator sunglasses — orange lenses. If you want to be on the safe side, ask him who paid him. He should say Archie. That's who we used."

Harry was contemptuous. "How much were you supposed to get for this little outing?"

"Ten grand."

Harry laughed. It wasn't a pleasant sound. "By the time the Old Bill's finished with you, it'll end up costing you ten years inside. And you'll need to keep your eyes open when everyone finds out you were kidnapping a child. No one likes a nonce." Harry snorted again. "I really wouldn't like to be in your shoes. I'd talk to the police very nicely, see if they can help."

Martha started to walk away.

Mummy's coming, sweetheart. Mummy's coming.

The words were playing on a loop in her brain.

CHAPTER 7

Doug turned out to be a laid-back teenager with greasy hair, his pale skin highlighting painful-looking facial acne. He smelled strongly of marijuana and, despite it being a warm day, he kept his hood up.

They found him sitting on his bike, leaning against a wall that gave a view of the ticket office and the steps leading up to the platforms. As they approached, a Kent-bound train thundered overhead, blocking conversation.

It took some prodding to get him to talk. Martha's palms itched with the desire to force answers from him. Instead it was Harry, showing a surprising gift for persuading a teenager to speak in full sentences, who extracted the information.

"They went into a house on the Milkwood Road. Two of them, the big man and a woman, with a little girl." He had a nasal way of speaking that did nothing for Martha's nerves. "They went into the downstairs flat — I saw them through the window. The woman was carrying the girl."

His description triggered an image of Betty, frightened and alone. It was so powerful she had to hold on to Harry for support for a second.

"OK to keep going?" said Harry, raising an eyebrow.

"Try stopping me."

* * *

The property had an unloved air. Martha shivered at the thought of Betty being inside. As she went to open the passenger door, Harry stopped her.

"Wait. Take a moment. Look at the place, check for traps."

Martha peered at the windows, looking for Betty. Nothing.

"We go in fast," Harry went on. He pulled some protective gloves from his back pocket, handing a pair to Martha. "Put these on. It doesn't hurt to cover your tracks."

As he spoke, he pulled the .45 from a holster under his left arm. "No point having a bloody big shooter if it's not ready," he said, holding the weapon in his right hand as he studied the front door.

Martha felt a sudden chill. All this activity, the gun, protective gloves . . . the frightening reality of what might be about to happen raced through her brain. Harry looked ready to start shooting and she couldn't risk Betty getting caught in the middle.

"Harry." Martha's tone was sharp enough to stop him in his tracks. "If Betty is in here, you can't go in waving that gun around. I know we can't be sure this kid is telling us the truth, but what if he is? You can't go in like a one-man SWAT team."

Harry didn't argue. Instead, he slid the gun into the gap between the small of his back and his trousers. Then he held his hands out wide. "Is this OK? No gun in sight."

If anything, her resolve hardened. "Sorry, Harry. Take my baton, if you like, but no gun. She's had enough trauma for a lifetime. And what if she gets caught in the cross-fire . . ." The sentence remained unfinished.

Again, Harry didn't argue. He took the gun and handed it, handle first, to Martha.

"I'm still going in first. You stay right here until I give the all-clear." Harry took a step back to give himself room to swing his steel-capped shoes. "These will make quick work of that lock," he said.

Two well-placed kicks and the lock shattered. He was inside before the door rebounded from the wall.

"Armed police, armed police!" he shouted, trying to cause confusion, which might buy them vital seconds.

The corridor was dark, with a door immediately to the right. Harry hurled himself through it, spinning around as he crouched low. But the room was bare.

He was back in the hallway as Martha stepped past the shattered door. Harry placed a finger to his lips and cupped his free hand to his ear. His message was clear. *The odds are narrowing. The kidnappers might be in the next room. We need to listen out for them moving around. The shock of having the front door kicked open will have worn off. They'll be waiting.*

They were both still as statues, although Martha's breathing sounded loud in her ears. She had to fight an urge to call her daughter's name. She imagined the kidnappers doing the same thing. Listening. Waiting. Getting ready to fight. Getting ready to hurt Betty . . .

From somewhere ahead came the faintest noise. It might have been from the next room along.

Martha was bracing to run towards it when Harry stopped her. He was going in first. One breath and he was moving fast through the door. He scanned left and right. To the left was a sagging settee, empty. The noise came again. Someone was behind the settee. Harry braced, his hands balling into fists.

Betty popped up, and laughed with delight as she saw Uncle Harry.

Then Martha was there, grabbing her little girl and hugging her so tightly that Betty wriggled to escape. Never had a moment been so special. Martha breathed in the scent of summer flowers that was her daughter. The wriggling grew more pronounced.

She relented, putting the little girl down.

During this emotional reunion, she noticed Harry carefully taking the gun back, holding it out of Betty's sight. He quickly vanished, but he soon returned, minus the Colt .45.

"Where'd you put it?" she asked quietly.

"Kitchen. I wiped it down. Something's off about this. The rest of the place is empty and the back door's open, but I don't see how they could have gone out that way at the same time as we were coming through the front. That tells me they left a while ago, which is weird. Why go to the trouble of kidnapping a little girl, risking a world of trouble, then just leave her behind? I've got a horrible feeling we might have been lured into a trap."

Martha went white as a sheet. "Are you saying we might be in danger? Have they set up a device?" She pantomimed quotation marks around "device", not wanting to worry Betty.

"No, no. I'm sure there's nothing like that here. But I don't think this is happening for our benefit." Then he beamed at Betty, who sniffled. "Let's get you two out of here. I'll fetch the car. We need to decide where we're going."

His words got through. Martha suddenly recalled they could not go home, not until it was properly cleaned up. Maybe Betty could never go back. What were the alternatives? Lucy would have them in a heartbeat, but perhaps they should go to a hotel, away from the place where her mother had been shot. Somewhere with a pool. Betty would like that. She spoke to her daughter. "Come on, let's go."

They were in the hallway when a police firearms officer raced in. He was holding a gun down by his side.

He shouted over his shoulder. "One woman, one child. One adult male. All three alive."

Harry called out. "I've got a baton. I'm placing it on the floor." He bent at the knees then stood up with his palms out to show his hands were empty.

More officers appeared and Harry spoke again.

"There's a gun back there." He jerked his head in the direction of the kitchen. "That was in here when I checked the back of the house," he explained in his best old-codger voice. "I put the safety on. I know all about that from my army days."

A voice crackled through on the officer's radio. "The property is clear. I repeat. Property is clear."

There was a moment of silence before Commander Shaw walked in, followed by a harsh-faced female officer who Martha didn't recognise. Martha pulled Betty close. The little girl sensed the tension and hid her face.

"Take the child," he said. Before Martha could react, he went on. "Don't make this worse than it needs to be. Especially for your little girl. I warned you. I told you not to get involved — but you knew better, just like your father." He hesitated. "The two men we found in Peckham are in a bad way. Your work, was it? The doctor tells me one needs intensive surgery. Given your upbringing, this may not come as a surprise — but Scotland Yard doesn't like vigilante cops. Bad for the optics."

Martha was too overwhelmed to speak. What was happening? How had Shaw been able to follow their trail? She felt frozen in place.

Even as Betty sobbed for her mother in the policewoman's arms, another plain-clothes detective appeared. Without hesitation, he pulled out a pair of handcuffs.

"Wait!" she said desperately. "Not in front of my daughter." She wanted to scream, to shout — but she couldn't risk upsetting Betty, who was watching with eyes wide open.

She took the hardest decision of her life. Managing to find a smile, she said, "Go with the nice lady, darling. Mummy has to work. See you soon."

Betty looked doubtful, but Martha kept smiling. "Give Mummy a kiss."

Betty planted a kiss on her cheek. "Is this a game, Mummy?"

"It's just work, love. See you soon."

With her daughter out of sight, the plain-clothes detective snapped on the handcuffs. "Martha Munro, I'm arresting you on suspicion of assault causing grievous bodily harm."

Part of her knew this was a holding charge. Part of her didn't care. She faced Shaw. "Whatever's going on here, I want to help clear things up. I need my daughter. That's all I care about."

He ignored her plea. "You've got a lot more to be worried about than that. If I were you, I'd be thinking very carefully about what you say. I was a huge fan of your father, and I'll try my best for you — but I warned you of the consequences if you went off on your own."

CHAPTER 8

Martha was taken to Brixton police station for processing. The public entrance to the station is set back from the high street, and the modernist-style building gives the impression of a reinforced office block — in fact, it comfortably survived a petrol bomb attack in the 1980s. Martha had visited in her role as a police officer, but this was quite different. The arresting officer left her in a grubby interview room with a female police officer to watch over her. Martha made no attempt to engage the woman in conversation — instead she gathered herself as best she could for what was coming.

Martha was aware of how easy it was to slip into a sort of fugue state, a sense that one was powerless against a higher authority. She'd sat on the "other side" of the desk often enough to have seen it happen. After an hour of waiting in silence she felt she needed to do something, no matter how trivial, to maintain her equilibrium and not hand the initiative to the police officers waiting to quiz her. She looked at her guard, who was standing by a wall and staring into the middle distance. The woman blinked, which gave her an idea. It wasn't the greatest — small victories would have to do while she was in a tricky spot.

"These lights are bothering my eyes. They're giving me a headache. Can we do anything about it?"

The woman tapped out a message on her mobile. Martha heard it swoosh as the message was sent.

About ten minutes later, they moved her to a new interview room. The lighting was gentler here. She was also given some water and offered food, which she declined. She wondered how much of what had happened that day was linked to her father. But why now, two years after his death? He'd established a reputation for his fearless pursuit of bent coppers. As the senior commander in charge of the anti-corruption team, he'd made countless enemies — both gang leaders and the police officers in their pay. There were people at Scotland Yard who hated her because of who her father was. And there was nothing she could do about that. She certainly wasn't going to plead special circumstances to earn an easier ride. If her dad had a reputation as a tough copper, she would show his daughter was made of the same stuff. It made her professional life more complicated than most but, as she was learning, John Munro had been more complicated than the official version.

And where was her little girl now? In some faceless Social Services office, waiting for her father to come back from holiday? Or would Justin be home by now, reunited with Betty? She was glad she still had a good relationship with Justin, even though they had argued so much when they had separated. She had never lost sight of what a good father he was. He could be relied on now in this moment of crisis. Betty needed both her parents after the trauma she'd just gone through — but at least she'd have her dad with her now. Betty was going to need help to process what had happened.

Martha's bleak thoughts were threatening to take over when the door opened to reveal Paul Avery, a solicitor and long-time confidant of her father's. Just five foot five in his handmade shoes and Savile Row suit, he looked like a bulldog — and could act like one if it would help a client.

He marched in, jowls quivering, seemingly disappointed that there was only a duty constable with her — not worth sinking his teeth into. "Where are they? Run away after they heard I was on my way down, I suppose. Pity, I was in the mood for detective on toast."

It was all bluster but done with one purpose: to lift her spirits. Which it did. Suddenly she could see there might be a chance of getting out of here.

Paul was eyeing the police officer.

"I want to talk to my client in confidence. Off you go. Quickly now."

Looking flustered, the officer departed.

"Right. Tell me what's going on. I want to hear it from you. In detail."

He was in his late fifties but moved as if he was a decade younger, with wide shoulders, big hands and meaty forearms that wouldn't have shamed a road-digger. While it would be an exaggeration to say he was the family lawyer, he was a solicitor and friend of the family. The first time he'd helped her father had been four years before she was born. She was twenty-five now, so he'd been around for nearly thirty years.

She talked him through what had become the longest day of her life, careful to start at the beginning and leave nothing out — including Harry's role in her predicament.

Harry and Paul knew each other well and got along even better. Their relationship worked because, when they first met, the lawyer had told him, "Never let me see you do anything illegal and we won't have a problem."

It was a rule Harry followed to the letter.

Martha carefully took Paul through the key events, starting with their arrival at the Peckham flat.

"We walked in to find these two guys chained to a radiator. One of them was in a very bad way; someone had done a real number on him. I didn't think it was life-threatening, but he was hurt badly, that's for sure. He was pretty much unconscious.

40

"The other guy was in much better shape. I'm beginning to wonder if he'd been left alone so we could talk to him. He admitted they'd killed Mum and taken Betty." She shuddered. "We like to think we're all civilised, but I came close to beating him then and there, even though they were chained up. But Harry stepped in."

Martha looked around the interview room, then carried on. "I'm glad I didn't do anything. It would have brought me down to their level. The one who was awake claimed they had been put up to it by a mystery man, someone he described as huge and vicious. He said this man had beaten them before taking Betty away. Bizarrely he tried to claim that Betty was safe with him because he'd made them promise not to hurt her, and Mum."

Paul shook his head. "You must have come close to punching him when he said that. Look, I need to ask this next question: are you certain you didn't touch these two? I don't know what I'd have done in the same circumstances."

Martha snorted. "No. Nothing happened. Nothing at all."

"What about Harry? He's incredibly protective of you and Betty."

"Again, no. If anything, Harry was a peacekeeper. Why are you asking?"

"Because the police are talking about charging you with GBH, or maybe even wounding with intent to cause GBH. I couldn't get a lot out of them, but that's the way they steered me. I have no idea what evidence they may produce."

"What!" Martha shouted. "How can we be charged with something we didn't do?"

They looked at each other, both coming to the same conclusion. Martha voiced their fears.

"Someone's trying to set me and Harry up. Where is Harry, by the way? I presume they have him somewhere in this building?"

"Yes, and that's the other odd thing," said Paul. "I gained the impression that Harry might be released. At the moment they're not even talking about charging him. Good for him, but why are you two getting different treatment?"

"I really wish I knew," said Martha.

"What happened when you found Betty?"

Martha had to fight back tears as she remembered her elation at finding Betty alive. "I thought I might never see her again, but there she was, smiling away. I hugged her so hard. I just wanted to hold her and take in that flowery smell she has."

She reached for her water as her mouth went dry.

Paul gave her a moment then asked, "Anything happen that I need to know about?"

"There was just Betty there, which made Harry nervous. He was like a dog with its hackles raised, sensing a threat. He started worrying it was a set-up, then the police turned up.

"But I can't see how they have anything. We didn't touch the first two thugs and there was no one to lay a finger on at the second place. All we did was rescue my little girl. Yet when the cops found us, it was like they were working from a script. Even Commander Shaw, who's supposed to have been a friend of my dad's, was acting like he was playing a part. It all felt unreal, as though the police expected to catch us in the act."

Paul puffed out his cheeks. "You may be on to something. I'm particularly interested that you say Harry got worried. He's got antennae for these things. Your dad said he was like a mobile alarm unit. It can be easy to get paranoid in these circumstances, but a bit of caution is always sensible. Anyway, we can do something to balance things out a little. You hinted that your dad left enemies behind after his death — well, he also had some friends. Perhaps it's time I called in some favours on your behalf.

"I'm not saying he foresaw this exact day, that would be daft. The last thing he possessed was mystical powers, but he did say the day might arrive when you and your mum needed help. Sadly it's too late for her, but not for you."

Martha's expression changed to one of total misery. "I can't get my head round the idea Mum's dead. It hits me every time. Even the joy of getting Betty back can't ease the pain."

"Do you want to take a break?"

"I'd love to stop the world, if I'm honest. But it sounds like this is far from over. If Mum thought I was allowing self-pity to get in the way of keeping Betty safe, she'd be furious. So, please, go on. Tell me more about my secret guardian angels."

"I don't have a great deal more. Just contact details for someone who might be able to help. In the first instance it's supposed to be me making contact, so apologies if it feels a bit high drama, but that was your dad's way — he just gave you a bit of the puzzle and left it there. I have no idea who these people are. Just that they have a bit of clout. I've never called on them and it was set up a few years ago. Maybe they've moved on."

He scribbled a note to himself. "While we're thinking of Betty, what do you want to do if you end up being held overnight? As you know they can hold you for twenty-four hours on the basis of your arrest. Have you contacted Justin?"

"Yes. I gave them his details when they brought me here. As far as I'm concerned, Betty shouldn't spend a minute longer here than necessary. It may be Justin already has her. Which is good."

"How are you two, by the way?"

"He's angry with me. Says it's my being in the force that put Betty and Mum in danger. But his feelings towards me would never stop him being there for Betty."

"Good. If things pan out for the worst, I'll get in touch with him. Let him know he's boss for a while."

She burst into tears. Paul patted her hand gently until she regained her composure. Wiping her eyes, she apologised. "It's been a bad day."

"Today is just the first round," said Paul. "The next fight is going to be the toughest. Something is going on here, something we can't see at the moment. But I'd bet my house it has something to do with your dad. So, from now on, be very, very careful. Keep Harry close and Betty closer. I won't pretend that we don't have a tough time ahead. But we can put a formidable defence together, and we have time. Time to get you an excellent barrister and, most important, time for you to be with your daughter."

CHAPTER 9

For the second time that day Martha had her eyes shut tight as she held her daughter close. When she finally let go of Betty, she saw that any hopes of a truce with Justin were premature. Although he was doing a good job of containing it in front of their daughter, he was radiating anger.

An argument was the last thing she needed. She was bone weary after such a long and exhausting day. She'd finally been released on police bail after handing over her clothes and shoes for forensic analysis. Harry had done the same, and they had both been told they still faced questioning. Now back home, she realised the day wasn't over. "Could you guys keep an eye on Betty for a moment?" she asked Harry and Paul. "Justin and I have things to discuss in the kitchen."

Not waiting for a response, she headed down the corridor with her ex-husband close behind. He closed the door.

"What were you thinking?" He sounded furious. "Betty could have been killed."

"I got her back, Justin. It was the only way. The police—"

"The police have teams of people, trained negotiators, which you know." He tugged at his hair. "You don't have to solve everything yourself, Martha. It's bad enough that her grandma was killed, she could have lost you as well. I can't

45

believe you just charged off, not after we'd already talked about the danger you put her — and yourself — in by being in the force."

She'd expected shouting — she might have coped with pure anger, but this was so much worse. Justin had tears in his eyes and was speaking in a low voice that told of his own exhaustion. She couldn't fight back. He wasn't saying anything that she hadn't rebuked herself for already. They were only standing a few feet apart, yet it might have been a chasm, until they both realised the same thing. They each saw their own grief and fear reflected in the other's eyes, and suddenly the tension went out of the room.

"Oh, poor Mum." Martha slumped against the counter. "It doesn't feel real. Has Betty said anything about . . . Did she see . . . ?"

"No. She was in her room when it happened. She heard Grandma shouting and a bang, so she guessed something bad happened. Then 'the scary men' came up and found her, and carried her out."

"Did they hurt her?"

"No — but they frightened her. She didn't dare make a noise. They gave her lots of sweets, which she didn't dare to eat, and she was alone for a long time. Then some other people — she calls one of them 'the nice lady' — came and took her to another house, and after that you were there."

Paul popped his head around the door. "Got a minute?" he asked. "There's something you should see."

Betty was drawing, very focused. The image she was working on was frightening, even in its childish form: a small girl and a woman, alongside a monstrously large man.

"Who's that, Betty?" asked Martha. But she knew. Even before Betty spoke, she knew.

"That's the big man and the nice lady. They left me in that room just before you came."

So that was them — the people who had hired her mother's killers, the people who had stolen her child. It wasn't much, but it was something. She'd get the bastards, somehow.

It seemed as if looking at the picture had made something click for Justin, that Betty's drawing was making him see things differently. "That man could have hurt our little girl. Maybe you and Harry are right after all."

* * *

Martha and Harry were on bail as the police waited for the results of the forensic tests. She had the added indignity of being suspended, albeit on full pay. She spent the days that followed in a bubble dominated by Betty. She was alert to even the smallest signs of trauma in her daughter and kept a sharp lookout for strangers in the neighbourhood. She even contemplated a new security system until she realised that the house already boasted a top-of-the-range model. Going any further would make her feel like she was hiding behind barricades. Justin's home system was quite different, and he readily agreed to an upgrade. She was giving nobody a chance to finish the job.

After a week she was back at Brixton police station, with Paul sitting alongside her. She was expecting a long wait, so was pleasantly surprised when a man and a woman appeared quickly. The woman, Detective Inspector Mary Holland, was in charge. Her colleague, a middle-aged detective constable, was there to carry the files and a plastic bag containing Martha's trainers, which, after a nod from the DI, he placed in the middle of the table.

DI Holland tapped the bag in a proprietorial manner. "These are very interesting, very interesting indeed. Would you like to know why?"

Before Martha could respond, Paul jumped in. "My client would like you to act in a professional manner. Not like a ham actor."

The DC erupted in a choking cough, earning him a narrow-eyed look from his boss. *You're going to be pulling night duty for a while*, thought Martha.

The DI carried on as if there had been no interruption. "Our preliminary checks have revealed blood on your

47

trainers, which matches to Hristo Dragov. Mr Dragov remains in hospital, where he is recovering from severe injuries sustained when he was savagely beaten.

"In previous interviews you have confirmed you found the Dragov brothers in the flat in Peckham. You claim they were beaten before you arrived and that you did not contribute to their injuries. In the light of this new evidence, perhaps you might like to amend your statement?"

The solicitor put a hand on Martha's arm to stop her responding. "I'm not sure what you are driving at," said Paul. "This new discovery — I can't call it evidence — seems to be very thin. The fact that a tiny amount of blood has been discovered on her shoe is hardly a smoking gun.

"From the crime-scene pictures we saw previously, there was blood everywhere. My client could have easily stepped in some. But that does not in any way undermine her statement that she did not harm either brother. If that is all you have, then I suggest you're wasting my client's time. I also note that you haven't found any blood on my client's clothing, at least not that you've mentioned. Perhaps it's time to look elsewhere for the real culprit."

The DI put her hands on the table, almost as a steadying gesture. "Our investigation continues and your cooperation is appreciated. That's all for now. You may go."

Martha didn't wait for any more — she was on her feet, ready to be escorted out. The DI led the way, and as the pair emerged into an empty corridor she hissed at Martha, "Don't think this is over." Then she was gone, leaving her underling to sign Martha and Paul out.

Outside, Martha enjoyed the calming sensation of the sun on her face. The incident, which she relayed to Paul, had been unsettling.

He listened intently. "This proves you're right. Someone wants you out of the way. That blood on the shoes bit was the thinnest 'evidence' I've ever heard. But I get a horrible feeling they may pursue it; they may try to charge you."

"That would be ridiculous," said Martha. "They've got no evidence, no witness, no CCTV — not that they mentioned. Surely no prosecutor will take that up."

Paul frowned. "Ordinarily I would agree with you. But after what that DI just said to you, I'm worried. Are they trying to get you in court any way they can? What do they have to gain? I hate it when you know the other side are up to something but you can't tell what."

* * *

A few days later she had a totally different priority. Her mum's body was released quickly. Elaine Munro had been an avowed humanist and hadn't wanted people to make a fuss. But she was also the widow of Commander John Munro. Old colleagues of her dad had got in touch with Martha and told her they would be there. In the end, more than three hundred people attended, most of whom she didn't know.

At the reception, she lost count of the number of people who had come up to her and told her she was "just like her dad". He would have been "proud" of the way she went to protect her family, they told her. By the end of the afternoon, she was exhausted and grateful to bid farewell to the last mourner.

After she had walked home with Betty, Lucy and Harry, the three adults opened a bottle of wine and drank a toast to her mum, and shared a meal of fish fingers, chips and beans with Betty.

The next morning, Martha woke up feeling better than she had done for weeks. She'd been experiencing a sense of dread on waking, but that had gone. She felt ready to get her life back on track, which was just as well because Harry turned up mid-morning with a pair of boxing gloves, some heavy-duty pads and a plan.

"Time to work on those boxing skills," he told her. "It'll be perfect for letting off steam and burning off a few calories."

She laughed, but then she realised he was serious.

"I'm not saying you're overweight, mind," he added. "I mean it's time to get in fighting trim."

"For prison, you mean."

Harry's eyes were sad. "I don't like to scare you . . ."

". . . but you want me to think ahead."

He was right. She was eating far too many treats, especially wine and chocolate. One drunken evening, she and Lucy had even come up with a recipe for a chocolate pudding with red wine sauce. And that was no preparation for a police officer likely to be jailed soon.

She had to make some changes. Events might be beyond her control, but that didn't mean she was helpless. There were questions she couldn't answer. Was she doing enough to help Betty? Would the people who had hired Betty's kidnappers return to finish the job? And, above all, why had they taken her?

The almost schizophrenic way the police were dealing with her helped her position. On one hand, she was being treated as a person of interest. On the other, she was being given updates about how the investigation into the attack on her home was progressing. Just as she was starting to hope the case against her was going away, she and Harry were both called in for more questioning.

* * *

They arrived at Brixton police station a few minutes before 10 a.m. the next day, the gloomy morning weather mirroring Martha's mood. Martha went in first, along with Paul, and they found DI Holland and her bag-carrier waiting. The DI seemed remarkably pleased with herself, which put Martha on her guard.

"If it's OK with you and your solicitor, let's get right to it, shall we? There's no need to delay. You'll be pleased to hear that Hristo Dragov has pulled through and last night was given the medical all-clear to give us a statement. He and

50

his brother have identified you as the person who inflicted a savage beating on the younger brother." She nodded at the DC, who handed over copies of the statement. "As you can see, they are in no doubt. They were defenceless and you brutally attacked them. I will give you and your solicitor half an hour to read this. It's quite short."

With the air of someone who feels their work is done, she was gone. Paul and Martha read in silence.

"This is total rubbish," Martha said, setting the papers down. "I did threaten them, but I made no physical contact. They'd been attacked before we got there. Think about it, they'd have found blood spatter on my clothes if I'd carried out the beating."

Paul finished his third reading. "This is their word against yours. And there is something that fits with the idea that you are being set up."

Martha looked at him expectantly.

"It's the way that the brothers only mention you. Someone reading this in isolation would have no idea that Harry was there at all."

Deep frown lines appeared on Martha's forehead. "I was too busy reading about my so-called 'starring role'. But you're right. What's that about?"

"I don't know, I'll need to think about it. It certainly improves Harry's prospects. How can he be charged if the only witnesses don't even mention him? He might as well be a ghost."

A short while later, Martha was on the pavement outside the police station waiting for Paul and Harry. On the solicitor's advice neither had answered any further questions, something which was greeted with indifference by DI Holland, who promptly confirmed they remained on police bail.

The two men appeared. Harry summed up the mood. "This is all messed up. Someone is so determined to get at Martha it's as though they don't care that a woman was murdered and a little girl kidnapped. It's a bloody disgrace."

CHAPTER 10

Throughout this period, Martha was kept on a rolling suspension, confirmed each month by her superintendent. After the second month, a man and a woman from HR visited her. There was something about them that put her on her guard, even before they told her she was now on full suspension until the investigation was over.

The woman took the lead. She showed no sympathy, going straight for the jugular. "Given your vigilante tendency, you are not to speak to any police officers. We don't need to see you get embroiled in unsavoury incidents. The Met is eager to be seen as above the fray. You'll need to be interviewed once the charges against you are finalised. Should you be found guilty, you will be stripped of your position and lose all benefits, including your pension."

The woman's lip curled. "Of course, it is possible you will either avoid being charged, or even avoid being found guilty by a jury of your peers." At this, the sneer grew more intense. "Should that happen, I need to remind you that you will still face an internal disciplinary hearing — which could result in your dismissal from the force and the loss of all entitlements."

She produced a flat stare; she was determined to have her say. "Officers like you, who think the rules are for others, drag the force down. The Met would be a better place without you. You should consider resigning."

Martha was not easily intimidated, but this performance hit the spot. It was as though she was getting colder and colder, to the point where she was frozen in her seat. She said nothing, avoiding eye contact with either of the pair as they stood up and left. She felt as alone and friendless as she had on the day her mum died.

She checked the time. Almost time to collect Betty from school. She had to get herself together. Despite trembling hands, she managed to make herself a coffee, enjoying the warming feeling as she drained her mug. The familiar ritual worked its magic, and she grew more focused by the minute. That woman had crossed a line and Martha was going to do something about it.

To her relief, Paul Avery answered the call straight away. When she explained her situation, he was outraged. "They cannot do that. They've effectively told you the Met has decided you're guilty, no matter what the jury says. Do me a favour and make a detailed note of what you can remember — as soon as possible."

They agreed to speak again the following morning — he was clearing his diary to give the matter his full attention — and, just before ringing off, he offered some reassurance. "This shows they're worried about you. And so they should be. This HR woman has made a major tactical mistake."

As Martha gathered her things, her phone beeped with a WhatsApp message. She didn't recognise the sender.

The message was brief: *You have more friends than you know.*

CHAPTER 11

That night, Martha tossed and turned until the early hours. Far from comforting her, the message raised a whole new set of questions. She needed support — but who were these friends? Former colleagues of her father? Or was it a trick — a message from Betty's kidnappers?

At 4 a.m. Martha gave up on sleep. She was going over and over the same territory, and she needed to give herself a break. Hot tea and CNN proved to be a calming mix. She wasn't really worried about the ins and outs of Washington politics, but the steady chatter of the glossy presenters served as a distraction. Martha couldn't begin to understand the effort that went into looking so sleek.

Just after 6 a.m., her phone rang. It was Lucy. "Hey, sweetie. I haven't been able to sleep either, and I saw your downstairs light come on a few hours ago. Are you ready for some company?"

Martha said yes without hesitation, and minutes later was enjoying the warm embrace of her friend. She guided Lucy to the kitchen. "I'll put the kettle on. Then you can tell me what's been keeping you awake."

Lucy, who was wearing a pink dressing gown over a knee-length top, was smiling.

"Just one of those restless nights — couldn't switch off. If we're both going to be awake, we might as well do it together — and I was so worried about you."

Martha laughed. "Let me get this straight: you were worried about something, saw my lights on and decided I was worried, so you came round here to worry about me."

Lucy shrugged. "That sounds about right." She held her mug up in a salute. "Cheers, Martha. Live long and prosper."

Martha returned the salute. "Make it so, Number One. Make it so." She looked around. "Do you ever wish you were out there, exploring the final frontier?"

Lucy nodded. "You can always rely on *Star Trek* to make the world feel like a better place."

She's right, thought Martha. Even their brief exchange had lifted the atmosphere. On impulse, she opened the WhatsApp message and handed her phone to Lucy.

"That's what's been keeping me awake."

Lucy's forehead crinkled as she read the message. "So, tell me why it's worrying you?"

"Well, it's good news, right? I've got friends. Lots of friends. So why is this one hiding their identity? And worse still, if I have lots of friends, does that mean I have loads of enemies?" Martha grimaced. "Actually, I need to rephrase that. I know I have enemies. What I mean is, does this mean I have even more enemies than I realised? And what do these 'friends' want from me? The more I try to make sense of it, the worse it gets."

Lucy raised her eyebrows. "I can see why you're wide awake . . . Have you mentioned it to anyone, like that lawyer, Paul Avery? I know he's working on your case." She drank more tea. "I met him here a couple of years ago when he came to see your mum. She asked me to watch Betty. This was when you were at work. I liked him. He was easy to talk to." Lucy shrugged. "At the time you were still furious with your dad. I thought that, if I mentioned the conversation, you'd have likely bitten my head off. After that, I just forgot about it. After all, he was here to see your mum."

"Yes, I take your point." She put her hand to her mouth. "My dad was a terrible one for secrets. I remember one conversation we had. I joked that he would avoid telling you what he had for lunch. To which he said, a bit weirdly, 'Paul Avery knows where a lot of bodies are buried.' I had no idea what he meant. I didn't want to be in on any of his secrets. Not then, at least." Martha paused. "I'm talking to Paul this morning, so I can ask him outright. It might help — but, knowing my dad, it will be one of his tricks, something he said to confuse the issue."

* * *

Later that morning she and Paul ran through her meeting with the HR team over the phone, and he congratulated her on the detailed notes she'd emailed to him.

"Your notes will stand up nicely in court as they were made contemporaneously, while the meeting was fresh in your mind. It was an obvious attempt to strong-arm you out of the police. But she made a real hash of it — showing her hand too clearly and opening up the possibility of you claiming compensation."

Paul said he would write to the Met that day, demanding an apology and a full retraction. "That should make them choke," he added, sounding so gleeful Martha could imagine him rubbing his hands together.

He was on the point of ending the call when Martha decided the time was right. "Paul, I received a message yesterday saying I had 'friends'. Nothing else, just that. I couldn't decide what to make of it. But, for some reason, the message reminded me of a conversation I once had with Dad about his love of secrets. In typical John Munro fashion, he muttered something about you, Paul Avery, knowing where the bodies were buried. I never followed up on it, but, like I said, it came back to me. It might have been Dad playing games — but does it mean anything to you?"

There was a long silence before Paul responded in the very deliberate manner he used when he was thinking hard.

"As we discussed recently, your dad left me with a contact number to call in case you were ever in deep trouble. Presumably this is a response to my call, although I've heard nothing directly — I was just put through to an answer machine. That's the way your dad liked things. There's stuff I have sight of, but plenty I don't. Maybe I should have told you earlier, but you had enough on your plate without me adding to the mix. I'll come over to your place later and talk face to face. It might take a couple of hours; there's a lot to get through."

* * *

Martha spent the next half-hour pacing around the house, too full of adrenaline to sit still. Her mind was a whirl. Did this mean that Paul was finally going to unlock the puzzle that was her dad, John Munro? The lawyer clearly knew more about her dad than she did.

John Munro had been a complex man, at times warm and generous, at others cold and withdrawn. The worst times were those rare moments when he was scared. He never talked about it, or admitted it, but sometimes she could tell that something was rattling him, despite him putting on a show that all was well.

Martha had mentioned it to her mother, but she'd always dismissed the suggestion, even if the answer always felt too readily prepared, as if she had agreed it with her husband. And that was odd, because they rarely agreed about anything and would always argue if they were together for any length of time.

The closest she had come to the truth was when she'd announced that she wanted to join the Metropolitan Police, not long after her father's death. Her mother had been instantly and adamantly against the idea, only backing down in the face of Martha's determination.

"You're so like him, in some ways. He could never shy away from a challenge — and, believe me, you are facing a challenge."

At this point, she had clammed up. Martha pushed and pushed, but all she got was an enigmatic, "I've said too much already."

Others were far keener to talk about him. At her first Met interview, Martha had been questioned about him, and in every part of the process she was asked again. It didn't matter that she'd told them each time: "My dad wasn't interested in me and I'm not interested in him." It was only a few years ago, and she could vividly remember the final interview, when she faced the most aggressive questioning of all. Was she joining the force because of her father? Did she know any of his old colleagues? Were any still in touch with him?

The interviewer, a detective chief inspector, couldn't disguise his eagerness. She had answered honestly: her father had always maintained a strict distance between work and family.

After the interview, Martha had tried to put the whole thing out of her head. But why, she wondered, was anyone concerned about who her dad was talking to?

It didn't seem fair. This was stuff for the top brass, for men and women with decades more experience than she could call on. So Martha did what she'd always done: she kept her head down and was extremely careful not to use the name of John Munro, shrugging and smiling when colleagues tried to discuss him. She was quite determined about it. After all, she was her father's daughter, not her father. Surely people couldn't hold that against her, could they?

Martha checked the time; a whole thirty-five minutes had passed. Her instinct was telling her in no uncertain terms that unpicking this mystery was the key to discovering who had ordered the attack on her home. Her father had made many enemies during his career, whereas hers had barely begun. Had one of those enemies instigated the moves that led to her mother's murder?

Everything was linked, including the police's determination to drag her through the courts, no matter how loudly she protested her innocence — and the more she thought about it, the more it showed what she was up against. These were not just hidden enemies, they were powerful people, able to manipulate events at will. She couldn't help wondering if Commander Peter Shaw was involved. He kept saying he was a friend of her father's. He used to be, as far as she knew, but did that count anymore? She shook her head. She had so many questions and maybe she would get some answers this afternoon.

In the meantime, she would talk to Harry. Like Paul, he knew more than he let on. Well, now was the time for him to come clean, to help her work out what was going on. Her only regret was that it had taken her mum's death and the kidnapping of her daughter to make her investigate her father's secrets.

* * *

She found Harry in his tiny front garden, puffing away on a foul-smelling nicotine inhaler. He said it helped him give up cigarettes.

She laughed. "Don't take this the wrong way — but you're in your mid-seventies, right?"

"Seventy-five, actually. These things matter, especially when you're my age . . . or Betty's."

She waved that away. "What I'm trying to say is that you've smoked like a chimney all your life without the slightest sign of a problem. So why now?"

"Never too late to stop. Did I ever tell you about my old mum? Smoked all her life, twenty a day. She lived to a hundred and four, and died making a cup of tea. She was bending down for the milk in the fridge and had a stroke. Just like that. She was gone." Harry kept a straight face. "That's why I'm giving up tea from next year. You can never be too sure."

"You're pulling my chain. Forget that, though. I have something to ask you."

Martha voiced all of her suspicions, and when she'd finished talking, Harry said, "I've got errands to run. Best bet is

59

that I join your meeting with Paul. I have a few secrets about your dad that I can share. He always said to me I would know when the time was right. It looks like the time is now."

She spent the rest of the afternoon trying not to think about the meeting. It was infuriating. Why did everyone have to be so bloody secretive?

CHAPTER 12

Tension was coming off Paul Avery in waves as he arrived for the meeting. They gravitated towards the kitchen — where Paul helped himself to a ginger biscuit from a plate Martha had just set out. The lawyer kept up a constant stream of chatter, further betraying his nerves.

Exhausting the weather as a topic, he sighed. "Sorry for the non-stop talking. I'll be honest, this is making me more jittery than I'd expected."

Before he could say more, the doorbell rang. Martha went to answer it, reappearing with Harry in tow. Paul was unsurprised to see the former gangster. "It's a good idea for you to be here."

He glanced over at the kitchen table, before opening the back door and walking to a bench at the end of the small garden. They followed him out.

"This is as good a spot as any," he said. "I doubt any microphones could pick us up out here. I'd like to sweep the house for any bugs, then work in the kitchen, where we can't be seen from the road."

Martha was incredulous. She decided Paul wasn't just tense; he had actually flipped. "You must be joking?"

He held his hands up in a curiously defensive posture. "I'm not joking, and maybe I should have suggested this a while ago. Just because your dad died, it doesn't mean his work died with him. I'm probably being overcautious, but better that than the wrong people listen in. Let me check the house and then we can start."

From an inside jacket pocket, he produced something that looked like a large mobile phone with a stubby antenna. He walked into the house. From the garden bench they could see him holding the device in front of him, sweeping the room with a series of slow half-circles.

Martha tried not to laugh. "Isn't he going over the top? I mean, it's all a bit cloak-and-dagger."

Harry didn't answer directly. "I've never told you about the first time I met your dad. I was acting as the muscle at a warehouse where the Johnson brothers had some drugs stashed. It was mostly heroin. Kilos of the stuff — must have been worth millions in today's money. Anyway, your old man was a sergeant in the drugs squad. He'd had us under surveillance for weeks. On the day of the raid, I was outside. Cocksure little git, I was. I never saw your dad, but he crept up on me, whacked me with his truncheon and had me in handcuffs quick as anything. He left me in the back of a squad car and wrapped up the arrests. Then he got in the car with me. He gave me a long look, as though he knew everything there was to know about me, and offered me a deal. Told me that, from now on, I was working for him. He'd get my charge reduced and I'd only have to do a few months inside. All I had to do was agree to be his man from then on.

"Well, inside I was laughing. Dozy plod, I thought, I'll just spin him along and tell him to fuck off once I get out of chokey. He could tell what I was thinking, of course. That was your dad; he could always see through the lies. The point is this: he said, 'You'll do this because you're one of those people who needs more excitement than other people. Working for me will make you a double agent. That should be enough to keep you on your toes. There'll be plenty to do. The world is changing. There's so much money in drugs now, they're attracting some very dangerous people. But I've been looking very closely at you, at the type of man you are. Take the chance to be better than an ordinary gangster, get your blood pumping and surprise yourself by doing some good.'

"I couldn't believe it. That morning, all I'd been expecting to do was guard a pile of smack. Yet here was this copper making an offer I couldn't refuse. He'd read me like a book. Word perfect, he was. Years later, I found out that I have a condition that makes it hard for me to feel fear the way other people do. I needed to live right on the edge just to feel normal. Your dad had worked all that out. And this was years before doctors came up with a fancy name for it. That was the beginning of an amazing friendship — one that started before you were born."

At that moment, Paul reappeared, waving his device. "All clear. Let's go. We should be fine, unless they're using some sort of new technology this thing can't detect."

CHAPTER 13

Paul and Harry sat at the kitchen table while Martha busied herself making drinks. Cold shivers ran down her spine. Had they really believed someone had been listening in to her life with Betty? Unexpected anger surged. What were these two playing at, leaving her so vulnerable?

She put the mugs down stiffly. Her rage was running hot and she didn't trust herself to speak. She might have said nothing, but Harry knew her all too well and sensed how furious she was.

"You're right," Harry said. "I should have said something as soon as you were released, but everyone's been knocked sideways by this. I wasn't thinking straight. Well, today, we can put that right . . . if you can give us the chance. I hope that, when you've heard us out, you'll understand why we made a mistake."

She breathed in through her nose and out of her mouth. The fury was still running deep, but something in his words got through.

She'd known Harry from childhood and would trust him with not just her life, but her daughter's life as well. He was part of her family. Looking at him properly, for the first time in ages, she saw the strain written in the lines on his face. This whole affair had hit him hard. Whatever she said to him, he would always blame himself for her mum's murder.

Fear, grief and overwhelming loss were a toxic mix. She forced herself to relax, dropping her shoulders, unclenching her fists.

"You're right, Harry. We need to talk. The last people in the world I want to fight with are you two." She pointed at Paul's device. "From what you've said already, it might be a good idea if you gave me one of those bug detectors."

Paul grinned. "Have this one. It's almost new and I can order another. I'll show you how it works when I leave."

Peace terms established, she passed around the plate of biscuits.

Paul Avery took a gulp of his tea and put his mug down. "Shall I begin?" He didn't wait for a response. "First, I'm assuming Harry told you how he met your dad?"

She nodded.

"That was John all over. He was a great judge of character and could read people as soon as he met them."

Harry laughed. "That's true. From that day on, he had me working as a snitch. I'd have been killed on the spot if anyone found out, but there was something about your father that stopped me worrying."

Paul took over. "The second thing I need to say is that your dad kept secrets within secrets. My information is based partly on what your dad told me, and partly on what I could piece together from my own sources.

"Let me tell you the first secret. He told me that, one day, you might find yourself in trouble. But he wanted me to react very carefully — told me that if I, or Harry, acted too hastily, we would risk making things worse. John told both of us that we had to wait for a signal, an unmistakable one, that would come when the time was right. He wouldn't say who the signal would be from, how it would be delivered, only that it would say, 'You have friends.' He said that, when that message came, it would offer you hope and tell us the time was right to talk to you."

Martha's anger bubbled up again. "Why couldn't he told me this when he was alive? Not being funny, but you just said you don't know everything and neither does Harry. So rather than tell me what the big secret is, he just left random clues." She clenched her fists and jutted her jaw. "I'd forgotten how infuriating he could be with his secrets within secrets. Go on, then. Let's find out what the great John Munro deemed I could be allowed to know."

"He was quiet for a reason — he wanted to keep you safe. Your father was dealing with the smartest and most dangerous criminals. He was so focused on the very top rung that he ignored the activities of those he thought of as lesser criminals. When I say 'lesser criminals', I'm still talking drug dealers and people traffickers. Bad, bad people."

Her eyes were wide. "I don't understand this at all. He was the head of the anti-corruption team, famous for putting away more bent coppers than anyone before or since. He was so good that the top brass worried he was undermining the Met in the eyes of the public." Sweat beaded on her brow. She was talking so fast the words almost merged. "But you're telling me this paragon of policing virtue was turning a blind eye to some real scumbags?"

Paul was sympathetic. "Your dad was a one-off. Yes, he was the man who hunted down corrupt cops. But he did more than that. He went after the very crime lords who were using their wealth to bribe and corrupt police officers. To borrow a phrase, he was tough on corruption and tough on the causes of corruption. But never forget how different he was from most police officers. Most cops, present company excluded, love the moment they make an arrest — the big collar. Don't get me wrong, he loved to nab villains, but if it suited his purposes he was willing to let someone else get all the credit.

"Your dad was in some ways waging a war, one in which he decided who the enemy was. He picked out criminals he could use as double agents, let some go free, even keep their dirty money, if they supplied him with information. In fact, Harry was the first person he did this with."

Martha was frowning. This was tough to hear, but she needed to know more.

Paul took a gulp of tea. "Now it gets complicated. He got away with his methods for a while, but eventually word circulated about what he was up to. At that point, some serious people, on both sides of the law, started paying him extra attention. Some criminals planted their own people, bent cops, into his team. It made him more secretive, and he began refusing to share information. This grated with the most senior Scotland Yard people, and pressure was applied to force him out."

Martha shook her head. "I had no idea. No idea at all. I thought they hated him because of his anti-corruption work. This is way beyond that. But if he was letting some people escape justice, was he on the take himself?"

"He never took a penny." Paul was emphatic. "He was the most honest man you could meet. Too honest, really. He argued that you could never catch every criminal or corrupt police officer, so it was better to focus on a handful of the big players — which reminds me of something your dad let out. He said to always remember that those with real power like to operate from the shadows. He didn't often give things away, but that day I got the sense he was locked in a struggle with a real player, someone who really got under his skin. I think he hated this person but could never lay a finger on him. Your dad didn't name him, I don't know why, but he did say he was very clever, always thinking several steps ahead. I probably should say 'is' clever. He — I know it was a man — may still be around. It's not impossible that with your dad gone, he has you in his sights. If John Munro was worried about him, we should be too."

"I've never heard of this man, whoever he is," said Martha. "Mind you, it wouldn't be the first time my dad kept something from me. Probably through some misguided notion that he was doing me a favour."

Paul held his hands up. "You're not alone in that. I have a few more bits. Your dad told me this bloke is also

67

very rich, so whenever journalists come sniffing around, he unleashes his own army of people like me. He's known as Mr Untouchable."

"You're getting quite close to describing a candidate for orchestrating this campaign against me," said Martha. "I just wish we had a name for this criminal genius."

Paul gave a short, harsh laugh. "How about we call him the Moriarty to your dad's Sherlock Holmes. We could talk about this mystery man all day, but until we know who he is, there's nothing to be added. I think we need to keep him at the back of our minds and focus on what we do know."

Martha gestured for him to carry on.

"Shortly before your dad died, he began to look beyond the police. He was confident he could find evidence to show that judges, MPs and more were on the take — even MI5.

"It was a problem that can be traced back to the early nineties, when there was a lot of illicit money swimming around. From drug smugglers, to people traffickers and money launderers, a river of cash flowed in. It was so big it simply shrugged off the broader downturn in the financial markets. In turn, this fuelled a massive expansion of smuggling gangs led by people who understood business principles. They had always been ruthless, but now the crime lords started copying the style of the most successful chief executives. They understood that change was needed if they wanted to protect their lucrative investments. Police corruption has always been a fact of life, but mostly it was low level: back handers and the like. Then it moved to industrial-scale bribery with one aim in mind — find out what the police actually knew by penetrating their security. The best way to look after their business interests was to gain as much intelligence as they could — in this case, from the police. There will be criminal plants around even now who joined the police in the mid-nineties. A few years later and they were in all sorts of jobs, and at every level. I'm not saying there are hundreds of crooked officers, but a small number in strategically important jobs makes a huge difference.

"Your dad was the first one to put it all together, and that put him in a dangerous position, although at first he didn't grasp how much of a predicament he was in. The more he scratched away at the layers of criminality, the more he became noticed. It was ironic, really. Over the years the bad guys observed him more intently than his own side. It's clear that his own family was considered fair game.

"He couldn't go to his superior officers because he couldn't be sure who was crooked. He needed to find a way to take the spotlight off him, and thus his family . . . you and your mum, to be preci—" Paul paused. "Rightly or wrongly, he set up his own team of loyal officers. All personally recruited by your dad and all sworn to secrecy. During one of our meetings, I once jokingly called it John's Army. He was furious. Told me that loose talk could kill. He said we should never underestimate how clever the gang bosses were. They were constantly on the hunt for infiltrators."

Harry looked solemn. "The crime lords were actually carrying out counter-surveillance, using people with proper training — ex-MI5, that kind of thing. As Paul said, money was no object. At first, their methods were successful at picking out who was a police infiltrator. Then your father turned the tables on them. He started laying false trails that pointed the hunters in the wrong direction. Instead of finding police infiltrators, they ended up targeting their own people without realising they were being tricked."

Martha was gripped. This was a side of her father she never knew. "When you say 'target', you mean kill, don't you? You're telling me that was on my dad's head. That must have been a burden for him to carry around."

Harry raised his hands. "It sounds bad, but you have to remember who we're talking about. People willing to smuggle children or women to be used as sex slaves. Rape and murder were all part of the scene. And they were only ever killed by their own side. They got what they deserved. I never lost a minute's sleep over it . . . and neither should you. As much as it did weigh down on your dad, he held to his convictions. He never lost sight of what was the right thing to do."

"Don't think that your father was some sort of vigilante. He was much more than that. He was a disruptor who was able to create confusion, distrust and downright hostility," Paul went on. "It kept attention away from what he and his team were up to in other areas. That allowed him to isolate some of the traitors within the force, saving countless lives along the way. It also reduced the risk you and your mum would be attacked.

"His determination to keep you safe can be traced back to the moment you were born. One of his enemies tried to pounce when your mum was ill, just after having you."

Martha was shocked. "When I was a newborn? I didn't know she was sick."

"Typical of your mum not to say. She was just as tough as John. It was a difficult birth, and she was in a bad way. Your dad was so worried. Harry was the hero of the hour."

Martha was seeing her father in a different light. This was filling in some of the missing details, the information she was going to need if she was to ever understand why he'd made the choices he had. He'd sanctioned people being murdered. OK, they were bad people, but it was still a revelation that left her conflicted. Harry had done a decent job of insisting the criminals deserved to die, and she could certainly empathise with the powerful urge to protect your family. Hadn't she just been motivated by the same thing with Betty? But did the end always justify the means? She needed more time to process that. Part of her wondered if she was intruding into something best left alone.

"I really hope you've got your cigarettes on you, Harry."

He grinned. "After all the grief you've given me over the years, I really should say no."

She laughed. "Come on, hand them over."

He passed her a pack of Marlboro Lights and his beloved Zippo lighter and followed her into the back garden. Martha lit up, inhaling the strong, bitter flavour as she took her first drag on a smoke in eighteen months. She had never really liked the taste, but she loved the buzz that the nicotine gave her. "Go on, then. Tell me why you were playing the hero when I was born."

Harry stared at the ground for a long moment then took a deep drag on his cigarette before carefully blowing the smoke into the air. "I don't know about hero, but I suppose it was just as well your dad made such a fuss about me being around. One of the gang leaders was on to him and wanted revenge. The word was they were coming for your mum, and maybe you as well. Hospitals are funny places; they can be great for targeting someone. Pop on a blue gown and it's an instant disguise.

"I told him no one would go after a copper's family. It would cause too much trouble. But he got angry with me — quite unusual for him — and told me the danger was all too real."

Harry took a sip of tea and Martha noticed his eyes were bright. Even now, all these years later, the emotion was still strong.

"He would not be talked out of it, so I promised. I took a book with me, thinking I would get bored on guard duty, but he'd got under my skin and I was restless. No time for reading. The nurses took the mickey. I couldn't sit still. I was pacing up and down outside the room you were both in."

He smiled. "On the first evening, I went in to check on you. You were both sound asleep. Then you snuffled. I can tell you it gave me an almighty shock! I actually jumped. It was so quiet in there and, suddenly, you surprised me."

He looked at her. "You're still surprising me now."

Martha smiled.

"After that, I went back to my seat outside where I could see the door. It was 3 a.m. when the killer almost got you. I was sort of dozing when this doctor appeared with a clip-board and walked inside. I was just drifting into a semi-doze when I did a double-take.

"He was wearing a blue overall and had a stethoscope, so he looked the part — in every way except one . . . his shoes.

71

He was wearing a pair of heavy brogues, really solid. Nearly every other member of staff chose more comfortable shoes, like trainers. Well, my body reacted faster than my brain. I ran in. He already had a pillow over your mum's face, pressing down. She was out cold anyway — couldn't put up a fight. I had a cosh on me, so I walloped him and he dropped like a sack of potatoes. I got him into the janitor's cupboard and left him tied up.

"When I went back to check on both of you, you were fast asleep with a great big smile on your face. Like you approved of what was happening. After that, I called your dad and he turned up with a couple of bruisers. They took the bloke away. He wasn't going to be having much fun."

Martha shook her head. "I wish they'd told me all this. What happened next? Did they try again?"

"Your dad made sure that was an end to it. A month later they found a body in the Thames. It was the gang leader your dad held responsible."

CHAPTER 14

Even the weather was taking its cue from the mood around the table. The previously blue skies had given way to thick, dark clouds. Martha switched the kitchen lights on.

Paul cleared his throat. "If you're feeling sorry for the assassin, then I can tell you what he told your dad: 'Kittens, puppies, babies, wives — it's all the same to me. That's why I earn top dollar. Anyone I get a contract for ends up in a bag.'"

Even in a day of shocks, the casual cruelty of his words would stick with her.

"Dad must have been beside himself with anger. Can you recall the mood he was in when he came to discuss this with you?" If Martha was going to accept her father as a cold-blooded killer, practically a vigilante, she was going to need these details about his humanity — she'd always accepted Harry as a take-no-prisoners criminal enforcer. Perhaps it was time to start giving her dad some of the same leeway.

Harry went on. "He was shaking with rage. You won't be surprised to hear this, but the event proved to be the beginning of the end of your parents' marriage. Once you were born, you became the centre of your mother's world. To her, your father's presence was a danger to you. She tried but

73

couldn't shake it off. Your dad started staying away during the week. Then he stopped coming home at the weekend. It took about eighteen months for their marriage to end.

"For a while, your mum asked him to stop visiting. He agreed, though it broke his heart. When he took you out on his own, she would have nightmares about you being hurt. Your father knew all that and, in the end, cut his visits down to a minimum. He blamed himself."

Martha didn't cry easily. She would not start now, but she was having a hard time fighting off the tears.

"For years I thought he never came to see me because he was a crap dad. Now I can see why he hardly ever came — and, when I did see him, why he was so aloof. I thought he couldn't wait for the visit to end."

She put her hand to her mouth. "One summer, he took me to Dulwich Park to get an ice cream. When it was time to leave, he suddenly got a handkerchief out and dabbed at his eyes. I asked him if he was crying and he said no, he just had grit in his eye. There was something about the way he said it that made me think he was lying. That's why I still remember it now. Oh, poor Dad, he must have been so upset."

She dabbed her own eyes with the back of her sleeve. "Thanks for telling me all this. It makes me see him as he really was, warts and all. Losing us was the price he paid to keep his family safe." She paused. "So why the attack now? He's been dead for two years."

The lines on Harry's face stood out in this half-light. "A few years ago, your dad told me he had cancer — he wouldn't say what type. He said you must never give your enemy a name. A bit bonkers, really, but it was his way. He had a year left, no more, and there was some housekeeping that needed doing. He had messages for me and for Paul. From me, he wanted one thing: to keep watch over you and your mum after he was gone. I failed him in that, no matter what you say. I was so caught up in his death that I underestimated his ability to detect things. You see, somehow your father had picked up that things were on the move again and that

74

this could place his family in danger. I should have worked that out."

Harry was carrying far too much, but Martha knew better than to speak. Instead, she patted his hand.

He didn't seem to notice. "He also told me that, if I ever needed to talk to anyone, I should try Paul Avery first."

The lawyer smiled gently. "Always glad to help." He spent a moment examining his shoes. "When your dad first told me about his cancer, Martha, he booked a nice restaurant; you might have thought it was a celebration. John had stopped drinking because the treatment made him feel sick, but he insisted on watching me polish off a couple of glasses of very drinkable red. He had quite a lot of undercover work still running, and it would far outlast him. He told me he'd put Harry on lookout for you, but he deliberately kept some details back because he thought low key was the way to go.

"He also told me two other things. The first was, as you now know, the instruction that, if you received a note saying you had friends, I was to tell you everything. Harry the same. The other thing was an email address. I don't know who it belongs to, or even if it still works, but your father told me I would know when to give it to you. It seems that moment is now."

He produced a card. "Those are the details he left me with. He said the person it belonged to would wait to hear from you."

Martha felt a surge of excitement. It was almost as though her father was reaching out to her himself — from beyond the grave.

"Did he say any more about this mystery figure? If I use that address, how do I know the right person will answer? Is this another police officer? Or maybe someone like Harry . . . a foot in both worlds?"

"All I know is that it's someone he trusted with his life. He said this person had sworn an oath to transfer their allegiance to you, and you could also trust them with your life." Paul puffed out his cheeks. "Your dad also told me you would ask for proof. In fact, what he said was, 'If she doesn't ask, tell her she's no daughter of mine.' He told you to ask them two questions, to make sure they're the right person: first, what name did your parents give you when you first started walking?"

On hearing the question, she went still. She had a powerful memory of being on the floor while her parents laughed.

"And the second question is: the first time you went to Dulwich Park with your dad, something happened that made you both laugh. What was it?"

She smiled at the memory. She turned to the two men but they both leaned back, holding their hands up.

"Don't tell us the answers," said Paul. "Those must stay secret."

She picked up the piece of paper. "What should I say?"

Paul said, "Keep it simple. Tell them who you are. Tell them you're seeking help because of your father. Tell them how they should reply."

There was no more hesitation. She tapped out the message on her iPhone and sent it off.

CHAPTER 15

Martha breathed out a lungful of smoke and sighed. Paul had gone, and now she was standing with Harry in the garden again. "Why are so many of the things I like bad for me?" she asked. "A few years ago, I had to do a lifestyle thing for the doctor. Part of it was to identify the type of food I was eating. I told him the truth — that my favourite food groups were beer, wine and crisps. To balance the books, I tried to start the day with a bowl of bran flakes."

She laughed. "The nurse was appalled and insisted on checking my blood pressure, which was perfect. I wouldn't have minded so much but she was very well padded, so it felt a bit like pots and kettles. To save time, I just lie now. I say it's nothing but vegan nut roast, lots of veg and decaf tea and coffee with almond milk. They all tell me I'm brilliant."

Harry laughed. "You get all that from your old man. John used to insist that going to hospital made you sick. He wouldn't trust a doctor until he got to know them."

Martha stubbed her cigarette out. "He listened to them when it came to smoking, though. I took it up when I was a teenager just to annoy him. The trouble is, I got to like it. I suppose I should stop bumming them off you."

A wistful expression crossed her face. "My mum was forever telling me that, one day, I would understand him better. Now it seems it took her death for me to get there. I just wish I'd known all this when they were alive."

She had always seen her father as a remote, authoritarian figure, steeped in the very heart and soul of law and order. But it turned out he was different, quite different. It was presenting her with a question that had to be addressed if she was going to carry on with this — and the man with the answer was quietly enjoying a fag in her garden.

Martha made herself look directly at the older man. "There is one thing I need to know. Was my dad a vigilante, Scotland Yard's version of Dirty Harry? I know Paul said he wasn't, but I can't quite shake the sense he might have been."

He surprised her with a smile. "Your dad was a complicated man, but he was no vigilante. He didn't go searching for trouble. He would rather see someone go to prison for a long time than die in a shoot-out with police. 'Death by cop', he used to call that. Idiots who think there's glory to be found dying in a hail of bullets instead of serving time.

"He certainly wasn't interested in the local punks. He always went after the organ grinder, never the monkey. That meant he took on the most demanding jobs. The ones where the other side were committed, had weapons and clever leaders. He used to say he was like a surgeon working on the most challenging life-and-death cases. The statistics might show he had a high death rate, but sometimes a high-risk operation is the only option.

"A lot of people didn't get that — or pretended not to. His enemies in the force liked to make out he was a gung-ho cop who took no notice of the law. Nothing could be further from the truth. Sometimes, he was the only thing standing in the way of anarchy. These gang leaders could buy anything apart from John Munro's integrity. Yes, people got hurt along the way. Yes, he broke some rules.

"Sometimes, I wondered how he kept track of who was who, with bad guys pretending to be good guys, and good guys pretending to be bad guys. But he managed it — and when he moved in on someone, they were always big players. The nasty bastards who would kill on impulse, or order someone to do it for them. John was no saint, but he did a lot of good — saved a lot of people like me for a purpose beyond a brutal life of crime."

A lot of the tension had gone out of her. Harry was proving a convincing advocate. She still had doubts; perhaps she always would. How else could it be with a man so complex, a man who had lived so many lives? If Harry had said her dad was without sin, she'd have laughed in his face. Instead, he had treated her with respect, given her the truth, as he saw it, and left her to make up her own mind.

"I can see that would make him stand out in the police. They don't like different. But tell me, Harry, how did you avoid getting tagged as an informant? People must have been worried about you."

Harry raised his eyebrows. "It worked because he was a clever little fucker and I was daft enough to spend a bit of time inside."

"OK. You've got me now. Explain."

"I left the big thinking to your dad. He had to do a lot of that — thinking. Part of what emerged from his brain meant me going off to the chokey every now and then. The first time I went inside, he was so convincing about it being in my best interests that I was sitting in a four-up in Wandsworth before you could say parole."

"A four-up?"

"Like it sounds, a cell with four bunks."

"I can't believe he made you go to prison. It must have been awful."

"I was a believer by then. I'd only drifted into the life because there didn't seem to be much else for a lad like me, from my background. He gave me better money and a sense of purpose. I enjoyed putting really bad people away."

"Did you just say he paid you?"

Harry looked innocent. "Have I never mentioned it before?"

She gave him a flat stare.

"I got a monthly wage, quite a nice one. God knows how he sorted it, and I never asked, but the police paid it. I couldn't live on dreams alone.

"Serving time wasn't too bad. I used the gym to keep fit and learned a few moves from martial arts experts who were also banged up." He paused. "Speaking of which, I'd like to step up your training routine as soon as possible. How about a few proper boxing sessions?"

Despite his words, Martha could see that Harry was exhausted. It must have been as hard for him to talk about her father as it was for her to listen. "Shall we call it a day? My brain is already stuffed to the brim. Any more will just go in one ear and out the other."

Harry stretched and sighed heavily. "Good call." And he left, telling her to ring for any reason.

With her brain gently spinning, Martha decided a little light housework was a good way to slow her thoughts down. She energetically tidied up and loaded the dishwasher and was about to punch the 'on' button when the doorbell sounded. She sighed but went to answer. A small man with a big grin was standing there.

"There's a lady what'd like to see you."

"What . . . ?" she managed to say, before an extremely elegant woman in her late thirties appeared at the gate. She had short black hair, brown eyes and the sort of cheekbones that wouldn't be out of place on a model. She looked at her phone and then at Martha.

"No question: you're the one we want. You've got your mother's looks — and your dad's build. He used to stand like you are now . . . looking like he was about to punch someone."

Martha realised her mouth was hanging open. "Who are you?"

"We're the good guys. The woman you're about to ring is going to confirm it."

CHAPTER 16

"Wait there."

Martha spun on her heel, pulling the front door closed behind her.

"What the fuck?" she asked the mirror in the hallway, deciding it might not surprise her if it answered. Harry had only left a few minutes ago. They must have been waiting and watching to be sure she was alone.

She made her way into the kitchen. Whatever the grinning imp and his companion were up to, she was going to see this through — but first she called Harry. When he heard about the pair who had just shown up, he told her he was on the way back. Now.

Next, she was going to ring the number they had provided. Depending on the answer, they could either come in, or Harry could toss them in the recycling bin.

She tapped in the "secret" number. To her annoyance, her hands were trembling. She gripped the phone tighter.

It was answered on the third ring. "Hello." The voice was female and cultivated — very BBC.

"This is Martha Munro, daughter of John Munro. I've been told to call you."

"And I'm very pleased to hear from you. Before we go on, I believe you have a little test for me, something that will confirm we are both who we say we are."

"I have two questions. What did my parents call me when I was little — before the toddler stage?"

"That would be 'Speedy Gonzales', the fastest baby in South London."

"OK. What happened the first time my dad took me to Dulwich Park?"

"You both had ice cream and sat at a bench to eat it. A big black Labrador sidled up to you and stole your ice cream. The owner was terribly upset, but you thought it was hilarious — especially when you discovered the dog was called Harry, just like your dad's friend."

She relaxed the moment she heard the answers. "So, what happens now?"

"I understand you have many questions. Not least being, why was your mother murdered? I do have some answers for you. But I suggest you invite my two associates inside. Sally's the brains and Quentin's the brawn. They work well together." There was a pause. "I gather your Harry's just returned. You work him hard, just like your dad. Might be best to invite him in as well. Quentin's rather good at his job, but I doubt he's ever encountered someone like Harry."

She didn't bother to ask how she knew Harry was there.

"What happens then?"

"Sally will answer your questions. After that, we should make arrangements to meet."

"But who are you? Who do you work for? How did you know my dad?"

"That will take a long time to explain."

"I've got plenty of time."

A soft laugh came down the telephone line. "If only everything was so simple. Before any of that, I need to decide if you're worth my time and effort. I'm sorry to be blunt — but you speak plainly, and it's refreshing to have someone say what they mean."

"At least tell me your name?"

"Talk to Sally first. Then come to see me — if she agrees. After that, we'll have that talk." There was another chuckle.

Martha was finding this irritating. She was about to say something sarcastic, but bit it back. Her father had gone to the trouble of creating access to this woman, and it was just possible she held the key to finding out who was behind her mother's murder.

"Many people who have come to know my name learn to regret it," the woman went on, steel-voiced. "Your father was a great man and I owe him many favours — so let's not rush things until we're sure about each other. That way, if things don't quite work out, we both get to walk away . . . safely."

The line went dead. It was a warning: all bets were off if she wasn't up to scratch. So this was her potential saviour. She shuddered. Maybe she should step away now; after all, she was running the risk of turning Betty into an orphan.

Her hands were sweating. Part of her was hoping the uninvited pair had disappeared, meaning she didn't have to deal with them. But they were still where she'd left them, with Harry standing close behind them and very much in their space.

She jutted her chin at her two uninvited guests. "I need to check on my daughter. She'll be worried about what's going on. So, if you could give me twenty minutes, I'm sure Harry could be persuaded into making you some tea."

He winked, and she relaxed. Harry always seemed to make things better just by being there.

CHAPTER 17

Walking into Lucy's house was like wrapping herself in a blanket of normality — one that smelled of freshly baked cakes. Giving Martha a quick hug, Lucy was beaming and relaxed. An appraising look followed this and an even bigger hug.

"You need a slice of the chocolate cake we just finished making. It was for you anyway, but now I get to have a slice too."

Martha smiled warmly. "That sounds like a perfect idea. I take it my little princess is watching TV?"

"She is, but to be fair, we got back from school about an hour ago."

Martha spoke in an undertone. "Anything out of the ordinary on your way home? Anyone watching the school?"

"No, I kept checking just like you said, and it was all fine, but . . . Martha," Lucy said, "if you're so worried that someone might try to take Betty again, why not get the police involved?"

"I have tried. They won't help. The school seems safe to me — they've got metal detectors and high fences — but the journey there and back . . . that's the weak point." She looked around the homely kitchen. "And here, I guess. I'm putting you in danger. I'm sorry I asked you."

"Try stopping me."

Betty was lying on her tummy on the floor, head angled up so she could see the TV.

"Mummy!" she shouted. She jumped up to give her mother a hug, her third in as many minutes. This was more like it. Betty thrust a piece of paper at Martha. "See, Mummy, you're the princess and you're saving everyone from the bad wolf."

The drawing showed a blonde woman wielding a sword as a dog-like creature ran away.

"That's lovely, darling. It looks just like me."

Her daughter beamed. "I made you a cake as well."

"I've just heard about it. Lucy's going to slice it up for us now. Do you want some? As long as you've had your tea."

The little girl nodded, suddenly serious. "I had fish fingers and chips with ketchup — my favourite. We've been waiting for you to come and eat cake."

The cake was great. Thick, gooey chocolate over perfect sponge. She declared it the best she'd ever eaten. Betty filled the space with bright chatter about school.

It was exactly what Martha needed. There were several points today at which she thought she had reached her limit — but she had kept going and that's what she resolved to do now.

"Are you two OK for a bit longer?"

Betty voted with her feet by grabbing her iPad and heading to the sitting room.

"As soon as I finish, are you up for a glass of wine?" Martha asked Lucy.

"If you're buying, I'm drinking."

CHAPTER 18

Sally and Quentin had made themselves comfortable in the kitchen. Sally moved with a feline grace — unlike Quentin, who was short with broad shoulders, making it easy to imagine him having to turn sideways to get through doors. He didn't so much move as barge his way around.

"This is a nice little scene," he said. "Like we're all playing a game of happy families."

Sally made an odd snorting noise. "I can't see your Harry here coming top in a competition to find the cuddliest grandfather. There's not many people Quentin is careful around, but your man is one of them."

Harry didn't react to that. Martha felt an odd sense of pride that he was worthy of respect from these two. While she still had no idea about their true capabilities, she was confident they would not be pushovers.

Sally was coldly appraising her. "Please, I know this is your home, but sit down. I've read the file about you. You're a woman who appreciates directness. As do I."

Martha shrugged and took a seat. There was no point in arguing the toss. Right now, this woman held all the cards, and it would be best to allow her to play them.

"Sally and Quentin — not your actual names, I take it?"

"They'll do for now." The woman gave her a hooded look. "We're not here to worry about labels. My job is to talk to you and get some feel for who you are. I don't pretend to be an expert on this. You don't need to watch your body language, and I don't do any of that tracking where people look. Up, down, left, right. Do it all. Makes no difference to me. So if you were planning a little display of special behaviour . . . I wouldn't bother.

"Now, as I understand it from my boss, her message last night means that Harry and Paul have filled you in on a few details. So here's the first question: what do you make of your dad after today? Has your view changed? Take your time. There's no rush."

Martha almost didn't answer. It was impertinent of a total stranger to walk into her home and ask questions like that. But if she was serious about getting more information, she was going to have to come up with something.

She kept her reply as neutral as she dared. "I'm a bit confused right now. But, above all, I have a much better understanding of him. I realise his depth of passion and his bravery in facing up to the choices he did. The rest? The rest will need time to process. Whoever said we're all flawed got it right."

Sally nodded. "We all carry the seeds of our own destruction," she murmured, just loud enough for Martha to hear. "I'd say that was a decent answer. I'll be honest with you, it's one that my employer is particularly keen to know how you answered. She's concerned that you might be a little rigid in your thought processes. It's important to be able to see the big picture, not to get bogged down in the details."

"I've learned quite a bit about both Harry and my dad today. It's safe to say that neither got distracted by outside influences."

Sally went on. "Do you have any thoughts about what happened to your mum?"

Martha was growing hot. "Aren't you here to tell me about that? But since you ask — I'm angry, really fucking

87

angry. I'm angry they killed her. I'm just as angry that it was an accident. I'm livid that my employers are blaming me and I can't believe that they're still having a go at my dad, even now. After all this time."

Martha took a breath before ploughing on. "But, most of all, I'm angry that Betty is going to grow up without knowing her grandparents."

Sally kept a straight face. "I have another question. What about your ex? Does he have a role to play with your daughter?"

"Justin has been brilliant since it all happened. He's done anything he could to make it easier for Betty. He drops his own work at a moment's notice to pick her up from school or just spend time with her. He's proved he's a brilliant dad. And I'm glad." Her final comment acted as a full stop to any more questions on the subject.

Sally sat back. "Sorry about that. I do have my reasons for asking but I don't intend this to be a marriage therapy gig. Shall we move on?" Martha got the clear sense that Sally was fishing, but what for? She held that thought as Sally carried on. "Going back to the crime. What are your conclusions about who's behind it?"

Martha took a long time with this one. She did have some thoughts, and none of them good. She almost didn't want to voice her fears out loud — just in case they came true.

Harry was sitting very still, like a statue of an ancient wise man. The sight gave her the focus she needed to carry on. "I don't think this is over. It's partly about revenge against my dad — they can't get him, so I become the target. But I think something else happened which has forced a move. Why come after us now? He's been dead for almost six years. Why send someone into our house like that? And why get those idiots to do it? I wouldn't trust them to steal a bike, let alone kidnap a little girl.

"Harry said to me at the time that he thought something was 'off' about it. Well, he's right. I'm just uncertain what.

It can't be an elaborate set-up to get me, surely not. I'm not important enough. But, like I said, I fear this isn't over."

To her surprise, Sally stood up. Her expression gave away nothing. "Thank you. You're done. I will set up that meeting. What happens then is a matter for the boss."

"How long will it be? Does she know what this is about? Why did you decide I was OK?"

"Just three questions? Everyone tells me you're a very controlled young woman. All I can say is she'll see you when it's right for her and you. How long that will be is a matter for her. But don't worry. Once she takes a decision, she sticks to it. I don't know how much she will share with you. But, as to your last question, my boss told me, 'Don't bother unless she's clever enough to be flexible in how she thinks.' Well, Martha, you passed the test with flying colours. It seems you do take after your father."

CHAPTER 19

Harry offered to stay and talk for a while, but an exhausting day was rapidly catching up with Martha. She needed to pick up Betty and then get some sleep — about three days should do it.

After he had extracted a promise that she would do some punchbag work, starting tomorrow, Martha watched Harry walk up the road to his house. If there was just one thing to thank her father for, it was ensuring she had him in her life. She wondered what he'd say if he knew how much she relied on him. Harry was a wise old head, a protector, a mentor, a father figure . . . a friend.

Talking of friends, she thought to herself and headed for the fridge. There were a couple of bottles of Sauvignon Blanc in there. She might be too tired to chew, but she could manage a drink.

The night flew by in a pleasant haze, with Lucy recounting dating disasters and Martha mostly listening and laughing. After putting Betty to bed, they started on the second bottle, managing to get halfway down the first glass before Martha's eyes became hooded with exhaustion. Lucy made her excuses, leaving Martha to check on Betty then slump into bed. She barely got her jeans off before falling into a deep sleep.

Daylight was streaming in when Martha woke in a cold sweat. She'd been having a nightmare about being chased by faceless pursuers. Suddenly thinking of Betty, Martha raced to her daughter's room, her heart pounding. She sagged with relief when she found the little girl fast asleep, lying on her back and looking as angelic as only a four-year-old can.

Tottering back to her own room, she checked the time. It was 4.45 a.m. and the sun was already coming up. That it was so light so early could throw anyone. Almost an hour later, she was running a bath, sipping a cup of tea as she watched the steam spiralling off the surface of the water.

Yesterday had sucked a lot of energy from her. Reflecting on what she had learned, she imagined her father using one of his favourite aphorisms, "Be careful what you wish for."

Well, she had wished for information about her dad, and details about his work. Martha was fighting to absorb it all. But she knew one thing: this was a morning for a really soothing, leisurely bath.

A couple of paracetamol to combat a tight little headache plus a splash of Jo Malone bath oil would help with that. The perfumed oil was especially precious, as it was the last present her mother had bought her. She stripped off and checked herself in the mirror. Her hair was a rat's nest, but that could be fixed. She was a bit blotchy and her eyes were puffy — but the upcoming boxing session with Harry would ensure she was too tired to worry about how she looked.

* * *

"I can't do any more," Martha panted, holding on to the punchbag for balance. "Let me rest for a minute. I'm going to have a heart attack if I don't stop."

They were in the little gym Harry had set up in what used to be his downstairs bathroom. Having always lived alone, he'd had the house remodelled to his liking. Upstairs were two bedrooms, both en suite, and downstairs was a

91

knocked-through living room with a kitchen just big enough to fit a microwave, hob and fridge. Just right for Harry.

They'd started the session with Harry taping her hands up and then fitting some lightweight gloves. She'd begun simply, punching the heavy bag over and over. Left hand, right hand. Now she was slapping the bag, not punching it. She had to stop; the muscles in her neck and shoulders were burning and she was losing sensation in her hands. He nodded, his eyes bright. "You've done well for someone out of practise. Let's get those gloves and bandages off, then we can do a bit of stretching." He was wearing a sleeveless shirt and she marvelled at the shape he was in for a seventy-five-year-old. She hoped she looked as good fifty years from now.

"Sounds like a plan," she gasped.

"Glad you like the idea. We can finish with a run and some more stretching."

She started backing away; her gloved hands held out in a warning. "A run? No way am I going on a run. Not today. Not any day. I hate running. That's my final word."

He looked at her slyly. "I went for a run with Betty a couple of weeks ago. She really enjoyed it."

Twenty minutes later, she was running, remarkably slowly, towards Belair Park. Alongside her, Harry was keeping up with minimal effort.

"You should try to glide across the pavement. You're slapping your feet down so hard you'll crack the flagstones."

"I'd like to crack your flagstones," she muttered, trying to conserve energy.

He feigned ignorance. "Sorry. Didn't catch that. Not far until we reach the turning point. Pick those feet up. You're aiming for a tea dance, not a clog dance."

By the time they were at Martha's house, she was moving at little more than walking pace. She fumbled the keys out of her pocket, handing them to Harry as she leaned, panting, against the porch wall. "Would you mind opening the door for me? I feel a bit wobbly."

Door opened, he stood aside to allow her in. "Same time tomorrow? We'll keep it gentle until you get a bit of fitness back."

She glared at him. "You're not my friend."

He trotted off. "See you tomorrow. If you need a lift up the road, text me." He didn't look back to see her flipping both fingers.

* * *

The next day, her legs, feet, back, shoulders, arms and hands were all sore. Especially her hands. Punching the bag had left them tender and raw. It was painful to make a fist, let alone throw a punch. Harry was sympathetic but businesslike. He had her run through some warm-up exercises that got her moving freely; then he worked the hands.

"Clench and unclench. Keep doing it. Now, make a fist. Not too fast and don't push too hard — the point is to loosen your joints up. Those hands are a sophisticated bit of engineering, so we need to treat them right. Flex those fingers."

She shot hate stares in his direction, which Harry happily ignored. A short while later, Martha was standing in front of the punchbag again. But this time, Harry wasn't on the opposite side, holding on. He was behind her, his strong fingers working out some of the kinks in her neck. The sensation was the most deliciously painful thing she'd experienced. He patted her shoulder. "Back to the punchbag, but this time don't worry about actually punching it. We're going to work on that technique and building your strength. Just go slow and aim every punch. I want to see good connections. Keep those hands nice and high, work your arms and shoulders. If punching the bag hurts, you're hitting it too hard. Big hits can come later. This is about direction and co-ordination."

Her first couple of blows slapped against the bag, sending pain shooting through her hands. She slowed down, working to just brush against the bag. It felt weird to be doing it like this, as though she was in a slow-motion action game, but Harry approved.

"This is much better. Keep those hands high, keep throwing those punches . . . left, right, left, right . . . we'll have you dancing yet."

She puzzled over that remark, then realised her feet were trying to match the rhythm of her hands. He kept her at it for another fifteen minutes, then called a halt.

"You OK to go for a run again? I'm hoping that feels a bit better today. Yesterday you needed something more intense."

She gave him a rueful smile. "Did I look like a woman who needed to punch someone?"

"You could say that. I have high hopes for you. I wasn't expecting to see any footwork just yet — you're weeks ahead of schedule!" He laughed. "We're not trying to create a new world champion here. I want to help you defend yourself. Learning to punch properly is key. Mike Tyson once said, 'Everyone has a plan until they get punched in the mouth.' But I reckon there's more to it than that. On rare occasions you get the chance to leg it without having to throw a punch at all . . . and that can be a real lifesaver."

She bowed to him. "It's almost like listening to the wisdom of a Zen master."

"Spoken with real sincerity." He smiled. "Tell you what, let's run a bit faster today."

* * *

They fell into a regular pattern. Martha rapidly built her strength and honed her boxing technique. As she moved more fluently she could feel the difference when she got on the front foot. All the hard work helped take her mind off the growing frustration at an ongoing radio silence from Sally and her mysterious boss.

Harry was helping with that by keeping up a running commentary as they worked together.

"Surprise is on your side," he told her. "You're strong, with fast hands, and a lot of men won't be expecting how hard you can punch. Even the toughest bloke is going to need a timeout if you break his nose and then thump him in the crown jewels. My advice will always be the same: hit, hit hard . . . scarper."

They were into the fourth week when she got home to a message from Paul Avery.

"The police investigation team submitted their findings to the CPS last week. I'm told the announcement will come at about 5 p.m., timed to allow it to make the evening headlines. The director of public prosecutions, the DPP himself, is making a statement. They're spinning it to make it appear like he's a champion of transparency and fairness, not someone in thrall to vested interests like the all-powerful Met Police. I hate this kind of manipulative politics. That a drugged-up career criminal killed a beloved mother and grandmother gets overlooked amid all the posturing."

His sigh of frustration was clearly audible in the recording. "I thought I could go over it all at your place. Get Harry there if you can. I'll be with you just after 3 p.m."

Listening to the message, Martha felt like the walls were closing in on her. She'd been in a bubble for a few weeks, working out, spending precious time with Betty, remembering her mum. The barriers she'd erected suddenly seemed flimsy.

CHAPTER 20

Harry arrived early.

He was wearing a suit, adding to her sense of foreboding. Placing a full pack of cigarettes on the table in front of her, he went outside to light up from another pack. Martha considered it for a moment then helped herself. To say she struggled with her conscience would be wrong. The battle was over before her conscience had even had a chance to get going.

Sitting down next to Harry, she sucked in a deep lungful of smoke, coughed and solemnly inspected the glowing tip of her cigarette.

"The condemned woman enjoying her last smoke."

"You're not condemned yet," said Harry.

After a moment, she said, "You're not given to whimsy, are you, Harry?"

"No."

"Comedy? Witty repartee? Banter?"

He shrugged, eloquent in his silence. Finally, he said, "What's the DPP like, then? Not sure they had one of those in my day."

She gave him an appreciative look. "Straight to the heart of the matter, as always." She took another drag, feeling the nicotine working through her body. "If you're asking whether

I've met him, the answer is no. I'm just a lowly detective. In fact, I'm a lowly, suspended detective, although I have heard a little gossip. He's said to be very smart and very political. He's not above using the post to polish his reputation."

This was greeted with a lengthy silence. Martha cracked first. "Penny for your thoughts?"

"I'm not sure what to make of it. Even back in the day, I didn't get too worked up about the legal stuff. For me it mostly involved saying 'not guilty' and hoping for the best. Your dad had the brainpower for that, so I left it all to him. I bet he'd have made sure this DPP fella would recognise that a dodgy case has been cooked up against you."

Martha decided that was too much to hope for. DI Holland had made it plain that they were determined to press charges, no matter how weak they were. Martha almost choked on her cigarette as a forgotten memory surfaced, one that she had thus far repressed.

During an interview a few months ago, the DI had shown her true colours. "Don't go thinking we're all mates," the woman had said to her. "My job is to make a case against you." Her curled lip and tightly crossed arms had told Martha that she had no friends here. "And from what I've read, it's more a case of how much ends up in the 'to be taken into consideration' column."

Martha couldn't believe the way she was being spoken to. The DI had noticed. She'd leaned forward, hissing into Martha's face, spraying flecks of spittle at her. "Don't like my attitude? Think I'm being a bit unfair? Not showing you enough respect? Well, let me tell you what's unfair. It's entitled little snots like you with their big-shot fathers running roughshod over the rest of us."

Paul Avery had saved her. He'd squeezed her hand, hard enough to make her look at him. He'd stared at her with a fierce intent as he spoke, never once breaking his gaze.

"My client is overwhelmed by the stress of this situation. Unless you're going to charge her, we're leaving now. You can resume tomorrow."

He'd stood up, guiding Martha to the door. The DI had winked provocatively, and Paul had had to use his full body to prevent Martha confronting the officer.

"Betty is waiting for you." He'd repeated it twice more until the message got through. "No need to talk, let's just get out into the fresh air."

The DI had looked disappointed.

Martha had moved in a haze of pure anger. Outside, Paul had insisted she get in the car as quickly as possible. "I want us away from here before we say anything."

Martha had been close to tears. "I'd like to kill that bitch. I'd like to do it slowly and then revive her and do it again."

"I agree. She's a deeply unpleasant woman, possibly quite mad. But she has done us one big favour. She's made it plain they won't be playing by Queensbury Rules. She confirmed you have enemies — and they clearly want you taken out. They won't thank her for being so direct and revealing their hand."

Sitting in the garden now, the memory rushed over her. She was about to start the toughest fight of her life.

Paul Avery arrived at 4.30 p.m., serious-faced.

"I've got an update for you, and I'm sorry that it's more gloomy news. I've spoken to a contact in the DPP's office, who tells me his man is throwing some big charges your way." He paused, seeing the way Martha's expression had changed. "But these are only the first real shots in the fight. We have a long way to go — and you'll have the best defence that money can buy, thanks to your father's friend.

"Which brings me to the good news. Charles Winter, a brilliant barrister — a QC, in fact — has agreed to take you as a client. Do you recall the case of the well-known phone billionaire accused of walking around with an unlicensed gun?"

She nodded. "That was extraordinary. Somehow he walked free, even though there was no question he'd had the gun. He was carrying it around in a custom-made leather holster. It was even studded with diamonds, for God's sake. Somehow, the jury found him not guilty."

"That's the one," said Paul. "As the judge said at the time, there was never any doubt about him having the gun. All he could say was that he had received death threats which he said were being ignored by the police. He claimed he got the gun to protect himself and his family. At best that should have only counted towards a reduced sentence, but that is to ignore the brilliance of Charles Winter. He put on a master-class, painting such a vivid picture of his client as the terrified victim that the jury were determined to see him walk free, whatever the judge said."

"In fact, that was two years ago, the last case Charles Winter took on. Nowadays, he spends most of his time at his vineyard in Portugal. I took a chance and wrote to him. I didn't want to get your hopes up, so I didn't tell you. But last night he emailed to say he wanted to get involved. He's on a flight back from Lisbon tomorrow."

She crossed the kitchen and hugged him gently. "Thank you. Thank you for being clever enough to pull it off — and thank you for being on my side."

Even Harry was smiling. "I've heard about him. He can wrap a jury around his little finger and run rings round the prosecution. You're in safe hands there."

Paul appreciated the comments. "My office will send over the charges once they're released. Then James Hill, the DPP, is doing a press conference. I believe the BBC are broadcasting live."

"Sounds like he has it all worked out," said Martha, a twist of acid evident in her tone.

Harry had other matters in mind. "Do you think the DPP is part of this plot against Martha? Is he one of John's enemies?"

"Instinct says not. Hill is young and has his eyes on political prizes. What we have here is a coincidence of inter-ests." Paul's phone rang. He listened and broke the connec-tion. "My office. Seems Mr Hill likes the limelight so much he's given the BBC the charge list now so that they get the 'exclusive'."

Martha called up the news on her laptop and they gathered around to watch. It didn't take long until the headlines appeared.

Martha was the lead item. The news presenter read from the autocue.

"Suspended Scotland Yard detective Martha Munro was today charged after being investigated for her actions following the shooting of her mother and kidnapping of her daughter. The move comes after the personal intervention of the DPP, James Hill. It was also announced today that Mr Hill is running for London Mayor next year."

Martha gave a shout of anger, but the lawyer quelled her. "There's more yet."

The presenter was saying, "Mr Hill told the BBC in a statement that he had become involved in the investigation into Martha Munro because it was 'critical that justice is seen to be done'. In the statement, he said that it was the duty of the DPP to get involved in the most difficult cases, ones where public opinion runs high, to be fair and scrupulous — especially when it involves the police investigating one of their own."

The programme cut to a reporter standing outside Scotland Yard. "I've just been handed the charge sheet. The detective is charged with two counts, including GBH with intent, and possession of an illegal firearm — a Taser."

"What sort of penalties does she face?" asked the presenter in the studio.

The reporter was nodding. "First, it needs to be stated that her legal team has already said she will firmly contest any charges. But, if this ends up in court, and Detective Constable Munro is found guilty, then jail becomes a possibility. Under sentencing guidelines, she could receive up to sixteen years for the GBH charge and up to ten years for the firearms offence."

CHAPTER 21

Harry couldn't keep his outrage bottled up. His voice came out as an urgent hiss. "He can't be serious? What planet is he on if he thinks that will stick? There isn't a jury anywhere that will convict her on that charge — they won't have it! Neither of us touched the little scrotes. All they've got is some blood on her shoe. There's no chance of you getting banged up for that. Which reminds me, why haven't I been charged? Or did I miss something?"

"I'll find out about you as soon as I can," said Paul. "As for you, Martha, Harry's quite right, and that's the point. This is a very weak case, and I'm surprised the DPP has associated himself with it."

"So maybe I'm right — he is part of this plot to get Martha," said Harry.

Paul made a seesawing gesture with his hand. "We need to keep our feet on the ground. I totally agree there's a lot going on here, but while it's tempting to see a conspiracy, we don't know that's the case. In the meantime, the most important thing to do is prepare Martha's defence — and find out what they have in mind for you, Harry."

Martha banged her fist on the kitchen table. "I'm going to fight this with everything I've got. There's no way I'm going to leave Betty. No matter what."

Paul smiled. "I couldn't have put it better myself. Another thing I'd like to know is exactly where this leaves the bigger investigation. What's happening with the Dragov brothers? We know you two didn't attack them, so who did? The DPP must be playing politics because, otherwise, it makes no sense to charge you while the murder and kidnap investigation is still ongoing."

"Unless he's bent," said Harry.

"It's getting harder to ignore the possibility," said Paul. "Let's get one mystery solved. I'll get someone in my office to sort out Harry's status in all this."

Call made, he turned back to Martha. "There's no escaping that perceptions around the Met are a little sticky at the moment. It was summed up by an article in *The Times* yesterday, claiming the public has lost faith in Scotland Yard. That video showing a bunch of officers dragging a mother out of her car was the latest PR disaster."

Harry was nodding. "That was the Old Bill at their worst. They tried to say she was a drug dealer, but she did voluntary work with her local church, handing out food to the hungry."

"Exactly right. And, coming after those two cops resigned before they could be quizzed over tasering another mother in front of her children, the public mood is ugly." He paused. "The DPP's enjoying his moment in the spotlight, and no one will notice when he eventually loses. It's not impossible that we get the charges thrown out in legal argument before the jury has to get involved. He might even get a few more votes by making out it was a soft judge that stopped him doing the job he wants. A real win–win.

"A genuine alternative is for you to plead guilty — which is risky, don't get me wrong — but if you take a plea, we can mount a strong mitigation based on your almost overwhelming distress at losing your mother and nearly losing your little girl. In the hands of an expert like Charles Winter we can chop that sentence down to a minimum.

"In my view, the best case sees you walking with a suspended sentence. At worst, you get six months, and we have you out in in twelve weeks, all being well. That's the thing about making a guilty plea; it strengthens your case because, despite having powerful mitigation, you didn't set out to abuse valuable court time. You accept you were technically in the wrong, but you were provoked beyond your control."

Martha was staring at him, her face fierce. "Are you kidding me? You want me to plead guilty? Twelve weeks is good? What should I do, thank the judge for sending me to prison? Making me see the error of my ways?"

Paul held his hands up. "I'm trying to give you options, not pass judgement or belittle your situation. I'm trying to help you make sense of it, but only you can know what level of risk you're prepared to take. I hate to say this, but pleading not guilty — and then losing — can be the worst of all worlds. You have Betty to consider as well, which, let's face it, the other side know as well. That's why I'm so glad Charles Winter is taking your case. It'll be fascinating to have his reading on this."

Martha gave him a brittle smile, somewhat mollified. "I'm sorry. This situation is terrifying me, but that's no excuse for picking on my own side."

She checked the time. "Can you excuse me for five minutes? I have to get Betty from Lucy's. I'll be right back."

Paul took the chance to call his office for an update, listening carefully as he was briefed about Harry's position, his only comment being, "We're sure about that?" He ended the call then looked at Harry.

"You're not going to be charged."

"What?" said Harry. In other circumstances his incredulous look might have been comical.

"They feel there's no solid evidence to charge you. They have the blood on Martha's shoe and the claims by the Dragov brothers that it was Martha alone who attacked them. They even say you tried to stop her. So, no blood, no claims . . . no charges."

"What about the gun?"

"No action, apparently," said Paul. "It wasn't fired and they can't disprove your original statement that it was there when you arrived. Off the record, the sense from the DPP's office is that Martha is being made an example to others. She disobeyed orders, attacked suspects and is now paying the price."

For a moment the two men were silent until Harry spoke. "I hate to add to the gloom, but this might tie in with something that's been bothering me — what if the judge has been nobbled? No amount of fancy talk will help then."

The lawyer sat down, exhausted. "That's the bit that's keeping me awake at night. The people we're up against are well connected. I fear they could easily get their own judge in place. Not even bothering to charge you is a blatant demonstration of power. It feels like they're saying, 'We only want Martha,' that you don't count." He stopped to think about it. "We would make an instant appeal if it was clear the judge was determined to find her guilty, but that would take months. Which is bad — because the longer she has to spend inside, the greater the chance that someone will get at her."

"That's what's worrying me too. She's a tough woman, but prisons are dangerous." Harry pulled up his T-shirt to show a nasty scar above his left hip. "That was back in the days when I was regarded as a tasty geezer, not someone to be messed with. I let my guard down and nearly died for it."

"How are the boxing lessons going?"

"Not bad. I need more time, but she can punch like a bastard already. I'm pushing her hard and she's soaking it up." He fixed Paul with a look. "How much longer have I got with her? She's young, strong and fit, so another month would do it at a pinch. Two would be much better, and three perfect."

This time, Paul did smile. "I can drag these things out. Assume you have the two months, and you can buy me a large scotch when I give you three."

CHAPTER 22

Elsewhere in London, the DPP's announcement was the focus of intense scrutiny.

In the top floor offices of a Mayfair-based hedge fund, Carol, the woman Martha knew only as a voice on the phone, was wearing a sour expression as the DPP finished speaking. It was clear that the other side had brought their A-game to this one. A cautious and pragmatic woman, she'd risen to the top because she never underestimated an opponent, and her default was to anticipate the worst that could happen.

She realised that Martha Munro was at high risk of being murdered. If she were a threat level, it would read "Critical". She was pretty certain the man driving the current threat against Martha was someone she knew all too well. If John Munro could have been said to have a nemesis, it was Neil Thompson. A brilliant and brutal man, he had the most to lose if he was identified. As far as she knew, he had the resources and motivation to go after Martha, but the man was preternaturally clever at covering his tracks, so she had no way of confirming her suspicion.

Carol wasn't sure exactly what she was looking for, but she had a shrewd idea. She'd known John Munro a long time and was well aware that he had a compulsion to keep secret lists. When he died it had been widely assumed that his secrets had died with him, but a year or so ago one of John's inner circle had let something slip at a police leaving party. After a few too many drinks he had muttered about his former boss keeping a detailed record of who was working for him, from police officers to villains.

The news spread fast and suddenly a lot of people were looking over their shoulders, each one terrified of being exposed as a rat. Appearing on John Munro's list was a sure way to reduce life expectancy. Which explained why the select few were after it, either to hide their involvement or give those not on the list the opportunity to exploit the vulnerability of those who were.

Carol had heard early and had acted fast. She had organised a specialist search team to break into Martha's home, but they had found nothing. Keeping the house under observation, she was startled to discover another team going in the next day. She had photos of the intruders but couldn't identify or link them to anyone. Even so, she remained convinced Neil Thompson was behind it. For all his alleged hatred of John Munro, it wasn't inconceivable that he actually worked for him. The crime lord would have been a perfect fit for John's operation — who better to provide vital information than someone seen as your mortal enemy? Carol knew it was the kind of double-bluff that John Munro would have relished.

Inevitably, word got out that the search teams had found nothing, and it didn't take long for a new theory to emerge: Martha Munro knew exactly where the list was. The only thing keeping her safe was speculation that John Munro had set things up so that if his daughter was hurt, or worse, the information would be released.

But that could only keep Martha safe for so long. Carol was sure someone would soon be willing to throw caution aside and go after her. When it came to the twisted ethics of the increasingly viscous gang chiefs, the murder of one woman — even a detective — would barely register. If killing

106

Martha got them the list, they would be in credit. The attack which killed Elaine Munro was clearly part of this new activity. Carol had long ago promised John that she would protect Martha and she intended to try her best . . . while at the same time looking for his secret list for her own use. It was invaluable information, providing the holder with significant leverage over wealthy and powerful people. She hadn't promised him she wouldn't go after that.

Carol needed to rip up her existing plans and come up with something new. Others might have delegated, but that was something she would never do — not with her own safety on the line. She began to reverse-engineer the problem. If she wanted to harm Martha, how would she do it?

A bullet in the head would be quick, efficient and permanent. Wait until the middle of the night and then break in? Two-man team — fast in, fast out. Say, a seven in ten chance of success. It was a good option, but maybe she could do better.

Ambush in the street? Two men again. A driver and a shooter. Less control than a break-in because of the need to wait for the target to come out . . . She judged it a six out of ten.

Ambush at a regular stop-off? Team needed to ensure proper surveillance and establish routine. Effective but time-consuming . . . Six and a half.

Bomb attack? High risk, likely to be high collateral damage. Need an expert bomb maker. Too blunt. Only in extremes . . . Five out of ten.

Then she thought: take her out in prison. It would be easy to set up. There'd be no shortage of willing volunteers. Maybe muddy the waters by making it appear gang-related. She considered this the best option. Say, eight out of ten.

She had no doubt Martha was heading to prison. The other side had shown an extraordinarily strong hand and were clearly pulling the strings. She was sure they would already have moved on from the DPP to making sure their choice of judge was in place. Fixing the jury would be easy with their resources.

She stretched a few kinks out of her neck. Even though she was confident they would attack her in prison, it wouldn't do to leave the back door open. It helped that Harry was working with Martha. It helped a lot. Hopefully, it would improve her awareness of danger. But more could be done.

From now on, Martha — and her little girl — would remain under twenty-four-hour watch. With mum and daughter following the same route to and from school, she'd need to be extra vigilant. Or her people would be.

* * *

Less than a mile away, two special advisers sat in a government office close to the River Thames. Their jobs were well paid, but even that income paled against their lucrative sideline in helping very wealthy criminals to exert pressure on 10 Downing Street.

One of them was checking the DPP's delivery against a print-out of the speech. When James Hill finished, the shorter of the two men counted any new or changed words. With a huge grin he announced, "Forty-three words. I think you'll be handing over that money now."

"With pleasure, dear boy," replied the taller man. "With such a pitch-perfect response from the DPP, ten pounds a word is well worth it."

"I thought today might bring good news, so I've been holding something back. Something good."

His companion sat up a little straighter and steepled his fingers. "I could guess — but I expect you're desperate to tell me."

He inclined his head. "You know me too well. We've heard from our friends. Bronzefield prison is ready to accept her."

In the background, the quarter bells of Big Ben had started to chime, marking the half-hour.

The tall man clapped delightedly. "For whom the bell tolls. It's an omen. This is a particularly good day, one that calls for something cold and fizzy."

CHAPTER 23

"Jab . . . Jab . . . Jab. Keep your feet moving. Up on your toes. Make each punch count . . ."

Martha was breathing hard, sweat pouring from her head and straight into her eyes. Harry had been driving her hard since the meeting with Paul. But now she needed a breather; her knees were turning to jelly, and she was missing more punches than she landed. Stepping back, she put her hands on her hips and gulped in air. Her heart was hammering so hard she leaned into the punchbag to give herself support.

"C'mon, Harry," she gasped. "Something's got you riled up. You've never pushed me this hard before. What's the big deal?"

Martha tried to make the last question sound casual — a hard thing to do when you're fighting for every breath. For just a moment, she saw a flash of emotion on his face. If it had been anyone other than Harry, she would have said it was pure fear. He glanced away, mumbling something about wanting to move things along.

She picked up a towel to wipe the sweat off her face. "You don't realise how hard boxing is until you try it."

Harry squared his shoulders like a soldier bracing for inspection. "Yeah, I suppose I have been pushing you. I'm not overdoing it, I hope?"

"I'm coping." She smiled. "But you've got me at my limit."

"Right, right. It's important you tell me when you feel stretched to breaking . . . the last thing we need is for you to pick up a training injury."

He grabbed the punchbag in a big bear hug before letting go and releasing a volley of punches, his hands a blur. She waited. He would talk when he was ready.

"Well, it's little Betty." He'd developed a sort of 'little boy lost' look. "What'll happen to her if, you know . . ."

"If they lock me up?" She sighed. "If this court case goes tits up and I get carted off, she'll live with Justin. It really isn't up to me — he's her dad. If I'm out of the picture, he has full parental responsibility. I'm just glad we're getting on better nowadays."

Now Harry looked comically relieved, provoking more laughter.

"Surely the fearsome Harry the Hat isn't scared of a girl and how she might react to questions about her former husband?" she asked, a grin on her face.

"Actually, I am. Especially when it comes to Justin. You've been known to throw things. Big, heavy things."

She held her hands up. "I confess he can irk me more than most. But, seeing how he and Betty get on, my bet is he will be delighted to get the chance to be a full-time dad again. Now we've got that out of the way, can we go back to normal training?"

"Normal?" He shook his head. "You and normal don't play that well. Anyway, what are you moaning about? You've done really well over the past few days. It's time to mix things up a little and get you learning how to kick properly."

She looked at him quizzically.

"You're doing well with your hands and that's great. It improves fitness and co-ordination, but in some ways, punching is the last thing you want to do. It's too easy to break something. But a swift kick? Now you can really slow someone down. And that might be all the difference you need . . ."

Harry checked his watch. "We can start thinking about that next time. Now it's time to get out on the run. It's the big one today — up to Crystal Palace."

Martha's heart sank.

CHAPTER 24

The text message was an instruction. "Watch the news on Channel 4 at 7 p.m." She knew instantly that it heralded nothing good.

It had arrived while she was getting Betty ready for school. With an effort of willpower she'd put her fears to one side, not wanting the little girl to pick up on her distress. It helped that Harry was now joining them on every trip to and from school, his presence acting like a soothing balm.

She waited until Betty was safely inside the school building before showing Harry the message. "Bloody hell, Martha. Someone's trying to put the frighteners on. Do you have any idea what they might be talking about?"

"I've been wracking my brain, but it could be anything. Anything at all."

"What about Paul? Have you told him yet?"

"Not yet. It only came an hour ago, so I waited until Betty was safe inside . . ." She gasped, her hand going to her mouth. "You don't think it might be a warning about Betty? That something's going to happen to her?"

She saw the fear in his face. When he spoke, he was obviously trying to sound cautiously positive. "I don't know, but it feels unlikely. Why would they boast about it in advance?

We should ring Paul when we get back. You don't recognise the number, do you? In the meantime, do you want me to stay here and keep my eyes on the school?"

"I did think about that," said Martha. "But we've checked out their security and know it's pretty good, all things considered. If you hang around all day that's going to make things more intrusive, which will only upset everyone, including Betty. Please stay on the school run, though."

When they got back to her house, Martha called Paul. He answered on the first ring. "How's it going?"

"Not good. I was sent a message this morning, I don't know who from, but it said I should watch the *Channel 4 News* at 7 p.m. tonight. Harry and I both think it's a threat, a sort of 'look what we can do' type of thing."

"You may well be right. Have you spoken to the police about it? I think you should, even just to get it on the record. Contact Commander Shaw, or at least someone on his team who can pass on the message. It may be nothing, but it's better he hears it from you in advance."

Paul rang off with a promise that he would tune in later. Martha tried responding to the message but it bounced back.

"Probably a burner," she told Harry, who nodded even though he obviously had no idea what she was talking about.

The rest of the day dragged, but finally it was almost 7 p.m. Martha had the news running on her laptop. The presenter started reading the headlines.

"*Channel 4 News* has learned that one of two brothers being held in connection with the murder of a police officer's mother has been found dead. Sources have told our reporter that he was found hanging in his cell. An inquiry is underway, but our source says the man was not considered a suicide risk."

The camera switched to a shot of a reporter standing outside Scotland Yard. "I understand that the Met has launched an inquiry. Remand prisoners are supposed to be closely supervised and questions need answering around how this happened.

"It's the latest controversy to hit the investigation. Early on, the detective was arrested after the Dragov brothers were found in a flat in Peckham. One had been seriously assaulted and remains in hospital. The police officer has been charged in connection with the incident."

Martha wrapped her arms round herself. She was badly shaken. "If they can do that to their own side, what chance have me and Betty got? What do the bastards want?"

Before Harry could speak, there was a loud knocking at the front door. Martha raced to answer it, throwing the door open to see a man standing there. With enormous relief she realised it was Hassan, a delivery driver she was now on first-name terms with after buying a flurry of presents for Betty's last birthday. He had a little girl of the same age.

"Got a special delivery for you. Had to get it here for 7.15 p.m., so I'm a bit early."

"Thanks, Hassan." She reached for the envelope and couldn't stop her hand trembling.

"See ya next time, Martha!" Then he was gone, moving fast as usual. She stared at the letter, mounting dread keeping her from opening it.

Harry reached to close the door. "Let's open it together."

She handed it to him, suddenly hating its feel in her hand.

"A bit late to worry about fingerprints." He opened it and scanned the contents, then showed it to Martha.

It read: *You have something we want.*

"Do you have any idea what this is about?"

Harry was frowning. "I'm not sure, but it has to be something to do with your dad. They must think he left something valuable. But why wait until now to come after it?"

"I can't think of anything that would be of interest. He left me money, he left this house to Mum, some personal stuff, but nothing that would bother a crime lord. Come on, Harry, you knew him. What's it about?"

"Well, I'd say it has to be information or money. Maybe lots of money. Apart from what you just said, did he leave you with a safe-deposit box? With jewellery in it, maybe?"

114

Martha almost smiled. "Harry, I do believe you're talking about something that's been stolen. No, nothing like that, I'm afraid. If there was, I wouldn't have kept it. I keep telling people I'm not like him."

"Maybe not in that way, but you are quite similar. I guess that leaves information, then. Which is the bit I'm not that clear on. Perhaps Paul would be better."

"I think it's going to take every scrap of what we all know, so tell me what you can, then I'll see what Paul comes up with."

"Fair enough. It's going back to what we mentioned earlier about your dad having his own private army. I do know he had a lot of people to pay, just don't ask me how he did it. If you twist my arm then I'd say he kept a list, showing names and amounts. If I'm right and that list is still about, then a lot of people will be well worried. Your dad never shared his secrets with me, it was better that way, but I knew there were some major faces he dealt with. Big names from both sides of the law."

She rang Paul, who confirmed Harry's account. "I wish I could tell you more, but he didn't share, like Harry said."

Ending the call, Martha felt a new sense of determination.

"I'm going to assume there's a list. We need to think about where it might be. I've been putting off going into Mum's room, but now is the time. What about you, Harry? Is there anywhere you can look?"

"There is, but don't get your hopes up. It's stuff he left with me a good ten years ago —a suitcase full of bits and bobs. He asked me to have a shufty at the time. He was looking for a receipt. I didn't find nothing then, but I never looked at it like it might be full of clues. I'll double check — it's worth a try."

CHAPTER 25

Every moment that Betty was out of the house Martha spent looking for the list. She looked everywhere — under every bed, under the mattresses, in the chests of drawers, then removing the drawers to look at them. At one point she even started checking behind pictures hanging on the walls. After three days she had found nothing but a mounting sense of frustration, along with a pile of documents which her mother had kept in her room. These would need checking in detail, a job she wasn't looking forward to.

A couple of times a day Harry would appear for tea and confirm he too was struggling. It was obvious from his harassed air that he hated what he was doing, but he turned down her offer to help. "He left this with me, so it's my job to sort it." It seemed his suitcase was filled with receipts for small amounts, accumulated by John Munro during his lifetime, which seemed to have no broader relevance. It was a mystery why he had wanted them kept. As Harry remarked, "It's not as if he going to put in a claim on his exes."

At the end of a week in which they had made no progress Martha called a break. She and Harry still needed to go through the documents and receipts, but she figured that could wait a couple of days. They already knew the killer document wasn't there, so what was left would only amount to clues.

Martha couldn't ignore the darkening clouds on the horizon. It wasn't just her upcoming court battle; the passing days did nothing to diminish the fallout of her mother's murder and Betty's abduction. There was a gaping hole in her life where her mother had been — the house was quieter, and she still couldn't bring herself to sort through her things, clear out the room. Her mother's beauty products were still in the bathroom; her favourite Turkish coffee, which Martha herself couldn't stomach, was still on the kitchen shelf.

And she was worried about Betty. Her teachers were reporting that the little girl, usually outgoing and inquisitive, had become withdrawn and unresponsive. The school therapist was giving her weekly sessions and said she needed time and patience.

The court case was a looming presence that was dominating the landscape with every passing day. Trying to put it to one side was impossible, since going to trial required active participation. Early on, Paul Avery had tried, without success, to have the case dismissed. Instead, Martha had been released on bail and told the next hearing to discuss preparations would be in a month's time, which had now elapsed.

With preparations now well underway, it was time for the more detailed pre-trial hearings. That started after the weekend — all the more reason for Martha and Harry to have a couple of days off. The good news was that on Monday, Charles Winter was going to be there. The barrister had suggested they set aside the entire day for formal hearings and informal discussions.

It was also something of a red-letter day in that the case against Martha was now formally transferred to the Central Criminal Court, better known as the Old Bailey. Martha was appearing in Court 18. Despite being a police officer, she'd never been to the Old Bailey, and while she appreciated the extraordinary history, she wished she was anywhere else. The clerk had reported that Martha would be the first case at 10 a.m. sharp. She and Harry would meet Charles and Paul an hour earlier.

The morning started well. Justin was looking after Betty for the day, including school drop-off and pickup. The pair left for school hand in hand, the little girl chattering away like her old self. School was early enough for Harry to tag along in his role as the "muscle" and Justin had agreed to allow a friend of Harry's to, discreetly, help cover the return home. The sight of Betty between Justin and Harry brought tears to Martha's eyes, and she reminded herself, again, that having Justin in their lives was an exceptionally good thing for Betty.

It was such a lovely day that she wanted to let off steam by walking to Herne Hill and picking up a Blackfriars train, which left a short hop to the Old Bailey itself. The two lawyers were waiting when they trotted up, Paul quickly ushering them into a small meeting room he had commandeered for the next hour. Charles Winter was in his legal outfit of a flowing black gown, worn over a dark business suit, and a traditional white court wig perched upon his mane of thick white hair. It lent him an air of gravitas that assured her she was in safe hands.

Introductions over, Charles was quickly down to business. He told her he'd been through the case papers and agreed with Paul's people about the fundamental weakness of the case against her, but he added a warning. "We need to take this very seriously. Just because the prosecution has holes in it, there's no guarantee they will fail. That's why we are going in as hard as we can. You've accepted that you were at the flat where the Dragovs were found, but you say you did not attack them. They say you did, which is your word against theirs — hardly the most compelling case. We can also call Harry to testify that you didn't attack either of the two brothers.

"I also intend to focus on your hands, or, to put it another way, that there was no damage to your hands, indeed no evidence of injuries to any part of your body. Yet the

Dragovs claim you punched them. Pretty difficult to do that without bruising your fists, especially given the sustained beating the younger brother seems to have suffered.

"Then we get to the last thread of their case. The blood on your shoe. This doesn't prove you hurt them, and it doesn't prove you didn't. It just proves you were there, something you have already acknowledged.

"Finally we come to mitigation. As Paul has already stated, it should be obvious to everyone that the shock of finding your mother dead and your daughter abducted was why you were armed with a weapon. A weapon we will point out was never discharged. I will argue that the intense distress briefly disturbed the balance of your mind. A state of affairs that was already subsiding by the time you got to Peckham, hence you did not open fire when you had the chance. My intention is not to try to use this as a defence, we can't do that, but I can send a simple and powerful statement to the judge. And if we're really lucky, the jury will buy into it and clear you anyway. I just need to get my speech right."

As pleased as she was by such a powerful statement, she couldn't shake off the fear. Her mind chose that moment to play a cruel trick, replaying Betty heading for school without her mother. One thing in particular was bothering her. "With all due respect to Harry, why haven't they charged him with anything?"

Charles was blunt. "It's a mystery. I know they couldn't find blood on his shoe, but he admits he was there. Then there's the gun he was almost standing next to. I know he claims he found it, but if I was a prosecutor, I would have tried it." He glanced at Harry, "Again, no offence. There's no doubt we're going to have to bring our A-game with us. But if the law were that simple, any fool could practise it."

Martha appreciated his attempt to lighten the mood, and really, what more could he say other than "let's be ready for anything"?

Despite it feeling like no time had elapsed, they were due in court for the latest remand hearing. After reporting to the court officials, they led Martha into the courtroom and told her to sit in the defendant's box. There was a brief delay and then the court clerk announced, "All rise."

In a few seconds everything was about to unravel. In the run up to today had been a handful of technical hearings to allow defence and prosecution to get up to speed. This included indications of how Martha was going to plead and bail applications. Until now, they had been dealing with a middle-aged male judge who had given the appearance of being scrupulously even-handed. Today, however, there was a different judge: a grey-haired, dark-eyed woman. Martha quickly broke eye contact at her cold glance. She could sense no sympathy there.

At first, matters went as predicted. Then came the question of remand. Paul, who was dealing with the details, requested a further remand on bail.

"My client will continue to live in the family home with her daughter. We would ask that you extend this until a trial date is set."

He was just sitting down when the judge said, "Just a moment, Mr Avery. You appear to be making a lot of presumptions here. I am concerned that proper procedure may not have been followed."

Alarmed by her tone, Paul rose to respond — but only managed one word before he was waved to silence by the judge.

"You may have your say in a moment. First, let us acknowledge the serious nature of the charges. The prosecution alleges Ms Munro carried out a grievous assault on a victim who could not defend himself. Not once, but repeatedly. Further, she is charged with possession of a lethal weapon. In my opinion, she poses a considerable flight risk — and I am minded to remand her into custody."

Martha felt the blood draining from her face. Where had this come from? They were right after all to be concerned about the power of her enemies to manipulate events. Up to this woman's appearance no one had mentioned she was a flight risk. Was she looking at a judge who had been, in Harry's words, nobbled? Even worse, if they were trying to have her remanded in custody, was the motivation to try and get at her? To hurt her? Maybe this was the stepping up of a campaign that had begun with the text message telling her to watch the news. She hoped Charles was going to prove as quick on his feet as promised.

Paul was about to start speaking but stopped when the barrister touched him on the arm. Charles stood up. He waited serenely for the judge to allow him to speak.

She inclined her head, staring at him intently.

"Thank you, My Lady. While you make a powerful case, may I take a moment to highlight issues which may allow you to reach an alternative conclusion? My client intends to mount a vigorous defence of the charges that have been levelled against her. She wants her day in court to deny allegations that, if left unopposed, will form an indelible stain on her character. Ms Munro is a police officer. Fleeing justice will not help, as she is acutely aware.

"Furthermore, I would wish to draw your attention to something that is not currently in any of the documents you have in front of you. Martha Munro's daughter, a child of four years old, is extremely distressed by events, and it would be potentially damaging to her long-term health if her mother suddenly vanished as a fugitive from the legal system.

"The third issue is that this case is engaging with a vast audience on social media and, as a result, Martha is extremely well known — this despite the best efforts of the court to keep her identity secret. In the circumstances, therefore, it is nigh on impossible to imagine how she could avoid being identified by the public."

He sat down, folding his hands in his lap, waiting calmly.

The judge shot him a glare of pure venom. She took her time before answering curtly.

"You present an efficient argument, Mr Winter. The court thanks you for supplying details that are pertinent to the case." She paused. "You have satisfied my immediate concerns. The defendants will continue to be remanded on bail until trial."

Martha's head was spinning as they reconvened in the meeting room. "What just happened?" she gasped. She sat down to stop her knees from shaking.

It was Paul who answered.

"The other side just flexed their muscles."

CHAPTER 26

Preparations for the court case were at a new peak of intensity. Every Thursday and Friday, just before noon, would find Martha being put through her paces as Paul and Charles recreated what she could expect to face.

Paul had arranged for a miniature courtroom to be constructed in a wood-panelled boardroom close to High Holborn. It had a raised platform for a "judge", a stand where the pair would face questioning and places for the respective legal teams. The cost was being met by Martha's still unknown benefactor. All Paul knew was that a large sum of money had been placed in his work account. He tried to chase it back, but the trail ran cold at a firm of solicitors in the Bahamas. They did not respond to emails or phone calls.

In mocking up the court, Paul had nearly gone the whole way, including a jury, a court clerk, a note taker and even places where members of the public could sit. It was Charles who voted it down.

"You can overdo these things — and I want our woman to have a little fear, a little respect. People who are fighting for their lives bring their own energy. When they take the stand, I don't want her looking too prepared. Juries can take offence at that. They think the defendants are being cocky

123

or disrespectful. I once had a client who was so relaxed, he started showboating. He got a laugh early on and thought that was it. By the time the prosecution finished, the joke was on him. He gave the impression he had to be guilty of something. The jury agreed and the judge gave him ten years."

Lesson delivered, Charles prepared to play the part of the lead prosecutor. Martha, in the dock, was wary of letting her guard down. This might have been a practice run, but a well-aimed barb still stung.

He began in low-key fashion.

Charles: "After you arrived at your home, what happened? Talk us through events."

Martha: "I identified my mum's body. Then I went straight next door to my friend's house. She made tea."

Charles: "You didn't go anywhere else?"

Martha: "No. I told you, she's my neighbour."

Charles: "You're sure about that? Maybe you spoke to someone? Had a look around? No big deal, it just slipped your mind?"

Martha (getting irritated): "Nothing about that day will ever slip my mind."

Charles: "You're really positive? I mean, stress has been proven to affect the way memory works."

Martha (not hiding her exasperation): "You keep asking and I say the same thing. I went straight next door."

Charles: "I'm sorry. I can see you're an emotional person . . . Let me put this another way. Did you speak to anyone?"

Martha (eyes blazing): "No, no, no, no."

Charles: "Thank you. I am sure you understand the need to check facts, you being a detective." He flicked through his notes. Then he pulled out a piece of paper. "Here it is. I understand that you are acquainted with a man known as Harry the Hat. Could you describe your relationship to him?"

Martha (thinking furiously): "I've known him all my life. To be honest, he's like a part of the family." She held her hand up. "I'm very sorry but I forgot. I did speak to Harry. It's the stress of this, it's making me muzzy."

"All the more reason to run through this. Get used to feeling this way," said Charles. "Are you ready? I'll carry on."

Martha sat straight.

Charles: "Would you say Harry looks out for you, worries about you?"

Martha (puzzled): "Yes, I suppose that's right. He's like a father to me."

Charles (thinking aloud): "A father figure? So, he would have been as distressed as you that day?"

Martha: "I don't get this at all. Harry was obviously distressed."

Charles (triumphantly): "And I put it to you that you wasted no time in contacting Harry and enlisting his support. The pair of you bypassed the police investigation and set out, intending to inflict harm on people you thought were involved. Yet you had no way of knowing if they were truly guilty — and, when you arrived, you attacked them immediately, inflicting serious injuries. Little wonder they 'confessed' — anyone would have confessed in those circumstances. Anything to make you stop."

Martha was shocked at the sudden switch in direction and how Charles was manipulating the evidence to make things suit his narrative. "It wasn't like you say, not at all. You're changing everything."

Charles clapped his hands. "Right, that's enough. Let's call it a day. I just wanted to give you a feel for what they might come up with. More importantly, what it's like to be in a packed courtroom under relentless attack. It can make you get flustered, which only makes things worse. If you appear fragile and emotional under pressure, they'll regard that as a result. The prosecution wants to implant an idea in the jury that you're unbalanced and can't be trusted."

She snorted. "You had me convinced you were the enemy there. I see what you did though. I have to admit that was clever."

"It's more about tricks of the trade than being clever. I set you up with some simple questions, then put you on the spot. I wanted to show you how easy it can be — and give you an insight into how you would react." He shrugged. "You got cross and almost let rip on a couple of occasions. The other side will love that. There's nothing better than a shouty defendant to convince the jury you're trying to hide something.

"It's perfectly allowable for you to get cross about a line of questioning. You just have to stay calm and dignified while pushing it away. That way you appear in control. With a bit of luck, you make them look like bullies."

Martha had been in court several times, but always as a police officer, either observing or giving evidence. Being the defendant was quite different. She was starting on a round of increasingly hard lessons. The experience frightened her more than she cared to admit. Would she cope on the day, or would she fall to pieces? Was she making it harder for herself by risking antagonising a judge who had already shown her teeth?

As a police officer, she knew full well that pleading not guilty was a two-edged sword. If the case went against you, then the risk of facing maximum punishment was magnified. Maybe she would be better off taking a guilty plea and trying to do a deal that saw her serve the shortest potential sentence?

As the idea wormed its way into Martha's brain, she could imagine being dragged off to prison while a weeping and inconsolable Betty cried out for her mother. It was a frightening image. Yet, at the same time, she needed to stay strong. As committed to the fight as she was, she had to consider all the options and do it with an open mind if she was going to make the right decision.

CHAPTER 27

Martha and Harry were walking back to Blackfriars station when she realised she was about to collide with a thick-set man talking animatedly on his phone. She nimbly jumped to one side as he brushed against her, seemingly oblivious to the near miss. *Idiot*, she thought, and turned in time to see Harry walk into a stocky young man.

"Oi, Pops, watch where you're going! You could get hurt, an old-timer like you."

She could see that her minder was going to teach the youngster a lesson in public civility and was about to intervene when she was hit hard in the stomach by a woman her own age, but much taller.

The blow winded her and left her bent forward, panting for breath. Harry, turned away, was still giving the youth a piece of his mind as the woman lent down and hissed in her ear, "Give us what we asked for and these problems go away." She could smell the woman's foul breath.

With that the stranger vanished, the stocky young man running after her, which is when Harry saw Martha was in distress. He offered support, which she angrily declined. Her sudden rage was not directed at Harry, it was against herself. She hadn't been paying attention because she'd felt safe in the crowd. If any of those three had been carrying a knife the outcome could have been disastrous.

Harry was just coming to the same conclusion. "That was a bloody set-up and I let you walk right into it. If you were paying me, I'd be resigning right now. I still might."

"Well, don't resign. You're the best I can get — which is better than I've just made that sound. Did you see the big woman who crashed into me? She just said if I want to be safe, I have to hand over what they asked for — which, we're guessing, is a list of people who were paid by my dad. But what if it's something else? How can we know that without having someone to ask?"

An idea slammed into her brain, instantly terrifying her with its boldness.

"Are you OK?" Harry asked, seeing her face. "Maybe you got hurt more than you realised."

She laughed, a brittle sound. "I've just had a thought. Please hear me out before you say I'm crazy. What if I change my plea? Make the big statement of pleading guilty. At the same time, you and Paul contact all the big players you know and say I'm willing to trade information so that I can put all this behind me. It would give us a chance to get this done with and find out what my dad left hanging over us."

"Martha, listen to me—" Harry was holding her gently by her shoulders — "I can only guess what you're going through, all the worry about Betty, your mum. No one should face that. And what happened just now, that was frightening. It scared me, and I don't scare easy. It could have been a whole lot worse. But you can't surrender or show weakness. Not to these people."

As quickly as the mood had hit her it seemed to break up. "You're right, of course. It was the weirdness of it. One second we were safe in a crowd, the next they'd cut us out of the herd. It terrified me. It made me think that I needed to find a way to make everything stop. The pressure is making me doubt myself. One minute I'm OK, then suddenly I'm not."

Harry kept his hands on her shoulders. "I once cried the night before a sentencing hearing where I knew I was going to be banged up. I thought I was OK but the night before I just bawled like a baby. Luckily, I was at home, so no one saw. It proper shook me up — I mean, men like me don't cry. I had to force myself to shed a tear when my old mum passed away, God bless her."

Martha relaxed. Sometimes she needed to listen to people who knew, and Harry was an expert when it came to crime and punishment. He had sixty-plus years to draw on. She looped her arm through his and they carried on walking in the sunshine. Neither was aware that this emotionally draining day had a lot further to run.

Their first hint that something was wrong sent Martha's heart into her mouth. As they turned into Idmiston Road she saw a marked police car parked outside the house.

"Betty!" she called out, breaking into a sprint. Harry was no slouch but she left him for dead. Unable to get the key in the lock, she banged on the door. Justin appeared, breaking into a big smile. "Just in time for pudding. We've got ice cream," he said.

She sagged against the doorframe. "I thought there was something wrong when I saw the car." She inclined her head at the vehicle and saw the driver starting to get out.

"I can see how you might think that, but actually he's been waiting for you. He got here about twenty minutes ago. I said you wouldn't be long."

"Martha Munro?" The officer, a grizzled-looking uniformed PC, managed to look both impatient and self-important. Martha was amazed at how much pomposity he could convey into saying her name.

"Yes — and this is my home. What can I do for you?"

"You can come with me to Brixton police station. Detective Inspector Mary Holland would like a word with you."

Martha was incredulous. "Am I being arrested?"

"No, Ms Munro, this is a request. The DI believes you can help her with her enquiries."

"Enquiries into what?"

"That's well over my paygrade. I'm just here to pass on the message."

"Well, since you aren't arresting me, I shall take a moment to speak to my daughter and make sure she has someone to look after her."

He pulled a face but kept his silence.

Martha dismissed him from her mind and walked to the kitchen, where Betty was demolishing her dessert.

"Hello, Mummy. Daddy got me ice cream."

"I can see. Listen, if Daddy can look after you a bit longer, do you mind if I go out again? It's boring old police business."

"That's OK. Daddy is reading to me after bath time, anyway."

"And you're OK, Justin?"

"No problem. I'd only be messing about on my computer, which I can do anytime. Much better to be with Betty."

Harry had come into the kitchen. "I'll get hold of Paul. He'll want to know what's going on. Why couldn't they just call you?"

"Because that would be the simple thing to do." Martha looked at Betty. "Can I have a hug before I go?"

"Of course you can, Mummy," said Betty in such a confident way it made Martha's heart swell.

* * *

Martha was processed quickly through the police station and then left, again, in an interview room. Kitted out with institutional-style hard chairs and a rectangular table that could fit two facing each other, it was not designed for comfort. All things considered, she was surprisingly calm, content to see what was going to be thrown at her, although she was glad Harry was tracking down Paul. She had a feeling he was going to be needed.

About half an hour had elapsed when DI Holland walked in. She was accompanied by the same dour detective, who looked like he was wearing the same clothes as last time.

The DI sat down and Martha tried to gauge her mood, but all she could deduce was that her eyes were a little brighter this time. Martha reminded herself to be cautious and say as little as possible.

The DI seemed in a mood to drag things out, opening a file she had carried in with her. It was short and she read it in silence before looking up.

"Thank you for coming in. I have a few questions to ask you about the death of Ivan Dragov."

Martha waited to see what came next. Nothing. She decided to make a statement of her own. "Can you confirm that I am free to leave at any time? That I am not under arrest?"

The DI placed her hands on the table. "At the moment you are assisting with enquiries. That could change, but you will be the first to be informed."

Martha restricted her reply to a curt, "Thank you." She was determined not to get sucked into a conflict. She was really coming to dislike this officer, and she hoped it didn't show too much.

There was another minute or so of silence, then the DI cleared her throat with an unpleasant phlegmy sound that Martha knew was intentional. "I'm hoping you can help me with a rather curious set of coincidences. Ones that seem to revolve around you." Her thin lips were set in a mirthless smile.

"Forgive me going over old ground, and some of it possibly painful for you, but this starts with the raid on your home which left your mother dead and your daughter kidnapped." She didn't look remotely apologetic as she ran through the terrible events. "In the immediate aftermath you and your accomplice tracked down the Dragov brothers to a flat in Peckham. You have already stated that you believed the brothers were responsible for the tragic events at your home.

131

It is also the case that you have been charged in connection with assaulting both brothers, Hristo Dragov very seriously, and possession of an illegal firearm."

She put her elbows on the table, linking her hands together. "I'm going to speak in general terms, so feel free to add any detail you think is important. Now, while the case against the Dragovs remains ongoing, the serious nature of the claims means they are being held in custody. Or I should say were, since Ivan Dragov appears to have been attacked and killed in his cell. Forensic enquiries will establish how it happened. Ordinarily you would be a prime suspect for ordering the killing. You had motive because you wanted revenge and, as a serving police officer, it could be argued that you knew your way around the system well enough to have commissioned his killing. As I said, a bit simplistic, but you get the gist.

"Now, bear with me, because this is where it gets interesting. On the day Ivan Dragov died, you called the police to say you had received a mysterious message telling you to watch the news. You told us you had no idea why this suggestion was made. Yet a few hours later, the man you say murdered your mother and kidnapped your daughter was dead. So, without me drawing you an actual diagram, you can see how all these events are connected to you. Indeed, some of my colleagues are concerned that you had advance knowledge of a man's death. I'm open-minded, but it is troubling. Perhaps you can help with this?"

Martha was incredulous. "That is a complete manipulation of what happened. Yes, I did say I had been alerted to watch the news. But I never said I knew what was going to happen, and that's because I didn't. Any suggestion otherwise is a complete lie and—"

A knock at the door interrupted her. The inspector stepped outside and when she returned, Paul Avery followed her in. He gave Martha an encouraging wink. Still standing, he began talking.

"My client voluntarily attended this meeting in order to help the police in any way she can. No one remains more concerned that justice is done than Martha Munro. But from what I just overheard, it's clear this is turning into a fishing expedition, one intended to try to put words in my client's mouth. Unless you intend to press yet more ludicrous charges, my client and I will be leaving. Immediately."

Martha walked outside on shaky legs. Never had Brixton High Street looked so welcoming.

CHAPTER 28

Despite a restless night, Martha was full of nervous energy as her mind kept replaying the events of the night before. She was back in the mock courtroom and Charles picked up on her mood.

"Would it be helpful if we rerun how we have arrived at this point? Or, at the very least, the events of yesterday, which Paul has made me aware of. You have had a formidable amount to process, both legally and on a personal level, and there is still more to come."

Martha was not a woman who wore her emotions lightly but was pleased at the suggestion. She recounted the moment when she and Harry had been accosted. "It made me feel the need to do something. The thought of what's still to come is making me want to run and hide."

Charles studied her. "You wouldn't be human if you didn't feel like jumping at alternative strategies. Pleading not guilty is often the toughest choice, but it is absolutely the right one for you. I will not insult you by claiming nothing can go wrong. It can. But I wouldn't be here if I didn't feel that you're entirely innocent — and fighting these charges is the sensible option. If something alters that view, I'll be the first to say so. We won't be guilty of a mindless determination to take your case to trial. Right now, we have a cogent, well-considered defence which is based on facts, not some wild notion of sticking two fingers up at the court."

Much as Martha welcomed his words, she steeled herself to see this through. It wasn't about trust; it was, if she was totally honest, about Betty and the best outcome for her. She needed convincing, and today was going to be the day.

She said, "I hope I'm not giving the impression I don't like your approach. I've seen enough defence teams to know a good one, and with you guys, I feel blessed. It's just that I'm so worried. Worried that maybe I'm the weakest link and will dissolve the moment I come under real pressure . . ." She trailed off, suddenly feeling alone.

"Take a seat," Charles urged her. "Of course you're worried. You should be — and so should I. Like I said before, this is as serious as it gets, and we need to bring our best game. I'm betting that your doubts were magnified by the behaviour of the new judge?"

Seeing her nod, he carried on. "Of course, there are challenges. I can't promise you that we'll prevail . . . Actually, I'll rephrase that. I can't guarantee we'll win at the first attempt — but win we will."

Martha was pensive. "I can't stop worrying about going to jail."

To her relief, he clearly gave her words serious consideration before he replied. "As I said, we have a strong defence. It should be an easy win, but sometimes there can be problems. Juries are made up of human beings. I'm not going to lie — we could lose because a jury doesn't like you or me. It happens. Just as bad, a judge may influence the jury unfairly. But if any of that happens, we will fight again, just as hard, and we will win because lightning does not strike twice — not in court. We would be starting again, with a new judge and a new jury. It would be a genuinely level playing field."

He paused. "But yes, even then, we might lose. But we would have put up such a powerful and justified fight that the sentence would be minimal. If we try to achieve

that through plea bargaining, we look weak, sound weak . . .
Martha, we would *be* weak. In those circumstances, our judge
would hang you out to dry.

"We all understand your dilemma, Martha. You have to
think beyond yourself and I admire you for that. It will not
offend me in the slightest if you want to take a plea."

Martha took in a huge lungful of air, hoping to calm
her fluttering heart.

"No need to wait. You just convinced me. I want to
fight this case, but I also want to do the right thing by Betty.
You've convinced me that doing the first helps the second."

* * *

At the next bail hearing, the judge made no attempt to reheat
the previous drama. She stated that the trial was scheduled to
begin in six weeks' time at the Old Bailey.

"What do you think of the choice of venue?" asked
Charles, as though he was discussing the location of a music gig.

Harry offered a view. "They don't like coppers at the
Old Bailey, I can tell you that much. Might work against
Martha, might not."

"I take it you mean that, since Martha will be a defendant, it might work for her." Harry was non-committal, so the
lawyer added, "As always, we'll have to wait and see. Only
the biggest cases get heard there. In normal circumstances,
our little case shouldn't get a look-in, but this isn't normal."

Paul interjected, "I've had some of my staff monitoring
coverage. They say the case against you is generating a lot of
comments on social media. Someone did a survey asking:
'How far would you go to save your child?' The overwhelming majority said they would do whatever it took."

Charles was interested in that. "I wonder if your people could see if there are any allegations being made online
against Martha? That might come in useful for jury challenges . . . or even help with an appeal, if we go down that
path."

"But juries aren't meant to look at anything relating to a trial, surely?"

"Not once the case gets underway, they're not. But you can hardly expect people to ignore all news just in case they get called to serve."

* * *

Making the most of a run of fine weather, Harry and Martha were in the habit of walking to and from the mock courtroom. It was Martha's turn to set the pace today — but, unusually, she was soon outstripping Harry.

"What's up, old-timer? Going a bit fast for you, am I? Perhaps a Zimmer frame might help you keep up?" She didn't get many chances to best him, and relished the opportunity when it arose.

"Ha, ha. Hilarious. You'll be a pensioner yourself one day. Then you'll be embarrassed that you used to mock a poor old man."

"Harry, you're one of the fittest pensioners around. I've seen you chase muggers just for fun. So, unless you've developed a sudden disability, what's going on?"

He looked sheepish. "It was talking about the Old Bailey. A load of memories floated to the surface, took me right back."

"You don't normally get sentimental over that sort of thing."

"It's not the place, not exactly. It's the people — your dad. A lot of his investigations ended up at the Old Bailey. That was where they tried to bring him down with claims he was taking backhanders from all and sundry."

Martha frowned. "I don't remember anything about that."

"That was thanks to your mum. You weren't much older than Betty is now. Your mum took you over to Ireland — she had relatives there. They put you up until everything was done and dusted. Your mum worked hard to protect you as much as she could."

They walked a little further on. "Your dad even sent me over there for a while, but I wasn't needed. All I did was stick out like a sore thumb. I was a South London boy in the middle of the Irish countryside. It was obvious the locals knew all about security. I was left to enjoy the Guinness, then come home.

"The Old Bailey's played a big role in our lives. Remember I told you I had to go to prison a couple of times? Well, the Old Bailey was one of the places I was sent down from. I can still remember your dad looking at me as they led me down to the cells. I swear he was hiding a grin. But he was as good as gold; there was a nice bonus waiting for me when I got out."

Martha hadn't quite got her head around the idea that good and bad guys were getting money from her father. "The less I know about that, the better."

"It was different in those days. No paperwork, you see. Made it much easier to hand out bundles of cash to those who preferred to get their hands on the folding stuff. Much better all round. Nowadays, they can do all this electronic monitoring. Bloody coppers — probably know more about your own money than you do."

He smirked. "What I'm trying to say is that when I got a little bonus from your dad, I used to keep the cash in a shoe box under the bed. I kept tabs by writing in a little notebook I kept in a kitchen drawer. It may not have been top-level security, but no computer is going to sniff that out."

Martha stopped walking. "You talking about notebooks has just reminded me of something. I must have been nearly twelve years old and Dad had come to visit me at Idmiston Road. At the last minute, Mum had got me to put on a new dress. When I came down to the kitchen, I found Dad writing in a pocket-sized notebook. It had a dark cover. I asked him what it was, and he laughed and said it was his little black book. I didn't dare to ask more. Anyway, we were off for ice cream."

Harry was nodding his head very slowly. "I never got involved with how he ran his operation. But you've just nudged a faint memory of him talking about his little black book. I never asked him about it. To be honest, it was usually a waste of time asking him about anything. I worked with him for a long time and never got the full picture."

CHAPTER 29

At the turning for Idmiston Road, they passed a family loading their car with suitcases, presumably to go on holiday. They took a few more paces when Harry stopped and grunted.

Martha looked at him quizzically and he said, "It must be a day for odd memories about your dad. You know I've got a suitcase of his, stuffed with receipts, which I've been trying to make sense of? He was always leaving stuff like that with me. I sometimes used to think I was his personal left luggage office. I didn't really think much of it when he turned up with this one. This was about six months before he died, making it the last thing he left in my care, not that I knew that then. He told me it was full of receipts, even opening it to show me. He called it his 'bits and pieces' case, asked if I'd hold on to it? He was always doing things like that, turning up with stuff for me to keep an eye on, usually just for a few weeks. I put it in the loft, and there it stayed, until recently."

As he was telling the story he'd slowed to a halt. "It's quite a nice case, really. Quality leather and never been taken away, as far as I know. What I'm trying to say is, would you like it? Maybe keep it for Betty when she grows up, something from her grandad? Aren't you always telling me old stuff is good?"

Martha patted his arm. "Vintage, I'm always saying vintage is good. Like a fine wine, or even you." She warded off the playful punch he threw. "I'd love to see it, Harry, but only if you're sure you don't want it? I just need to see Betty and have a bath. Can you pop down with it in half an hour or so?"

They parted outside her house and Martha walked in, looking for her daughter. Betty was already home — Martha had recently given Justin a set of house keys, so improved was their relationship, and he had started to bring her directly home from school rather than going to his place. Betty had been offered the chance to stay at Justin's place but was reluctant, and Martha deduced her daughter really needed the comfort only her real home provided. It didn't matter to Justin; he was happy to be where he was needed. Martha was drawing great comfort from his being around, even though it was in preparation for an event they both hoped wouldn't happen, but it was nice to come home and find Betty there — almost as if Martha's mother was still around and doing the school run, before all of the trouble. After a cuddle and a chat with her daughter, Martha went to the kitchen to speak to Justin, who was washing up Betty's dinner things.

"Betty's in a lovely mood. Sounds like you two had a great day."

Justin grinned. "We had a great time at the park. How are things going with the case?"

"It's been a tough day — we were told the case is going to the Old Bailey. Hearing that brought things home. Listen, I know it's cheeky, but do you mind staying on for fifteen minutes while I have a bath — keep Betty company for me?"

"No problem. Take as long as you need. I love hanging out with Betty." Justin poured her a glass of wine. "I can tell you're feeling the stress. Who wouldn't?"

"Thanks. I must admit that the only time I ever risk a bath now that Mum's gone is if I'm up early and Betty's still asleep. It's silly, but I can't help worrying about her hurting herself."

* * *

A couple of hours later, Martha was feeling much better in her baggiest clothing and Betty was tucked up in bed. Deciding against more wine, she made a cup of tea and was taking her first sip just as the doorbell rang. Harry was outside, holding a small suitcase.

"Going on holiday?" she asked.

He followed her to the kitchen, placing the suitcase on the table. It looked vintage. At a guess she thought it was from the 1970s, but she wouldn't have bet on that. It bore similar dimensions to a standard airline cabin bag, the type you can take on board, with a lock either side of the leather handle. Both were open.

Martha studied it closely, even giving it a suspicious sniff. "This looks like it might share a birthday with you, Harry."

"This is the case I told you about. The one I've had in my loft. The one he said had only receipts in it. The one he even said I should check for myself."

Martha waited patiently. Harry was going somewhere with this.

"Your dad always did things for a reason. And he was clever. Like leaving me with this. I thought it was just something he'd done dozens of times before. Well, I guess the old bastard got one over on me again. I should have spotted the clues from him being so careful to tell me what was in it. As you now know, he never told anyone anything, if he could avoid it." He stared at her. "Care to guess what I think I've found?"

She no longer felt tired. "Have you discovered his little black book?"

"Maybe. Let me show you something first, because if you agree, we may have to damage this case."

"You think there might be a secret compartment in it?"

In answer, he pulled a small plastic ruler from his back pocket. He placed the ruler against the suitcase.

142

"Seven inches deep. Now, inside . . ." He read the measurement and then took it again to be sure. "Six and a half inches. I'm terrible at sums but that's half an inch different. I think this case has a false bottom."

Martha beamed as she held the suitcase up to examine it more closely. "I can't see anything by eye. Whatever made you think about it?"

"It was something Paul said a few days ago, while we were in the mock courtroom. He said your dad once thought about doing something similar, but decided against it because it would have attracted too much attention. He reminded me how much your dad loved things to be mysterious. This evening I was looking at the suitcase when it hit me. How much more mysterious than a case with a false bottom?

"That's when I knew he'd done a 'find the lady' on me. Taking my mind off the suitcase itself by showing me it was full of boring receipts. Would you like to do the honours?"

Martha spent a little time looking for concealed catches, but there was nothing.

"We'll have to cut the bottom out," she said.

Harry had come equipped and handed her a sharp-bladed box cutter. "This should do it."

She carefully cut the bottom free of the suitcase then used the blade of the knife to lift it free. Her heart was beating fast as she lifted it away to reveal the notebook she could now recall seeing it all those years ago. It was covered in black leather and taped firmly in place to stop it rattling around. There was also an envelope addressed to Harry. She released both and made to hand the envelope to Harry, which he declined.

"Would you mind?"

She tackled the letter first, opening it to extract a sheet of paper. The handwritten note was in her father's distinctive hand:

Thanks for being a good friend, Harry. And apologies for misleading you. I needed somewhere safe to keep this book,

and who better than you? I'm sure that, one day, you will
need it, and am equally sure you will work out my little ruse
when you really need to. I know you will put it to good use.

She read it again. "He didn't even sign it." She leaned
over and picked up the notebook, cradling it in her hands.
"Before we go any further, do you want a drink? I know I do.
I've got wine and lager in the fridge."

They both chose a beer. Martha drank a couple of
mouthfuls before looking at the notebook again.

"What do you think?" she asked.

He threw his hands wide in a "who can say?" gesture.

Taking a breath, she opened the book, staring unblink-
ingly at the opening page. She flicked through some more
pages and then laughed as she showed it to Harry.

"You've always said he had secrets in secrets. So, no
change there. It's in some sort of code. I got it in my head
that he had his own private army, but there's only one entry
per page."

Martha counted the entries. The individual pages contained just numbers and letters, nothing more. "Twenty-
eight entries. I guess these must have been the important
ones." She handed it to Harry. "See for yourself. It's not the
smoking gun we thought. At least not until we crack the
code."

Harry flicked through. "Nothing about this code makes
sense. I mean, this one, 'LEMI 2', or this one, 'DOG 1'.
None of it rings a bell."

Chastened, Martha said, "It was daft of me to expect it
was going to be easy. I was wondering if we'd see Peter Shaw
in it. Ever since he had me arrested, he's just disappeared. If
I didn't know better, he's using the charming DI Holland to
keep his hands clean while she does the dirty work. It's been
bothering me that he turns up claiming to be a friend of John
Munro's. He hasn't done anything to prove it." She pursed
her lips. "I guess we're going to have to do this the hard way
and work out the code. Which is something I am totally out

of my depth over. Maybe we give it to Justin? He's into hacking — he might have the right software to crack this." Even as she spoke she felt more doubtful than hopeful.

Harry shrugged. "You lost me at 'software', but this is your dad all over. He never liked to make things simple. Why would he let a little thing like death impede his philosophy?" Harry sighed. "Whatever we do next, we need to be careful before we get someone else involved. We don't even know how current the contents are. My guess is that many of the people listed here may still be around."

He turned the notebook over in his hands. "I only knew a fraction of what your dad was up to, but if this book contains his biggest secrets, then that information is going to be extremely valuable.

"I did hear rumours about it — from time to time. But nothing solid. I kept my ears open, but nothing I heard made sense. One minute everyone was convinced the list existed, the next they were certain it didn't. From time to time, people would say he must have left something behind, something hidden away, but it never developed and there's been nothing for a while now. Can you imagine what will happen if word leaks out that his daughter has got her hands on a secret notebook? I hate to think who might come out of the woodwork."

"Well, that's just it, Harry. They already have." She took the notebook from him. "This is the reason Betty was taken."

CHAPTER 30

Justin stared at the little notebook in horror.

"You think this list your dad kept is what killed your mum and got Betty kidnapped? It's too horrible, I can't even bring myself to touch it. Oh, Martha, if only we'd known. Do you think we might have prevented what happened?"

"I doubt it," said Martha. "We think the contents of this notebook are so important and so valuable that certain people would move heaven and earth to get at it. Harry believes it's a list of the most important crime lords, or policemen — which might turn out to be the same thing — that Dad kept on his payroll. Reputations could be ruined if he's right."

"Just knowing about the list is potentially dangerous."

"I couldn't agree more," said Martha. "The more I think about it, the more it seems like something triggered a panicked scramble. The kidnappers didn't even have time to demand a ransom, remember? And if they've been asking for Dad's little black book since the kidnapping, they've been far too subtle about it."

"At the moment they acted you didn't even know about the notebook. Do you think they realised that?"

"It's impossible to know, not without asking them, and I don't see that happening any time soon." And then a thought occurred to her. "Commander Shaw. He asked me if my dad had given me anything the shooters might have wanted. He was leading the investigation — he was the one who said this had something to do with Dad. I can't say for sure he's behind any of this, but I'm trying to be logical."

Justin looked thoughtful. "Your mum was convinced this house was broken into a few times following John's death, but nothing was ever taken. Does that throw any light on things?"

She nodded. "Don't remind me. Mum said people had been in the house, and I didn't believe her. I thought it was some sort of weird grief thing. I hate thinking that if I'd acted at the time, then this could have been avoided. Harry says I'm wrong — how could I have known about something my dad deliberately kept secret from me? Anyway, he says that after Dad died it went quiet, and more recently the rumours started up again. Best guess? Something happened very recently which brought the notebook's existence to light and gave people the impression that I might have it."

Just saying the words made her tense up and she flexed her hands. "I've got a working theory based on the little I do know. Whoever hired the Dragov brothers was taking a risk because they were in a rush. I think they were only supposed to get Betty, and then only so that she could be used as leverage over me.

"Let's face it, if I had known anything I would have talked straight away. But instead, the operation was bungled, Mum was killed and while the brothers took Betty, she was taken off them and left for me to find. I don't think the intention was to hold Betty that long, just enough to send a message to me to cough up the secret list. Then, when it unravelled, the people holding the real power took off."

"So, who are these people? Any clues?" said Justin.

"That's the million-dollar question. There have to be at least two separate groups: the person who ordered the kidnapping and a faction within the police itself.

"Harry and I both think there is the possibility that no one is quite sure what they're looking for. Obviously, it's a list, but is it a smoking gun? How big is it? Is it online? Who features on it? All these questions need answering. We need time to crack the code so we can identify who's coming after us — before they find out I have the damn list."

Justin looked grim. "It's beyond irony that we can't go to the police with this."

"Tell me about it. The only thing I do know is that John Munro was juggling a lot of balls when he died, and it's now up to all of us to get them back in the air."

Just running through the different scenarios was taking some effort, but she still had areas to cover.

"I know telling you all this drags you deeper into this conspiracy, but I didn't think it was fair to leave you in the dark. If you want me to stop, I will totally understand. Just say the word."

Justin reacted like she'd slapped him. "You are kidding, right? You think I'm going to run away?"

"Oh, Justin, forgive me. That's not what I meant at all. Knowing you're here for Betty is helping to keep me going. I don't know what would happen if you weren't here." She looked down as tears pricked her eyes.

Moved by the passion in her answer, Justin smiled gently. "I'm here to stay, to the bitter end."

"Thank you. Just one thing, then I'll make the tea. Do you understand anything about code-breaking?"

"Nope. Not my field. I can look into downloading some code-cracking software, but don't hold your breath. Let's talk to Harry later — I'm thinking we could bring in a specialist on that front."

* * *

Harry slammed his hand down hard on the table when he was told Justin's suggestion the next day. "No, there's no way we can do that. We can't bring new people in on this. Secrets have wings."

His dramatic intervention took them by surprise. Harry never lost his cool. Ever.

Justin was unapologetic. "Harry, I get what you're saying, and this is only an idea. I don't need to tell you how important my little girl is. I'm floundering here, looking for ways to keep Betty safe. It may not be the best idea, but I won't apologise for throwing it out there. Martha's explained this notebook is the reason she was taken from us. And that it's the key to keeping her safe. New eyes on this notebook would give us an advantage — it'd only be one other person."

"But that's the trouble with secrets. The only real secret is one no one knows about. Once you start sharing them, they take on a life of their own. Trust me. I've seen too many people get hurt because they shared some big secret with someone they trusted — and the next minute, gone."

He stopped to let the finality of that statement sink in. "It's human nature. Once someone has some information, they just have to share it. You can't stop it."

CHAPTER 31

As any decent military historian will tell you, the best laid plans only survive first contact with the enemy.

In this case, the enemy was the judge at the Old Bailey. For a few weeks the case had been gently meandering through the system until the new judge intervened to turbocharge proceedings. She wanted a jury selected and all sides ready to go on the coming Monday.

Martha poured her efforts into making sure that she, Betty and Justin could enjoy the weekend. She kept the thought to herself but she couldn't escape the idea this might be their "final" weekend together.

Fortunately, Betty was in a lovely mood, still enjoying the novelty of having Justin sleeping on the sofa each night. Martha had offered him her mum's room, but he'd very gently turned it down. "Let's leave it for a little while longer," he'd said. She was pleased. She knew she'd have to get in and sort the room out eventually, but this postponed a job she was quietly dreading.

Martha was pleased her daughter was coping so well and was deeply grateful to Justin, who had stepped up without any hesitation. But a tiny part of her wished she could wrap Betty in her arms and keep her safe forever.

All too soon, Monday morning came around. She and Harry travelled to court together, but neither felt like indulging in their usual banter. The stakes felt too high for jokes.

Martha sat in the defendant's box as the assembled legal teams made their final preparations. Then the jury filed in and Martha felt like someone had thrown a switch as the prosecutor rose to his feet.

Although the hearing was under strict legal safeguards that prevented discussion in the media, the wood-panelled courtroom was packed with expectant reporters. The press box was so full that the court had set up an overflow room with a live audio and video feed. The jury was absent, being sent out by the judge during legal arguments.

Martha tried to pretend to herself this was an everyday event. She wasn't doing a very good job of it. Now and then a sense of panic overwhelmed her, and she was dreading giving evidence. She wished she could be more like Harry. He'd been accredited to the defence team and was sitting on the bench behind Charles. He was the picture of relaxation and positivity.

The next thing she knew, she was saying "not guilty" when asked how she was pleading. She thought her voice sounded weedy.

The crown prosecutor, George Grylls, a stocky man with ginger hair visible under his wig, was on his feet. He finished outlining the case: "It is clear to me that this defendant acted in a pre-meditated fashion as she set out on a revenge mission. No one disputes the appalling situation that Ms Munro found herself in, but no one can be above the law — especially not police officers. If we cannot trust a police officer to follow the rules, then the very walls of society are at risk of tumbling down."

As the man sat, Martha narrowed her eyes. Hearing him outline the case really grated as it underlined how unfair this was. Even though she was innocent this man was trying to have her jailed. She didn't even know if he was part of the conspiracy against her. She caught herself beginning to slump and sat up as straight as possible, trying to radiate innocence. Harry had reminded her that the jury would be watching her like hawks, looking for clues to her guilt or innocence.

Charles was already on his feet, waiting for the judge to grant him permission to begin speaking.

She inclined her head. "You may proceed, Mr Winter. I would appreciate your brevity."

"Thank you, My Lady. I will not be long."

Martha was glad she was sitting down. This was it: the first chance for her team to get some points on the board. Discreetly, she wiped her hands on her trousers and took a sip of water. Charles clasped his hands together in front of him.

"It is our contention that the prosecution has utterly failed to make its case. They have presented no evidence to support this charge other than, and it grieves me to say this, a rather sensationalist account of events. The truth is remarkably simple. My client received a phone call at work warning her that a serious event had taken place at her home — her mother was dead, and her daughter taken by the killers. Beside herself with grief — exactly as any other person would have been — she asked a colleague to drive her home. During that journey, she made no phone calls, as the officer who drove has already testified.

"Once at the scene, she confirmed the terrible news and was then, unprompted, given information that her daughter was being held captive. A man she trusted implicitly and had known all her life provided that information. She felt she could count on this information and left with him to find her daughter.

"She had only just identified her mother's body. It was foolish to set out on her own, but she was in shock and acting on impulse. She was in no state to conspire with her companion. I hope My Lady agrees with me that to pursue such a serious matter on such flimsy grounds would hold our legal system up to ridicule."

As he sat down, Martha had to resist putting in a round of applause. She was feeling confident — until the icy gaze of the judge lingered on her.

"The case will continue in one hour."

Charles jumped to his feet. "One thing, My Lady, we are still waiting for your ruling on allowing the statements from the Dragov brothers to be used. For reasons we are all aware, neither can attend or face cross-examination."

The judge glanced down. "The statements will be allowed, I am satisfied they were taken using correct procedures."

As Charles made to object again, she stood up and left. It was a clear demonstration that she was operating to a drum beat only she could hear.

Outside the court, Harry shook his head. "You'd think the judge's knickers were on fire, the way she legged it out of there."

Martha asked Charles what he made of it.

"To be honest, she's acting like she only has one goal, to find you guilty. I especially don't like her allowing the statements. We don't get the chance to cross-examine, which is wrong, but in the short run we have no choice. Her court, her rules. It means we have to play this out before we can launch a formal protest."

Martha felt her mouth go dry. This wasn't shaping up well.

CHAPTER 32

"All rise."

As one, the occupants of the courtroom stood up. Gripping the sides of the defendant's box as she waited for the judge to appear, Martha had never felt so alone. She was painfully aware that she was the focus of intense scrutiny from the public gallery, which seemed to have become the most coveted seats in London.

George Grylls proved to be a methodical man, laying out the details clearly and slowly. He made a great play of the Taser the police had found on Martha, repeatedly labouring that it was a significant weapon, a more powerful version than the police would use.

"The fact that she was, to use the language, 'tooled up' with such weaponry — well, that might imply a degree of forward planning."

"Objection. That is a blatant attempt to prejudice the jury."

The judge seemed irritated. "I agree. Strike the remarks, although Mr Winter would be wise to avoid making constant objections."

This brought a smattering of sycophantic laughter from the jury, and even Martha smiled, until she noticed Charles looking worried.

Grylls wasn't giving up. "I am demonstrating that the defendant was armed with a weapon that was more powerful than she used in work situations. I believe this shows a state of readiness on her part. A readiness to use violence."

Charles was on his feet. "Objection. Same point as before, minus the phrase you don't like."

The judge responded. "You both need to be careful with your wording, Mr Winter."

Charles surprised Martha by requesting an adjournment until after lunch. "We are almost at the point where we would break, so if My Lady agrees?"

She did, informing the court that proceedings would resume in one hour.

Martha's team met up in one of the rooms in the bowels of the ancient court building. It had a table and some plastic chairs; privacy rather than comfort was the intention. Martha fired a question at Charles the moment the door shut. "Something's rattled you. What is it?"

He didn't deny it. "I don't like the way the judge is behaving. She's making little jokes at Grylls's expense, but it feels put on. When I raised the second objection, she appeared to agree with me — but then she didn't instruct the jury to ignore the information."

A plate of sandwiches arrived, together with some tea and coffee. They all took a drink, but no one seemed hungry — not even Harry.

Once again time seemed to speed up and Martha was back in court watching Commander Shaw lay out the police case. He was wearing a dress uniform and positively glittered as he spoke. If anything, his manner was even more pedantic than Grylls, although to Martha's worried eye the jury seemed impressed by his every word, especially his final remarks.

"It was clear to me that Ms Munro was extremely agitated. She was bouncing on her feet, and I noticed she was clenching and unclenching her fists. I became concerned that she might be thinking of taking matters into her own hands and I reminded her of her position. In my opinion she took no notice, and I took the additional precaution of formally ordering her to stay out of the investigation."

Charles was on his feet. "I would ask that you rule against this evidence. Commander Shaw is making a series of claims about my client which he could not possibly have known."

The judge waved her hand. "Objection denied. I shall allow it."

Charles sat down quickly and silenced Harry's grumble with a glare.

Grylls then read out the statements of the two brothers, addressing the opening remarks to the jury.

"I just wanted to remind you that because of the unfortunate death of Ivan Dragov, one could say these words are spoken from beyond the grave."

"Objection." Winter was back on his feet. "That remark is irrelevant and melodramatic."

The judge didn't wait. "It may not be to your taste, Mr Winter, but I shall allow it."

This time the QC reddened. He sat carefully, bracing his hands on the table; he needed to be ready to present Martha's defence. Soon Charles began setting out his argument, giving no sign of the worries he'd expressed a short while ago. When he finally turned to the jury, he was oozing sincerity.

"I do not believe it possible to find my client guilty. If my client had launched the alleged assault, she would herself have suffered injuries, especially to her hands and feet. Hristo Dragov describes being punched, repeatedly, in the face. Yet when Martha Munro was examined, no trace of injury to her hands could be found. Since there is no suggestion she was wearing gloves, how is this possible?

"The answer is that it isn't possible. And if this basic element is wrong, the rest of the prosecution's case is too. This is a tissue of lies designed to discredit a fine young officer. I ask you to find her not guilty."

Martha watched the jury intently, hoping for clues about their intensions. She hoped that they were inclined to believe her, although the one time she made eye contact with the jury foreman, the woman looked away. She reminded herself to be cautious — she couldn't afford to be accused of attempting to intimidate a jury member.

The moment Charles sat down, Grylls was on his feet. "If I may, My Lady? I would like to present some new evidence to the court, evidence we have only just received."

The judge looked at the jury. "There will be a short period of legal debate which need not detain you. I shall recall you when this matter is concluded."

Charles waited impatiently for his chance to speak. "This is the first I have heard of new evidence. You cannot allow new evidence after the jury has been presented with concluding statements."

The judge was imperious. "I decide what is fair, Mr Winter. I alone decide what is allowed in my court. I remind you not to challenge my position. Mr Grylls, I take it you have sufficient copies of the new material?"

He bowed. "I do, My Lady. It is quite short, as you can see for yourself." He handed her a stapled copy of two pieces of A4 paper.

The judge read it with a professional eye, then handed it to Charles. "That won't detain you very long, Mr Winter — and I'm sure your client will have an answer. Just to be fair, I will give you a thirty-minute break. Then the evidence can be submitted." Standing up, she walked off.

From her position, Martha could see Grylls was smirking. She felt sick.

Soon, they were all back in the room, reading the new document. Martha could hardly believe her eyes. "None of this is true. I would never say that. And why aren't they revealing their source?"

Charles sighed. "It's an old trick and only works when you have the judge on your side. You introduce damning new evidence, claiming your source needs protecting. The judge agrees and suddenly you have evidence that is impossible to answer."

He gave Martha a very direct look. "I'm afraid this means you're going to be portrayed as unstable, manipulative and calculating, with some sort of father fixation. It's just mad enough for the jury to go for it. We'll win easily on appeal, but this judge worries me. It's quite wrong to be allowing this evidence. She knows we'll appeal, and win. But in the meantime she might say this evidence provides a reason to remand you in custody. So be ready for anything. Above all — do not lose your temper."

As they trooped into the courtroom, Martha was thinking furiously. She was up against powerful opponents who were well organised and well funded. Was she crazy to have ever thought she could win?

The prosecutor was already waiting. Soon, the jury shuffled in. Then the nightmare began.

* * *

Martha was soon back on the stand, despite another attempt by Charles to halt proceedings. After he finished the judge rounded on him. "That was your last intervention along those lines. Next time, I will hold you in contempt of court."

Grylls waited with all the patience of an attack dog smelling blood. "You are the daughter of former Commander John Munro, a man who ran the anti-corruption unit at Scotland Yard?"

"I am."

"Did you know your father was one of the most feared officers at the Met?"

Charles jumped in. "Objection. How can she possibly answer a question like that?"

"Be very careful, Mr Winter, and that is hardly a difficult question, it merely requires yes or no, I would imagine. Carry on, Mr Grylls."

"For the record — did you know your father was feared?"

Martha nodded.

"Out loud, please."

Her voice was faint. "He was only feared because he—"

"Because of your father," Grylls interrupted, "you were determined to make a name for yourself. You wanted to build on the family legacy. Martha, isn't it true that you set up the whole thing? It was a tragic accident that your mother was killed, but it might as well have been your finger on the trigger."

Martha felt hot and dizzy.

Grylls was driving on. All traces of the pedantic lawyer were now gone as he charged into the attack. "We have a witness who says you wanted to get yourself talked about. That it had to be something big enough to get everyone talking about you."

Even though she had been coached to face such an attack, the reality still stung. She glanced at Charles, who jumped up. "Might my client take a brief break? We had no warning of this line of attack. She needs to compose herself and answer these questions as honestly as she can."

He wasn't expecting a positive answer, but he hoped his intervention allowed Martha a few moments to process the new accusations.

To his surprise, the judge nodded. "You may have ten minutes. No more."

There was no time to get to their briefing room, so they grabbed a quiet space just outside the courtroom, Harry making sure no one got close.

Charles spoke to Martha. "I'm sorry, Martha. I underestimated them. I thought I'd seen it all, but I hadn't. I won't make the same mistake twice, but for now—"

She finished the sentence: "For now, they win. Are they going to produce this 'witness'?"

He put on a tired smile. "I fear that is exactly what they're going to do. The best thing we can do now is attempt a little smoke and mirrors. When we return, I will say a promising new line of inquiry, one that could help you, has emerged. I'll say we need this afternoon to pursue it." He paused. "There are only a couple of hours of court time to go today, so she should grant us a delay. But a delay is all it will be. This judge is not on our side. I expect the witness will appear tomorrow morning and the jury will be sent out shortly after."

"What about this new line of defence?" asked Martha.

Charles shrugged. "We'll say it didn't work out and thank her for her indulgence."

Paul Avery couldn't keep the anger out of his tone. "This is as big a disgrace as I have ever encountered in court, but I feel helpless to stop it."

"You're right. I'll carry on the fight with every bone in my body, but you need to start taking notes for our appeal." Charles gestured at Martha. "I'm fearful that their entire strategy is based around getting you taken into custody while we go through the appeal process. There's no doubt that you'll be freed once we get in front of an impartial judge — but until then we're at this woman's mercy. If I challenge her head on, it may make matters worse. She's itching for a fight."

Martha was already mentally putting up the shutters. She had to get ready for what was coming. Until tomorrow morning, she was going to be Betty's loving mother — but, once she arrived at court, her chances of avoiding custody were vanishingly slim.

CHAPTER 33

To say it had been a tough day in court was an understatement, but every step away from the Old Bailey lifted her mood. She and Harry headed wordlessly towards Blackfriars, enjoying the anonymity of walking along crowded pavements. Crossing the River Thames at Blackfriars Bridge, she enjoyed the cool breeze and felt calmer about what might happen. They stopped at the halfway point, Martha gazing down at the river and taking comfort in the familiar sight of one of the sleek river taxis crossing underneath her. Looking up, she ticked off some of her favourite buildings — Tate Modern, the Oxo Tower and even the dome of St Paul's. A street sweeper went by, his dreadlocks covered by a woollen hat.

She silently dismissed the thought of jumping on a train; she needed this chance to stretch her legs, so they headed slowly towards Elephant and Castle to find a bus. Nowadays, this was very much an up-and-coming area, boasting expensive new apartments. In her father's time, it had been a place to be avoided, even during the daytime.

She called Justin to let him know what was going on and he suggested they all meet up in Dulwich Park. There, Betty could have an ice cream and play on the swings, while Martha enjoyed a few moments of much-needed normality.

* * *

Betty squealed with delight when she saw her mother. Martha scooped up her daughter and held on tight. The little girl was quick to seize the opportunity as she spoke into Martha's ear. "Mummy, Daddy says I can have ice cream before dinner tonight."

Martha laughed. "That's why I'm here. I want to see my little girl eat the biggest ice cream in the world."

Betty looked solemn. "Don't be silly, Mummy. I need to leave some room for the chicken and chips I'm having later."

An hour flew by. Harry left them there, wanting to go home and change out of his court clothes, but promised to drop in later for dinner once Betty had gone to bed.

Back home, Martha knew she needed to talk to Betty as soon as she had eaten. Far too soon, the moment was there. She recalled the teacher's advice: "Keep it simple, not too much detail. Make it sound like there's nothing to worry about."

They were sitting on the floor of the front room, Martha watching her daughter drawing pictures of a dog — a large black blob with four uneven legs, lop-sided ears and an enormous tongue. Martha welled up, thinking it was the best dog she'd ever seen. She tried to get a grip. She was in danger of being too emotional and making things worse. Her mouth was bone dry.

"You know Mummy is a police officer? And my job is to stop bad people?"

"Of course I do," Betty said imperiously. "I'm nearly five years old."

Martha smiled and ran her fingers through the little girl's soft blonde hair. "What I'm trying to say is that, sometimes, my job makes me very busy. I may not be around for a bit. I might have to visit a prison, but it will only be for a few days. It's just a silly rule. If that does happen, Daddy will stay at our house with you."

For just a moment, Betty showed no reaction, but then her eyes met Martha's.

"You are coming back, Mummy?" There was no mistaking the fear behind the question. Martha felt something break deep inside her, opening her arms wide to cuddle her daughter. Betty had lost so much already, she didn't deserve more pain. "Yes, I'm coming back. I double, double promise and cross my heart."

Betty said nothing, but the little squeeze she gave Martha spoke volumes. They stayed locked together for a few precious moments, giving Martha the chance to inhale the scent of her little girl, before Betty wriggled free and stood up in front of Martha. Her big eyes were bright and serious. Martha worried about what was coming next.

Betty said, "Daddy always lets me have ice cream. I like it when he's around."

Justin had the grace to blush. "What can I say? I'm just a four-year-old's bag-carrier."

CHAPTER 34

Martha woke at first light. She wanted to have a long, hot bath. She might not have another chance.

All too soon, she and Justin were getting ready to drop Martha at school. Everything seemed nice and normal. Except her ex-husband was going off script. As they stood in the hallway, he wiped his eye. "Just got some dust in it. Nothing to worry about."

The happy little bubble she had created burst the moment she and Harry reached the Old Bailey. A huge mob of photographers, reporters and TV crews pounced, all yelling her name and shoving each other to get into the best position.

Harry was at his fiercest as he battered a path through the crush. She passed people shouting questions: "Did you kill your own mother . . . What's it like to have a bent cop as a father . . . ?"

Other reporters were trying a different tack. It was being reported that following the death of Ivan Dragov, who had fired the fatal shot, Hristo, his younger brother, was being offered a deal: take a guilty plea on kidnapping and receive a sentence on the lower end of the tariff. That could see him out after twelve months. Some journalists were trying to draw comments from her.

She wanted to turn and confront her questioners — but Harry was determined to keep her moving, desperate to avoid confrontation. Fighting on the steps of the courthouse would win her a slot on the news and do her no favours.

As they reached the sanctuary of the court building, she noticed Harry shaking his hands. Martha said, "I thought I saw you land a couple of punches."

He smiled grimly. "A few were getting a bit personal."

Security meant they couldn't take their phones into the building. One of Paul Avery's paralegals had been tasked with looking after their things while they were inside. Finally entering the quiet bustle of the court building acted like a balm for both of them, allowing their minds to settle and focus on the day ahead. Martha and Harry made their way to the meeting room to find Charles was already there, deep in some document. He didn't look up, but Paul, sitting alongside him, did. After a quick greeting, he explained why Charles was so engrossed. "We got the witness statement, twenty minutes ago. Charles is going through it now."

"The one from the mystery witness we talked about yesterday?"

"It's from an Olivia Chambers. She was a temporary admin worker at Croydon police station. She says you opened your heart to her over too much alcohol."

Martha was shaking her head. "I don't know her — and even if I did, I wouldn't have that type of talk with anyone. Least of all a stranger. What am I supposed to have said?"

Paul pulled out a chair. "Sit down."

Feeling sick, she threw a helpless glance at Harry and then did as Paul suggested.

"Do you want to read it, or shall I read it out loud?"

"Out loud, if that's OK?" She glanced at Charles.

"Don't worry about him," said Paul. "It would take a bomb going off to interrupt him. I'll paraphrase the start and then read out the key detail . . ."

He cleared his throat and began. "So, Olivia Chambers said it was a Wednesday evening, just after 6 p.m. on the tenth of March, when she encountered you in the Croydon Arms. I believe that's the pub favoured by officers and staff at the Croydon station? Chambers says she'd been invited to a leaving party and went along, even though she hadn't really met most of the people there. She wanted to be part of the team. She says it was very boisterous and, as she was not drinking, she drifted away from the main action. That's when she noticed you. Her statement reads:

> *I saw a young woman, my age, sitting on her own and just staring into space. I felt she was lonely, and my natural empathy drew me towards her. I introduced myself and she told me to call her Martha, no surname. I asked her why she was drinking alone, and her answer surprised me. She said she was always alone. No one understood the pressure she was under, and no one ever would. By this time, I was worried for her and asked why she felt under pressure. She started crying and said it was because of her father. I gathered she was a detective and her dad had also been in the force. But she wouldn't be drawn. She kept saying he cast a big shadow.*
>
> *At this point, she insisted on having another drink, even though I tried to talk her out of it. She had a double vodka and swallowed it down. After that, she sat in silence. I eventually offered her a lift, but she refused, so I went to leave. She stopped me. She leaned right against me and said she had a plan. She was going to do something that got people talking about her and not her father.*
>
> *I was troubled but didn't know what to make of it, so I left her. Not my finest hour, I suppose. It was only after that poor woman was murdered in Dulwich that I realised who she was. Even then, it took me a while to come forward. I didn't like to think about it. But the court case has made me realise I have a duty to speak out."*

As Paul finished reading, he handed her the copy of the statement. "Read this thoroughly. From your expression I can tell this is all news to you."

She took the copy, surprised her hands weren't shaking. "This is total fiction. I don't suppose you have a picture of her? Maybe that might jolt a memory."

"No, but you'll see her in the witness box soon."

"Have we checked she was really working at Croydon?"

"They've supplied documentation. She was covering a maternity leave and was there for four months. Apparently."

Charles interrupted. "We need to get into court. This judge isn't our friend, so we can't be late. I'll try for another delay, argue that you have no memory of this conversation, but it won't work."

Martha gasped, "Because they've already said I was drinking. They'll say I've suffered a blackout."

Charles gently cajoled them out of the door. "Let's find out what's in store."

CHAPTER 35

Martha was in Court 18 at the Old Bailey, waiting, brooding and watching the public gallery steadily fill with members of the public. She'd heard people insisting the courtroom was cramped — but it was plenty big enough for the impact it was about to have on her life. In a few minutes, the judge would appear, and from that moment, her right to freedom was in the balance. She hoped to catch sight of this so-called witness, but the woman was being kept somewhere out of view until they called her to give her bogus evidence. At least Harry was there, giving her a sly thumbs-up from his position with her legal team. He had somehow talked his way into the part of chief cheerleader.

The judge came in and Martha stood. There was no point in antagonising the old cow — much as she would have enjoyed that.

Charles was quickly into the fray, standing up with an intent response. "A point of order, My Lady." He was polite and respectful, but firm.

The judge sighed loudly enough to make the jury take an interest.

"Yes, Mr Winter."

He pushed on, apparently oblivious to the hostility. "We only received our copy of the statement this morning. There is a lot to absorb."

"You don't strike me as a slow reader, Mr Winter. You're certainly quick enough to raise objections. A lot of objections." She considered him coldly. "Perhaps you think we are all here at your pleasure? Myself, the court officers, police officers, prosecution, witnesses and the poor jury who have to sit through all this before passing judgement?"

It was all quite wrong, Martha knew. As Charles feared, the judge had one goal — to put her in prison. She glanced at the jury, wondering how many of them were bought and paid for. The judge wanted them to think her barrister was a fool and a time-waster.

Martha was already thinking about what would happen next and how tough life in prison would be for her as a former detective. It would be even worse that she was the daughter of a controversial copper.

Martha was glad Harry had driven her hard in the training sessions. She flexed her knuckles. They were bruised from constant sparring. Over the months, he had been unstinting in what he taught her, including every dirty trick he knew. His eyes were on her now. She remembered his words. *You're tough. You're strong. You can punch, wrestle, bite or kick. Never give in.*

Her strength returned, just as the judge refused any more delays.

Grylls announced triumphantly, "Just the one witness, My Lady. I call Olivia Chambers."

There was a delay before Chambers appeared and took her place on the witness stand. She was of average height, slim, with an oval face framed by black hair that touched her shoulders. Martha was quite certain she had never met her. She wanted to jump up and shout, "Impostor, liar, cheat! How much have you been paid?" Instead, she contented herself with some hard staring, which Chambers countered by not looking at her.

She appeared, Martha thought gloomily, like a super-efficient filing clerk who would rather swallow broken glass than tell a lie. Whoever was behind all of this, the level of detail and planning was outstanding. Even down to finding an innocent-faced witness to tell the biggest lies of all.

A sort of fugue state enveloped Martha as she listened to the woman go through her evidence. She was perfect, even looking at Martha in a worried but caring way as she described her downing vodka. It was Oscar-winning stuff.

Grylls played his part to perfection, keeping his interventions to a minimum as he led the woman through her evidence.

Now it was Charles's turn. He rose, mustering all his natural authority as he studied Chambers and then his notes. When he spoke, his voice was firm; any doubts were being kept well out of sight.

"Ms Chambers, you seem to have a remarkably excellent memory of something that happened quite a while ago. Are you quite sure about your recollection? Many of us, myself included, might struggle to recall events so precisely."

A faint smile flashed across the woman's face. She glanced at Martha before turning to the jury.

"I have an excellent memory. I play a lot of quiz games and do quite well with them."

"This is no quiz, Ms Chambers. The evidence you have provided is essential."

Chambers was almost contemptuous. "I realise how important this is. I was trying to answer your doubts about the accuracy of my recall. May I continue?" She glanced at the judge, who assented. "That night has stayed with me because I was shocked by what the accused said, and the amount she was drinking. Women need to be so careful with how much they drink."

Several members of the jury nodded along with this, and Martha's heart sank even lower. "I recall the night, and the accused is very attractive, something those of us less blessed tend to notice."

Once again there were nods from the jury. Chambers was doing an outstanding job.

"Obviously I didn't know who she was then, but when her picture appeared in the papers, I recognised her as the woman I'd spoken to. I understood exactly what I needed to do — step forward and give evidence."

Charles had little else to offer. He didn't want to risk looking too hopeless. "No further questions."

He sat down, and was done, the evidence given. The witness was asked to leave the stand.

Now it was time for the closing statements. The prosecutor was even more self-assured than before. After a long-winded resume of the evidence, he returned to the topic of his new witness.

"Here we have a woman, Olivia Chambers, of outstanding integrity, who was willing to stand up and be counted — despite this case involving a police officer. Any reasonable person would agree with me that there can only be one conclusion: in a cynical attempt to improve her own standing, Martha Munro orchestrated the abduction of her own daughter. An abduction that tragically led to the death of her own mother. The savage assault she carried out on Hristo Dragov was an attempt to silence a key witness to what she had done — not, as you were told, the act of a desperate mother."

Martha felt sick at the way these lies were being wrapped around her. His remarks provoked a roar in the packed room, as everyone seemed to start shouting at the same time. The judge was furiously shouting for order. An uneasy silence followed, before the judge issued a warning that any more interruptions would see people taken to the cells.

Grylls carried on, almost rushing in his eagerness. "You may be tempted to think the defendant has paid a high price, but the prosecution says this was a disaster waiting to happen. It will be hard for some members of the jury — but there can only be one verdict. You must find her guilty."

From their expressions, Martha was certain that a majority of the jury did indeed agree with his demand.

But Charles wasn't going down without a fight.

"The prosecution has come up with a ludicrous suggestion for which there is not the smallest shred of evidence, apart from the blood on her shoe, which only goes to show she was there. Something she has never denied. As to the claims of assault, I urge you, again, to consider how she could have inflicted such damage without damaging herself. With regard to the firearm charge, my client admits this but points out it was never used, which you might have expected to happen given the claim that she beat a defenceless man. Why not taser him as well? Because she never touched him.

"This case is a serious mistake. And so is the account you have heard this morning. A brilliant young woman is having her name trashed based on a brief conversation between strangers, a conversation that my client has emphatically stated did not take place. Martha Munro has already suffered. But the only thing she is guilty of is trying to save her daughter. Nothing else. You must find her not guilty."

Before sending the jury out to consider their verdict, the judge offered some guidance that made Charles turn bright red with fury.

"This morning you have heard evidence which the defence has done its best to discredit. Well, I ask you this: of these two women, which one would you trust?"

She pointedly looked at Olivia Chambers and gave her a broad smile.

Martha's barrister was on his feet, objecting to this "unfair guidance". The judge retaliated immediately. "The defence will withdraw those remarks immediately, or you, Mr Winter, will find yourself cooling your heels in the cells."

Charles replied, "As My Lady directs, I allowed emotion to obscure reason. I withdraw the remark."

The jury, six men and six women, filed out. They didn't seem to have a care in the world, yet they would decide her fate based on evidence that was stacked against her. Martha glanced at her watch. It was only 11.06 a.m. At home she'd be thinking of having a coffee, putting out the biscuits if Harry was there.

She shook herself. She needed to be strong, not distracting herself with pleasant daydreams. In a short while, she could be heading off to prison. She needed to find her "fight head".

Less than twenty minutes later, she was standing again as the jury filed back in. The judge was quite inscrutable. An outsider would never have guessed at the way the woman had blatantly manipulated the jury.

Martha turned to view the back of the courtroom. Olivia Chambers was making her way out. The woman turned and, for just a moment, made eye contact, her expression blank, before bowing her head and scurrying away. Much as she'd have cheerfully liked to put her hands around the woman's throat, Martha stayed very still. She would have her revenge — but right now, she needed to get out of this mess. If she could.

The forewoman of the jury rose. She might have been a teacher or a bank clerk. She was wearing sober clothing — black trousers and a cream top — and her hair was short and neatly styled. She looked confidently at the judge, giving nothing away. Martha's mouth was dry.

"Have you reached a verdict on all the charges?" the judge asked.

The forewoman nodded. Martha felt sick.

"Might I trouble you to answer out loud, so that everyone can hear?"

The forewoman inclined her head. "Yes, we have." This time, she stole the briefest glance at Martha. It didn't fill her with confidence.

"What are your verdicts?"

"We find the accused guilty as charged."

Martha sank back into her seat, clenching her fists. The world dropped away as each charge and guilty verdict was read out. There was more uproar in court — but this time the judge seemed content to let the noise run on.

As the room quietened down, all eyes were on the judge. She looked at the two legal teams. "Does the prosecution have any remarks?"

"No, My Lady."

"The defence?"

"We shall be demanding a retrial and intend to pursue this as a miscarriage of justice."

Watching intently, Martha realised the judge no longer needed to be openly hostile. She had won this battle, which was all she had needed to do.

The judge inclined her head at Charles. "You may do as you see fit, Mr Winter. That will be in the hands of others. Today, I need to conclude these proceedings."

She turned her gaze on Martha. "Please stand, Ms Munro. In the ordinary run of events, I would have set an immediate jail term. However, there are issues I should like to know more about. I am going to ask that we remand you in custody for the next month until reports can be carried out into the circumstances of this case. I am especially concerned that you have a young child. I want reassurances that you are a fit and proper mother."

It was as if the life was being sucked out of her. Martha grabbed the sides of the stand to stop her falling to the ground. Charles was talking urgently to Paul, then he asked to speak to the judge again. She inclined her head.

"My Lady must act as she sees fit. But I may be able to offer some assistance. I rarely take cases anymore, and then only when I have examined carefully the background of the potential client. In my opinion, Martha Munro is an excellent and caring mother. Furthermore, she is appealing this conviction and it is my opinion she will be vindicated."

He might as well have not spoken. The judge simply ordered she be taken down to the bowels of the court to begin the process of transitioning to the prison system.

* * *

The holding cells in the Old Bailey were clean and quiet after all the bustle of the courtroom. Martha sank onto a chair, wondering how long she would be there. Soon she heard footsteps, and Harry appeared at the bars.

"Harry!" she said in surprise. "I thought only the lawyers were allowed down here?"

"I've got a friend on duty," he told her, but his voice wasn't as cheerful as usual. "I'm told they're taking you to Bronzefield, out near Heathrow."

Martha recognised the name. "But that's a high-security prison. Why there, for a pre-sentence report?"

Now that the worst had happened, she was back in control and answered her own question before Harry could reply. "Because that's where someone wants me to go."

Harry looked as fierce as she had ever seen him. "They'll be waiting for you — so be on your guard. From now on, trust no one. Not the screws, not the other prisoners. In fact, you can't go far wrong if you assume that anyone who speaks to you is a liar."

Sensing his concern, she touched the bars in front of her. She couldn't get her hand through, so it would have to do.

"Look after Betty and Justin. Tell them I'll be home very, very soon. Thanks to you, I'm as ready as I can be for what happens next."

"We've had a bit of luck," Harry said. "Turns out the driver knows who I am; he can be trusted. It's not much, but I've been able to make sure you'll be safe in the van taking you there."

Martha just nodded.

"Get yourself organised and keep safe. I've already started calling in every favour I'm owed, so one way or another we'll keep you safe."

Despite her predicament, Martha's thoughts were dominated by one topic. "That bitch threatened my little girl."

Harry frowned. "We expected this. She hasn't got a shred of evidence against you. Charles says it's never going to happen, she's just rattling your cage."

Martha managed a weak smile. "At least Betty's got Justin, if the worst comes to the worst."

"It won't. Now, time's running out. Do you remember the code we came up with?"

"Yeah. 'Marcus sends his love.'"

"Good. Only someone who says that is delivering a message from me. Now, what else?"

The smile was a little stronger. "Keep my hands up."

"That's it. You're ready. I'll be in touch as soon as I can."

"Tell Betty I love her."

"The moment I see her — and then we start planning the party for Mummy coming home."

A guard appeared and told Harry his time was up. He stepped back from the door then stopped. "I'm getting old. I almost forgot to tell you . . ." The guard was becoming insistent that Harry go.

"Tell me what?" said Martha.

"The person inside, her name's Julie."

The guard was tugging his arm. "You're out of time . . ."

CHAPTER 36

The transfer to the prison van gave Martha her first sense of what the immediate future had in store. Now she was on her own.

Everything she'd done had led to this point. As Harry would put it, she was in the boxing ring and waiting for the bell to signal the opening round of a fight to the finish. Thanks to Harry, she was fit and strong and her experience as a police officer would help. She would do whatever it took to keep safe and get back to her little girl in one piece.

She was locked into a tiny cell in the prison van that just about gave her stretching room. It had a blacked-out window which she knew to stay away from, otherwise she would risk being "lit up" by the flash guns the waiting photographers would use to target the blackened windows.

Before locking her in, the guard had told her she was the only prisoner in the vehicle. Then he added, "Sounds like they're looking forward to seeing you at Bronzefield."

He'd closed the door before she could ask what he meant. After a brief wait, they started moving. Martha shrank into a corner, the furthest she could get from the window. The van turned to the left and then a cacophony of screaming and shouting erupted. People were slamming their fists against the sides of the vehicle, making it rock back and forth. Even above the sound and fury, she heard a woman's voice shrieking, "Burn the witch!" The demand had a medieval quality, which added to the sense she was trapped in a nightmare. It was surprising how fast mobs could gather at the Old Bailey, especially with social media making court reporting almost instantaneous. Perhaps the protestor believed the claim Martha's actions had led to her mother's death, or perhaps she held Martha responsible for all the police violence in the world.

All Martha could do was strengthen her resolve as she rested her gaze on the tiny window and the blur of flash guns.

The van finally got clear of the crowd and sped away. The journey would take her towards Windsor Castle, but her destination was far less salubrious. She had the odd thought that the Queen might, even now, be watching the story unfold on TV.

Martha settled down for the journey. She had packed a "prison bag" of clothes and a toothbrush, but she didn't know if she'd be allowed to keep it. She'd added a paperback in case she got the chance to read. The book, along with the bag, was being held securely for the journey — or so she'd been told. Her mobile was still in safe-keeping; she hoped Harry remembered to pick it up.

An hour later, the van came to a stop. It waited a moment, pulled forward, then stopped again. She guessed they had arrived. Martha knew very little about the prison other than it was a fairly modern building and, from the outside, looked like a warehouse or storage facility, which she supposed it was — a warehouse for human beings.

It had a wing devoted to inmates regarded as having the highest potential for violence. Martha was sure there would be killers inside. People imprisoned on the most serious charges sometimes felt they had the least to lose. Had someone like that been supplied with her name and details in return for money and a promise of a better life inside? More privileges, better food, cleaner clothes?

The doors opened and Martha blinked in the light. The van guard ushered her out to where a pair of female guards were waiting. Both guards had short hair. Long hair was easy to grab hold of, she remembered, pulling you off balance. They were about her height, powerfully built and very professional. If anything, this calm indifference made her feel all the more isolated. Inside these walls, she really was just a number.

As they passed through the outer reception, Martha could smell the prison: a warm, musty concoction, with hints of disinfectant, food and other things it wasn't worth dwelling on — although it was better than some places she'd visited. In total silence, they led Martha to a room marked "Reception". They went inside. Here she was ordered to sit at a table while the two guards remained on their feet, arms folded.

The darker-haired one spoke. "Just waiting for the doctor and the nurse. If you've got anything stashed where the sun don't shine . . . now would be a good time to mention it."

Martha shook her head, holding her arms out. "What you see is what you get."

The guard curled her lip. "A comedian. It always helps to look on the bright side. Not sure you're going to get much chance of that."

Martha tensed. She hoped she wasn't about to get a beating from these two, but she wouldn't go down easily. If she got a few shots in, it would send out a message that she was no easy touch. If there was one thing her police experience had taught her, it was essential not to come over as a victim. That just alerted the predators, who were always after the weakest prey.

An unspoken communication seemed to be going on between the guards. The first woman was in charge, and now her arms were down by her side, her hands balling into fists.

She was stepping forward, no doubt intent on attacking her, when the door opened and two women walked in. Both wore blue cotton uniforms and one had a stethoscope round her neck. Clearly medics. The guard instantly resumed her pose of innocent indifference as the two women introduced themselves: Dr Woolard ("Everyone calls me Doc") and Nurse Ball. They took her into a small side room, leaving the guards outside.

The nurse produced a blood pressure kit and expertly attached it to Martha's right arm. Pressing the start button on the machine, she inflated the cuff until it bit painfully into her upper arm.

Her reading — 110 over 70 — produced a whistle of approval from the Doc. "That's very good. You'd have been forgiven for being a little raised in the circumstances." She added, "No history of low blood pressure?"

She rattled through a list of questions and asked permission to take a blood sample for "routine screening". A few more tests followed. If this proved to be the worst the day threw at her, she'd settle for it. The procedure was helped by the attitude of the two medics, who did not treat her as a prisoner but as a person.

"You're good to go," said the doctor. "You're in good shape and the blood tests will tell us if anything needs looking at."

Afterwards they returned her to the guards in reception, who took her photograph and fingerprints. ID in prison was of prime importance. Now she was settling down she was vaguely surprised to find the prison wasn't dark and dungeon-like. Instead, the walls were painted in pale pastel colours, and it was illuminated with a combination of electric lights and natural light through barred windows. The furniture was cheap but functional.

She stayed on high alert, having seen an account by a former prisoner who claimed fighting among inmates was almost routine — mostly scuffles, but people got hurt — and that there were never enough guards to go around.

A man in his thirties, with a hipster-style beard, walked in. Pulling up a chair, he started reading through a list of rules. She switched off; most of what he was saying was common sense. It was the unwritten rules she was most concerned about. He stopped talking and looked at her. Now she paid attention.

"At present, you have no telephone privileges until we review you."

"When will that be?"

He shrugged indifferently. "Over my pay grade. You can ask the warden's office — oh, and you can keep your clothes."

With that, he was gone.

"Come on," said the guard. "You get to see your room now. A nice little pad for one."

Martha followed the woman out. But she had barely taken three steps when a starburst of pain erupted and she hit the floor in fiery agony.

The other guard had sucker punched her in the kidney.

"Let me help you up," she said. "It's so easy to fall over in new places."

She pulled Martha up. "Now, that's just a little something for you to think about. Some people want to have a much longer chat with you when they get the chance. Unfortunately, they'll have to wait as you're in a cell on your own. But asked me to say hi and tell you they'll be with you real soon."

Martha was seething. Not only had she been caught flat-footed, she was utterly powerless. She needed to get up to speed fast. She hoped this "Julie" Harry had mentioned showed up soon. If nothing else, she could act as a guide to the people she needed to avoid.

CHAPTER 37

As Martha lay on the thin mattress in her tiny cell, it was all too easy to imagine that the last occupant had died in here. She'd been locked in since shortly after arriving, having refused the offer of food. Never a big eater, her appetite had vanished.

Every time Martha fell into an exhausted sleep, the guard outside — a piggy-eyed blonde — crashed her baton against the door to force her awake. It was now almost 3 a.m. and, to add to the misery, the woman in the next cell had started loudly weeping. Martha's eyes were painfully gritty and itchy.

Her brain raced with multiple scenarios, all of them ending in violence. Her body felt weak and lifeless and her hands were throbbing. The guards had claimed this isolation would keep her safe. The police officer in her said that made no difference. If someone was coming, they would come now. This night stretched on without end.

Just before 5 a.m., there was a sound she had been dreading: a loud click. The lock on her cell door had been deactivated remotely. Martha sat up and quickly fought down the fear. She waited and watched to see what would happen. Someone, and it wouldn't be a friend, was coming through that door — and then there would be violence.

If she was going down, she was going down fighting. She stood up, making sure she was balanced, and her hands were held high.

Martha was still scared — but now her fear was under control. At least she was doing something, getting on the front foot. She would not be defeated before the start. She stared at the door. Nothing. She listened hard, but all was silent. No breathing right outside. Even the weeping woman had shut up.

The atmosphere was oppressive. As the wait went on, she felt herself being pulled towards the part-opened door, like a needle drawn towards a magnet. She had a straight choice. Fight out on the landing or in the cell. She would stay in the cell. That way they came to her, to her patch. She was going to defend it.

A piercing scream shattered the silence, the sound bouncing off the walls, making it impossible to pin down distance or location. Then the silence returned. Martha could imagine that every woman in the prison was lying on their bed as they waited for what happened next.

Then she heard the noise. It was a low noise, the sound of someone walking very carefully, one step at a time. This person, it seemed, had all the time in the world. The footsteps carried on, the soft sound becoming more distinct. They were getting closer. Closer to her cell.

Adrenaline was surging through her body. Her mouth was dry, and her hands were flexing into fists. The noise was quite audible now. It was right outside. Her eyes were glued to the door, and she tried to control her breathing. She had to be calm. One big punch, maybe two. She had to give it her best.

The door opened to reveal the biggest woman she had ever clapped eyes on. She had huge shoulders, fists like small hams and towered over six feet tall. She was all muscle. The woman had short, thick hair, dyed bright orange, making an eye-catching contrast with her dark colouring. Intricate tattoos covered most of her exposed skin.

She had piercings everywhere Martha could see, and probably more where she couldn't. For a fleeting moment, Martha wondered how this was allowed, then decided there was no one daft enough to make her take them off.

With a chill, Martha noted the woman's hands again. She was holding a short blade, which was covered in bloody gore. Did that explain the scream? Martha needed to react or risk being frozen to the spot by fear. Shouting at the top of her voice, she hurled herself at the enemy, throwing punches in a blur of hands.

The first blows landed with a satisfying smacking sound — but the big woman was insanely quick. Bobbing and weaving, she evaded the next flurry, except one which grazed her ear.

She didn't flinch, just grabbed Martha with one meaty hand and raised the other above her head before smashing it like a club on top of Martha's skull.

* * *

Martha came to lying on her back.

The giant woman was reaching towards her, a horrible grin on her face.

CHAPTER 38

"When Mummy has a day off, she puts the washing on before taking me to school," Betty told her father as he set out the cornflakes, a corrective note in her voice. "It means she has time to dry and iron anything that's important before I get home. If the dishwasher is full, that goes on as well — so you need to check."

It was the morning of Martha's last day in court, and Betty was taking events in her stride. Unexpectedly, she reacted to her mother's absence by stepping into her shoes. This mostly seemed to involve close supervision of Justin and making sure all the household chores were being done properly. An almost-five-year-old can be a surprisingly tough boss.

The stream of instructions continued at a steady pace as they walked to school. Dropping her off at the gate, Justin waved at her as she disappeared inside with her friends. As he turned away, he froze. Two women across the road were snapping a selfie, their backs to the school. *Why would anyone want to take a selfie just there?*, he wondered as he walked home. It was hardly a tourist hotspot. Were they taking pictures of parents and children? He worried away at it, wishing he'd stopped to say something to a teacher. Was he being paranoid? Seeing enemies everywhere?

He spun on his heel and walked back to examine the spot where the mystery women had been standing. It was a great location for photographing children arriving at the school gate. This was too much of a coincidence.

Harry had been very clear about one thing. "If something's not right, call me. There's no such thing as a coincidence." Harry was probably still in court with Martha, but he sent a text.

A couple of hours passed before Harry finally returned his call. He sounded strained. "It's bad news. Martha's been remanded in custody. The lawyers think they can get her out on appeal, but it'll take a few days."

Justin sat down, the news making him feel shaky. "My news sounds a bit trivial now."

"If it's about Betty, tell me."

Justin explained.

Harry was all business. "If you don't mind, we'll get there early this afternoon, scout the situation. Then, if you spot them again, we can decide what to do."

"You can't do anything in front of Betty. She's been through enough already. We can't let her feel frightened about school."

"I may be ancient but I'm not daft." Harry sounded a bit put out. "If we spot them early, I might be able to frighten them off before Betty comes out. But I'm not going to start fighting people in front of her. Did you get time to take a photograph of them? It might be useful if they do come back."

"Sorry. After the abduction I've got tunnel vision when it comes to Betty's safety."

They arrived at the school half an hour before classes finished. They were the only people there. Ten minutes before the children were sent home, parents started arriving, chatting at the gates. But Justin saw no sign of the suspicious pair.

Right on time, Betty skipped out — and, in that same moment, the women were back, once again pretending to take a selfie. Justin nodded at Harry, who, moving in front of

Betty to block a picture, made a show of turning and looking at them. The women pretended not to notice.

"Funny place to take a selfie," Harry said quietly to a nearby teacher, as Betty chatted to her father about her day. Alerted, the teacher moved towards the women, who were already walking away.

* * *

As he walked with Justin and Betty towards Martha's house, Harry tried to think strategically. The women wanted a picture of Betty — but why? Were they working for the person who had ordered Betty's abduction? Was another attempt on the way? Or did they just want to scare Martha to give up the notebook? But nobody had asked Martha for the notebook, ever. It was a puzzle — one he couldn't solve alone. He needed some extra help.

As the thought entered his head, he looked up and saw a man and a woman standing outside Martha's house, waiting for them. Sally and Quentin.

Harry studied them. "I didn't see you down at the school — so that suggests this owes more to chance than anything else."

Sally pulled a face. "It's not chance at all. My boss found out that there would be another warning move against Betty, just to add to the pressure of Martha being in prison."

"You mean you knew those women were going to be there and you didn't even warn us?"

"Relax, Harry. We didn't want to alarm you until we were sure. But we were down there and since you never spotted us we did a good job of staying out of sight. I recognised one of the women — she's freelance, very low level. But they've done what was wanted — they put the wind up you."

Justin had been holding Betty out of earshot. Harry made eye contact.

"I'll explain what's going on in a minute. It might be easier if I talk to these two at my place, while you get Betty

187

settled." Betty needed little prompting to race into her house, eager to put the TV on. "Don't forget to put the security system on," he added.

Once they were in his home, Harry didn't waste any time. "Who are these people? Why are they targeting Betty like this?"

"The honest answer is that neither Quentin or myself have that information. Our boss knows, or I think she knows, but she's not sharing anything with us, not so far. All I know is there are secrets within secrets about this and your Martha is right at the centre of it. We've been told to offer you our support until the danger to Betty, and Martha herself, is over."

Harry was far from mollified. "You must know who's behind this."

"Actually, I don't," said Sally. "There aren't many people who could orchestrate something like this, but I couldn't say which one it is. I just don't have all the pieces." She stopped, and Harry sensed she was weighing up telling him more.

"Look, what I'm going to say is a guess — well, a bit more than that, really. My boss is a big player; she squashes anyone who gets in her way. If she's keeping something from me, then it's because she doesn't want to get into a conflict . . . And that's all I know."

She pulled out her mobile. "Let me talk to my boss and let her know she was right about the situation that's going on here. Then we can talk about Martha."

She was back inside ten minutes.

"That was quick," Harry said. "I thought you'd be gone for ages."

Sally picked up a glass of water, taking a small sip. "From now on, we're stepping up security around Betty. Basically, we'll have more people on the ground. Obviously you should walk Betty to school as well as Justin."

"Try and stop me being there. That little girl means the world to me," said Harry.

"I sort of guessed that. Just so you know, we'll have enough people close by to step in if something goes wrong. Our team is going to be in the area twenty-four-seven until this is over. In fact, I'd be very grateful if you could put up with one of us being at your place for the odd cup of tea."

"In the circumstances, how could I refuse? One more question though — you started off telling me your boss was trying to get out of a straight fight. If she's now getting more involved has she now told you who we're up against?"

Sally raised her eyebrows. "Nice try. And the honest answer? I still have no idea, but it's complicated, very complicated." She paused. "I'm concerned those women were so easy to spot. They wanted to be seen. It's like the judge — they're sending a message that says they're holding all the cards."

"They're sending a lot of messages," Harry said in frustration. "Messages like child abduction and murder. But they haven't asked for anything. What's it all about?"

"I can't speak for them, Harry," she said. "Now, Bronzefield — that's the danger spot for Martha. If someone wants to harm her, they'll attack there. We've alerted our people. It's privately run, which limits us a little. We've asked for extra officers to be put on duty, although I'm told that's unlikely."

Harry nodded. "Which worries me because we don't have a lot of time. I've put some calls out."

He kept the details to himself. Sally claimed she was on their side, but he didn't have to trust her. The fewer people who knew about his plan, the better.

"She'll have to get through until lunchtime tomorrow on her own," Sally said. "Can she get to a phone?"

"Not a chance." Harry spat out the words. "They've put her on a forty-eight-hour communication lockdown. She can't call us until late tomorrow."

CHAPTER 39

The pain jerked her awake. It felt like someone had hammered her neck down between her shoulders before her head was put in a clamp and screwed down tight. She was lying in a comfortable bed. Daylight streamed in through a window. Instead of the gigantic woman, she saw Dr Woolard at her side.

"Welcome back to the land of the living. You've been in and out for about five minutes now. I'm told you fell out of bed and hit your head — did rather a lot of damage for such a short fall. Yours isn't the only weird injury today. One of the more dangerous prisoners is next door. She also fell in her cell, cutting herself quite badly and breaking the fingers in her right hand. Strangely, some fingers have gone forwards, others have gone backwards — one even went sideways. I dread to think what will come next. Somebody accidently punching themselves in the face, probably."

Martha was bewildered, not helped by the sensation she was underwater. It must have shown on her face.

"Sorry, I should have mentioned that 'falling out of bed' has given you a concussion. You'll need to stay on the medical wing for observation. Probably until lunchtime."

At that moment, Martha spotted the huge, ginger-haired woman. She was striding towards them, her expression fierce.

Martha shrank back in her bed. The doctor turned to see who was there. "Oh, that big lump is Julie. You were lucky she found you. She's one of the best medical trustees we have. She'll be helping to look after you."

With a reassuring smile, the doctor was off, leaving Martha alone with Julie. That was the name Harry had given her. If this was a friend, she'd hate to see her enemy. The woman stepped up to the bed, managing to loom and leer at the same time.

She leaned so close that Martha could smell soap and the hint of mint on her breath. She wanted to shout, but the pounding in her head took on a new urgency. Julie's lips were moving — but now Martha's ears were ringing. Her vision slowly closed in.

* * *

Martha came around again a few moments later. The pain had lessened, and the ringing in her ears had gone.

"I'm supposed to say something to you . . . 'Marcus sends his love.' Does that mean anything? I feel a right tosser saying it."

Martha went from terror to happiness. Her entire body relaxed. "I think that means you're not going to kill me. At least . . . I hope so."

The giant threw her head back and roared with laughter. "I'm your knight in shining armour, your protection. There's a lot slobbering over getting a piece of you. They all seem a lot less keen now they know you're my bitch." She grinned. "I got the message to look after you last night, just before you arrived. I got wind that one of the crazies in here was coming for you, so I was waiting for her. When she saw me, she was overcome with emotion and fell down. Broke four fingers and cut herself with the shiv she was carrying. I had to take the blade off her for her own safety."

Julie leaned in conspiratorially. "To tell you the truth, a lot of people seem to get emotional when they see me. I only have to walk past one of the screws and he bursts into tears."

Martha was trying not to laugh, desperate to keep the daggers in her head at bay. "I wonder if it's the way you introduce yourself. I mean, do you bash many people on the head? Or just the ones you're supposed to be looking after?"

Julie winked at her. "Only those who go all ninja on me. I couldn't believe the way you moved in that cell. Where did you learn to box like that?"

"I've got a fantastic teacher. He's the man who organised getting the message through to you. He's called Harry; he's practically family."

"Harry the Hat? Lives in Dulwich?"

"That's the one."

"Very resourceful man, your Harry. I spoke to him last night after he got the message through. Turns out he was pals with my grandad. Everyone called them the 'Twin Terrors' . . . no one in South London would take them on. They were up for anything. But my grandad died suddenly, very young — my grandma was devastated. Cutting a long story short, she moved to Tottenham. By the time I came along, Harry was still in touch, but seeing him upset my gran. I knew about him, though. 'Uncle Harry' always sent a card and money for my birthday.

"He knew I was in here and was able to get in touch. When he told me who he was, well, it was like being introduced to a long-lost member of the family. And when he told me about you, and the trouble you were in, I was up for it straight away. Even with you being a copper." Julie rubbed her huge hands together. They made a dry, rustling sound. "From now on . . . well, my life is your life."

Martha was silent for a moment. "Is that some sort of North London bad girl talk?"

"Very perceptive of you. I think you'll go far. Now, I need to leave you be for a little while. Just take it easy. This is the safest bit of the prison — well, it is when I'm around — so you can relax a bit for now."

Martha was glad to follow that advice. The pain was creeping up again and she wanted to close her eyes.

* * *

Sometime later, Julie was by her bedside again.

"Hello there. You had a nice little nap for half an hour. Doc says she's hoping you'll stay awake for a while now."

Martha risked a gentle nod and was pleased it didn't hurt.

Julie was studying her. "You look well on it — just no boxing for a while. Doc says concussion is a funny thing, hits some people harder than others."

She glanced around, double-checking no one was within earshot. "I need to find out more about which of the inmates wants you hurt. If I can do that, I might be able to head problems off at the source. That crazy woman I had a run-in with didn't just wake up that morning and decide to attack you. Someone put her up to it, probably supplied the shiv."

They broke off as another orderly approached and placed a plate with a sandwich on the bedside table. Martha's stomach rebelled at the thought of food, and Julie said, "If you're not hungry, I'll have it."

Martha waved her hand to indicate she could eat it, and Julie picked it up with one of her outsize hands before taking a huge bite. The sandwich disappeared impressively fast.

Scratching the tip of her nose, Julie went on: "How did you end up in here? Harry told me the general story. The more I know, the easier it will be to keep you safe."

Martha didn't hold back. She was prepared to trust Julie completely, and not just because of her extraordinary connection to Harry. There was something about her which suggested she would be a loyal and steadfast friend. Martha instinctively understood that sharing all the information with Julie was the right thing to do.

After explaining about her father and how she had discovered his many secrets, she said, "I have at least two groups after me. I think. Both are well organised, and both have high-level connections. One group seems to want me dead or sidelined at the very least. The other side is claiming they can protect me — but first I have to meet their boss and prove I'm worth the effort. This could all change in a heartbeat.

"And, to make matters really interesting, I have no idea who any of these people might be, or why they're after me. I feel like I'm wearing a blindfold while trying to walk through quicksand."

She stopped. "There is one more thing, but it's dangerous information."

Julie had a smile on her face. "You mean, you'd tell me but you'd have to kill me?"

"I sound like a drama queen and, a few weeks ago, I would have made the same joke. But some of the secrets my dad left behind are deadly, and this is one of them."

She glanced around for the umpteenth time. There was still no one close enough to listen in. "My dad paid money to a lot of informants. I don't know all the details, but it looks like he wasn't worried about morality; he just wanted hard information. He was willing to deal with the devil himself if it was the only way to get it. We think he kept a record of who he was paying. A secret record. I only found it a few weeks ago and it's in some sort of code.

"You don't need to be a rocket scientist to work out that a lot of people would be very keen to see that information buried. What we've managed to piece together is he had informants everywhere — drug dealers, people traffickers, fraudsters . . . even corrupt police officers already receiving backhanders. Sort of triple-agents, I suppose. Just knowing about this book could be extremely dangerous. I'm not sure how many people in it are still alive, but they must be powerful. I'm sure it's the reason Betty was abducted."

Martha sank back against her pillows. The only bit she hadn't mentioned was Harry's role as a police informant. That was his story to tell.

Julie's face was serious. "That's quite some story. I mean, I sort of guessed that powerful people were after your arse. It's not that easy to get someone attacked inside prison. Judging from who they sent after you, they weren't that bothered about whether you took a beating or were murdered."

She stopped. It seemed, to Martha, that a thought was occurring to her. "If they're as well organised as you say, then they'll have a backup plan. If I can get you moved within the next couple of hours, are you going to be OK? I've already fixed it that you can move into my cell. I want you close and I want the rest of the prison to know that as well."

She smiled. "I even have a bit of a crew myself. Someone once told me I was a 'bitch from hell'. The name stuck, so my crew are 'The Bitches'. I took the precaution of having a couple of them nearby. Glad I did. Let me make some more arrangements. It may be that I have to 'talk' to some people."

By talk, she meant hit. "No problem," Martha said. "I might have made a fuss before, but now . . . do whatever it takes."

Julie stood up and nodded at her. She walked off without further comment, but U-turned at the door.

"In all the excitement, I forgot this." She pulled a mobile out of her pocket. "I heard they took your communication privileges away. Use this — it's untraceable. Just wait a couple of hours and then Doc will go on her rounds, so you'll have a good sixty minutes to make any calls."

Martha gratefully took the phone, tucking it into her sheets. According to the small wall clock it was noon — in a couple of hours, she could tell Harry that Julie had already headed off one attempt on her and was making sure Martha stayed safe.

CHAPTER 40

"When is Mummy going to call?"

Justin smiled as his daughter slipped her hand into his. "As soon as she stops being busy, she's going to call you," he reassured her.

Betty didn't know it, but she was walking to school under military-grade protection. Harry and Justin would be the last line of defence if things went sideways, but the chances of that were slim. The house and route were under Martha's mysterious benefactors' surveillance from first thing that morning and had been declared clear as Betty and her minders set off.

A couple of hundred metres ahead was a new point man, Eric. He'd taken over from Quentin at 6.30 a.m. that morning and was the leader of the new team that their mysterious benefactor had put in place, as promised.

He explained that he had a dozen people working with him. Moving between home and school was going to be hardest. "Could she go by vehicle rather than walk?" Eric asked. "It would make the job easier."

Harry actually blushed. "I'm afraid I put the kibosh on that a couple of months ago."

Eric's face creased with puzzlement.

"I told Betty that, if she walked to school every day, she would grow up big and strong. Like her mummy. Now she won't go any other way, even in the rain."

Eric sighed. "You know that thing actors say? Never work with kids or animals. They should say the same about close protection." He shook his head. "Still, it is what it is. If anything kicks off, your only duty is the little girl. We'll do the rest. I've been told to hold nothing back, so, between ourselves, my team are all armed — guns and Tasers — and if needed we'll use them. Obviously not legal, but if it comes down to it, we will use them."

Seeing Harry about to protest, he quickly went on: "Yeah, yeah. Not in front of the kid. It'll only happen if she's in real danger. Even then, there's a standing instruction to keep her out of a kill zone. There'll be no 'friendly fire' incidents. I've done this all over the world and never lost a client yet. Trust me — failure will not be tolerated."

Now Harry was pondering for the thousandth time: what exactly were the secrets that John Munro had taken to his grave? And more importantly, why couldn't they stay there? Life would be so much better without having armed mercenaries on the school run.

The journey was incident free, although Harry couldn't shake off the feeling that they were on the brink of disaster. He didn't see any of Eric's people. The man had promised his team would do their job and so far . . . well, he wasn't going to think much beyond that.

They were met at the gate by the head teacher, Jeanette Brown. The small woman was so anxious she was hopping from one foot to the other. Once Betty had walked into the school building, the head pulled Justin to a quiet corner, Harry following.

"This man, Eric—" judging by the way she pursed her lips, he'd made a poor impression — "the one who calls himself a security consultant, has told me he wants to station guards in the playground and inside the school. Well, I'm very sorry, but that is quite impossible. Eric is suggesting that there's a significant threat to Betty. If that is the case, I have to ask why she's coming to school at all?" Her voice had risen sharply while she was talking, betraying her concern. "Surely you'd be better off dealing with this matter elsewhere? I have a duty of care to all my pupils and staff. If Betty is here, does that put everyone else at risk?"

Justin knew the head teacher was genuinely concerned, but hearing it was tough.

"Mrs Brown, you're quite right to raise this," he said. "I apologise for not putting you fully in the picture. This is all new to me. We've taken action to ensure that there's no risk to Betty, and certainly not to anyone at the school, pupils or staff. Eric is part of that process, but he has far exceeded his authority in approaching you before I had the chance to explain.

"I was going to tell you this morning and I can assure you that there is no danger. In fact, I suspect we have massively overreacted — but better safe than sorry. There is no need for Eric to post people inside your school. I can understand why you found that alarming."

The head remained doubtful. "I'm not prying, but is this about her mother's court case?"

"It is. I'm hoping Betty can stay at school for now, especially after what happened to her grandmother."

He let the sentence hang. The head was a clever woman; there was no point in soft-soaping things. If she wanted Betty out, that was it.

Mrs Brown's expression hardened. "OK. But I will review it daily. I want your word that you will tell me if the threat increases. And—" she pointed at Eric on the other side of the street — "if I see him, or any of his men, so much as looking at the school, I'm calling the police."

They shook hands.

As they walked away, Justin sighed. "This school is one of the only stable things in Betty's world. But am I doing the right thing leaving her here, Harry? Martha said it was safe. Now I'm not so sure."

"It's as safe as any home," said Harry. "But that Eric bloke . . . he's a bit too keen on showing off. I'll have to talk to him, get him to rein it in."

Justin cleared his throat. "Any thoughts about how Martha is getting on? Do you think your messages got through to the right people?"

It was the second time Justin had asked, but Harry didn't complain; he understood what was going through his mind. At the same time, he was reluctant to discuss any details. Not that he had a problem with Justin, but there was so much at stake, silence was his best option. "The only thing I can say for sure is that, if something serious had happened to her, I would have heard by now. But I'm not going to dress this up for you, Justin. It's a worry that Martha hasn't been allowed near a phone. She's not allowed a mobile in prison, but she should have been given a phone card.

"As to my trying to get protection for her — I've said before, it's a long time since I've needed those sorts of contacts. But I do know some faces, and I've been rebuilding my network over the last couple of months. Don't give up hope, and remember, if anyone can get through this alone, it's Martha."

They had slowed to a stop at a crossing for the South Circular road. Justin tapped his foot on the pavement. "I suppose that, with time, Mr Winter will be able to get involved through official contacts. What do you make of him, Harry?"

"He's a top man, I would say. Never much liked lawyers — but he's the business. He took the defeat hard, even though the case was stacked up against her. I've seen a few things in my time, but they threw the kitchen sink at us." He looked thoughtful. "Stop me if it sounds like rubbish, but if they're going to so much trouble to get Martha, do you think that makes it less likely they want to kill her? If they wanted her dead, there are much easier ways of doing it."

"That sounds sensible, in a clutching-at-straws kind of way. So why are they doing it?"

The lights changed and they crossed the road, Harry following Justin. "We've been talking about the enemy sending a message. Perhaps we should look at it differently. Are they getting worried because something has happened, or is *about* to happen? Maybe connected to that book? Something that would worry them?"

Justin stopped. "I'm not sure I agree with you and Martha that all this has anything to do with the book. For years its existence seems to have been a secret. From what you're all saying, no one was looking for it because no one knew it was even around, no matter how well hidden."

"You're right. I'm clutching at straws," said Harry. "The problem is, we're so in the dark. Even me finding the book owed more to luck than judgement." He sighed in frustration. "We need Martha back home to work this out. Like her dad, she is. He had a genuine talent for spotting stuff that everyone else missed, and she seems to have it too."

Arriving at Martha's house, Harry turned down the offer of tea. He wanted to go for a jog, clear his head and break up some of the tension.

He was getting ready when his mobile rang. He didn't recognise the number, but his heart leapt as he recognised the voice at the other end.

"Harry," said Martha. "It's me. I'm safe and it's all thanks to you. I'm being minded by a woman who'd give you a run for your money."

He choked up at hearing the good news. "I won't lie, that's the best thing I've heard in a while. We've all been really worried. I expect you know I've spoken to Julie, but you talking to me is the proof that she's the right woman for the job."

"Well, you don't need to worry about me anymore. She's already stopped one attempt to hurt me; now she won't leave my side. I may not even need those boxing lessons. She's so tough she scares the pants off everyone, including the guards. I'm told you and her grandad were known as the Twin Terrors . . . You kept that quiet."

"She told you that? That was a long time ago! We're talking forty-plus years ago. Jerome Bateman . . . He died suddenly when he was only thirty-five."

He heard her sharp intake of breath. "I don't mean he was shot or anything. It was a sudden death brought on by an undetected heart condition. He was lucky, in a way. He never suffered, just went to make a cup of tea and fell down dead on the kitchen floor. I still miss him. I only have to close my eyes to see him. Always laughing, he was."

"Hah, always punching people from what I've heard!"

"Well, only the ones who deserved it."

"Yeah, yeah . . . back in the days when you had gruel three times a day and men were real men."

"I can't believe it was only yesterday when we last spoke."

Martha agreed. "It feels like forever. Any news from the lawyers on when I might get out?"

"Nothing yet — but Charles could call anytime. How are you fixed for more phone calls?"

"Good, I hope. I'm going to call again tonight and talk to Betty. How about 6.30 p.m.?"

"Should be fine. I'll get Justin standing by his phone."

"If there's a problem, I'll text."

"Yeah, nothing to worry about." He had his fingers firmly crossed.

Swiftly changing the subject, he said, "I've been wondering about something. Knowing what your dad was like, do you think he might have left some message for you, something related to the book . . . but done it really obscurely?"

She gave it some thought. "I'm sorry, Harry. Nothing springs to mind. But you're right, he did like to have a backup plan, just in case."

CHAPTER 41

The official prison induction covers the sort of things you might expect. The rules and regulations, time in your cell, free time, exercise, the canteen — all the little bureaucratic details that can fit onto an A4 sheet of paper. But if you're really lucky, there's another induction: the unofficial, off-the-record and strictly need-to-know tour conducted by the inmates and not intended for the ears of the guards.

For a lot of prisoners, especially those entering the system for the first time, it can be a simple exercise: keep your head down and work out the unwritten rules before you find yourself headfirst in the toilet.

Martha, however, was on a VIP tour. The rarest of all. The moment the doctor had given her the all-clear, Julie had her up and ready to go. "I need to show you around, make sure that everyone sees you're mine." She eyed her charge. "You're not going to throw up, are you? That will really spoil the look I'm aiming for."

Martha took a few exploratory steps. She had a faint headache, but nothing a couple of paracetamol wouldn't fix. "I'm good to go. My mum always said I was thick-headed."

Julie set off at a leisurely stroll, undergoing an extraordinary transformation. In the hospital wing, she had been a careful assistant for the nursing team. Now she was acting like a lioness protecting her young. Martha shivered slightly as she recalled seeing Julie for the first time. What had she been thinking when she'd attacked? Harry had told her repeatedly that fighting was always the last resort. Sometimes the enemy was just too powerful.

Trailing in her wake, Martha felt like the new girl at school. Not just any girl, but the one who was being talked up as a rising star. The one people would enjoy taking down a peg.

Their first stop was the main recreation room. There was a TV on, showing one of the myriad chat shows which dominate daytime schedules, and some chairs and tables for people to sit at. About twenty people were there. There were two guards in the room, but they melted away when they saw Julie. Julie took Martha on a very slow and deliberate circuit, ignoring the fact that all eyes were on them. Then they got back to the entrance and Julie started off again.

Once again, they were watched in silence until they were about halfway through the circuit, when suddenly a voice called out, "Cop bitch!"

Martha had only the vaguest sense of who might have said it, but Julie slowly turned and walked over to three women. Martha followed, ready to fight, if the giant woman started something.

Now they were close, Martha could see the three women were mean. They had hard eyes — eyes that said "no mercy" if anything kicked off. Their right arms were tattooed, sleeve style, which she guessed showed some sort of gang allegiance. Closer still, she could see the muscles in their necks, arms and shoulders. Julie showed no fear as she stopped in front of them. She looked each woman in the eye. The first two broke under her gaze, but the third wasn't cowed. She wasn't going to back down.

Martha didn't take her eyes off the three women; she was expecting them to act at any moment.

Julie moved with lightning speed. Her huge right hand shot out, grabbed the woman who had taken up the staring challenge, lifted her off her feet and slammed her face-first into the ground. Still holding the woman by the neck, she picked her up and put her back in her chair.

She wasn't finished. In a display of strength, she grabbed another of the women and threw her at the third. There was the sickening sound of bones breaking, and in the next moment the two women were on the floor, screaming in pain.

In a matter of seconds, she had unleashed a level of violence that saw one woman with blood streaming from a broken nose and her two companions needing urgent medical treatment.

"Anyone else like to say something? Anything you want to get off your chest?"

Her voice boomed out. Every other woman looked away.

Julie dominated the space. She pointed at a woman sitting on her own. "I've seen you making eyes at these three. Do you think what I did was unfair? Or do you think they were right to call my woman a 'cop bitch'?"

The woman was more than big enough to take care of herself. At least she would have been, if it was Martha she was up against. But Julie wasn't just big; she was a force of nature. The woman shrank away as Julie walked over. Julie eyed her coldly. "Speak up. I can't hear you."

The woman mumbled something, clearly too frightened to get the words out of her mouth. Julie grabbed her and lifted her on to her tiptoes. The victim's eyes were bulging, her face glistened with sweat and, Martha noticed, she had wet herself.

Julie remained coldly detached. "I asked you to speak up."

The woman managed to gasp out a few words. This time they were audible. "They shouldn't have said that about your friend."

Julie shook her none too gently. "Well done. No one likes to hear bad things said about their friends, and Martha is my friend." She noticed the pool of urine and curled her lip. "You've pissed yourself . . . stupid cow. Best go and get changed."

The woman blushed and headed out. As she went past Martha, she shot her a glance that was pure venom. Martha winked at her, making the woman develop a suddenly waxen appearance. Even so, Martha made a mental note. If she was ever alone with that woman, she would need to keep her guard up.

With a nod of her head, Julie indicated they should leave. Outside, she turned to Martha. "Sorry it all got a bit medieval, but I didn't like the buzz when we went in. There were a few too many in there who clearly thought getting at you was worth the risk of coming through me. I didn't have time to warn you, but I needed to act fast. Those four women are the nastiest in here."

She cracked her knuckles and stretched her neck muscles. "It's been a few years since I had to go as hard as that. I'm quite pleased to find I could still do it."

Martha couldn't help the little worm of fear that appeared in her guts. "Do you think I should expect them to just keep coming?"

An unreadable expression flashed across Julie's face. "The faster your people can get you out of here, the better all round. I find it a bit too easy to get carried away." Seeing Martha's face, she hugged her, squeezing so hard she forced the air out of her lungs. "Don't worry. The whole jail isn't against you. Although, even if they were, we wouldn't give up without a fight. That nutter who had an accident with her hand told someone, who told me, that she was offered big money to 'hurt you but not kill you'. What's bothering me is how determined these people are to reach you. Someone, somewhere, really wants to send you a message."

"Everyone keeps saying that. I wish they'd just say what they want."

Martha followed Julie through the prison to the cell blocks. Here, they stopped outside one of the doors.

"Welcome to your new home. I'm on the top bunk, by the way."

Two older women appeared on the landing. "I've got a few more rounds to do, so these lovely ladies will keep an eye on you." She paused. "Anyway, I'll be back in time for dinner at five. We can make a bit of an entrance in the dining hall, although hopefully a bit more low key than earlier. I can show you around and make sure people know they mustn't touch."

"I'm hoping to call my daughter tonight at about half past six, just before she goes to bed. Can we be done with eating by then?"

"That should be no problem at all."

* * *

The dining hall turned out to be a non-event. None of the women eating wanted to interrupt their meal by looking at Martha, and even the guards seemed more interested in studying their shoes than her. At 6.30 p.m. sharp, she was in the cell, punching in her home number. Betty answered on the second ring.

"I was waiting by the phone, Mummy. I've missed you."

"Not as much as I've missed you, darling. Tell me what you've been up to." She listened contentedly as the little girl chatted through her day. Then she finished, sending Martha a "special kiss", and was replaced by Justin.

"Harry filled me in, so keep safe and see you soon. Harry also has a message from the lawyer."

She smiled as she imagined the scene at the house. Betty would have the two men wrapped round her little finger.

Harry was next up for the phone. "We might have some good news. Your barrister knows a few people and got through to the senior adviser to the home secretary. It meant he could talk him through what happened at your trial. Apparently, he was horrified. The powers that be don't like to think how easily criminals can get at the justice system.

Charles said this adviser got a bit squeaky when he was told what the judge did."

Harry snorted. "Now, this is where it gets slippery. Apparently, the minister is about to go big on law and order — so the last thing they want is a high-profile miscarriage of justice. But a lot of the public also support what you did. If we sit on our hands for now, he'll get a pliable judge to hear your appeal in the next forty-eight hours — and make sure you're freed, pending a full appeal. Charles said he snatched the offer with both hands. We get you out and home where you belong, and we can fight the case another day."

Martha was delighted. Events were moving more quickly than she had dared dream. She lay back on her bunk, savouring the moment. This was the fightback. There would be more to come, but it was important to put your marker down.

The fight was coming to her enemies.

CHAPTER 42

Harry never got anxious. In a long career on the wrong side of the law, he was famous for holding his nerve under any circumstances. Not today. Today he was anxious. Martha's situation had him on edge. Feeling he was up against a superior force was a novel experience, and not one he was enjoying.

It was the waiting that was the problem. It gave him too much time to think, and try as he might to stay calm, he actually jumped when his phone went off later that evening. He was relieved to see it was Charles.

Wiping his suddenly damp hands on his trousers, he answered. Charles had a deep baritone voice honed by years of court work. "Harry? I've got some wonderful news. My contact has come through and a friendly judge is holding an emergency session in the High Court, first thing tomorrow.

"At the same time, they'll release Martha on bail. They'll deal with the formalities via video link, then she can go home. I gather we're getting what we asked for. The new judge will cite misdirection by the trial judge as the reason for acting so quickly."

"That is brilliant news," said Harry, grinning from ear to ear. "When can I collect Martha?"

"You can pick her up from Bronzefield in the morning and take her straight home to Dulwich."

Harry was about to say he needed to be on school duty when Charles added, "By the time all the paperwork gets done, it's going to be 11 a.m. at the earliest. I used to know your part of the world — I imagine a couple of hours will get you there with a bit to spare."

Harry walked back down Idmiston Road to tell Justin and Lucy the good news. Then he spent the rest of the day willing Martha to ring so he could be the one to tell her. Lucy had an extra reason to be happy. She needed to spend some time with her elderly mother, who lived in Devon, but had been waiting to ensure Martha was OK before going.

It was a long day, but finally, at 6.30 p.m., Martha was on the line. She shouted with delight when he told her what was happening. Then she listened avidly as he explained the details.

"Charles has really come through," Harry said. "He must know some top people to get this done so fast. I was worried it would take a lot longer."

She laughed. "I feel the same. It's a funny thing, though — I will sort of miss this place."

"Like a hole in the head," said Harry. "I'll see you tomorrow."

* * *

The following morning, Harry thought that their plans to ensure Betty's safety were either a brilliant success or there had been no threat in the first place. The latest morning run safely completed, Harry raised the issue with Eric.

"My boss has assigned a high threat level to both Martha and her daughter. If Martha is being released, there's no way she will cut down the protection. Now you've given them a slap, the other side will be keen to get back with a marker of their own. This might be time for more security.

"Why don't we talk before the afternoon run? That gives you plenty of time to raise it with Martha. She might have a view. In my experience, mums are keen to get involved. And that's an understatement."

Eric looked around. He seemed unable to be outside without scanning the immediate area. "The boss sends her congratulations to you."

"She does? Why?"

"You beat her hands down at the prison. We got someone inside last night, but only on the guard roster. Then we discovered your woman had already saved the day. She says to let you know that if you ever want some consultancy work . . ."

Despite himself, Harry was flattered. He worked hard to hide it. "Do I look like a consultant?" he said, spreading his arms wide. "I'm a pensioner. What can I do? Tell your boss it must be 'no thanks'. I made an old friend a promise that I would look out for his family. Turns out it's a full-time job."

* * *

Ninety minutes later, he was in the car park at Bronzefield, waiting for Martha to emerge. It took another hour before she appeared. Harry was sincerely wishing he hadn't had that last cup of coffee and took off the moment she was strapped in, heading for the next service station as fast as his little Ford Focus would take him. A lifetime of knocking around with the sort of mechanics who primed getaway cars for bank robbers had given him the skills to get the best out of his car.

Martha laughed at him as he hobbled off to the find the toilets while she cheerfully went to get herself a coffee. He declined an offer for more.

Back in the car, they filled each other in on what had been going on.

"When I said goodbye to Julie, it felt like I'd known her all my life. She's out herself in ten days — and was hoping she wouldn't have to punch a guard to extend her stay to watch out for me. I've told her to come and see us, me and you, as soon as she gets out. She's got no plans apart from staying out of prison. Honestly, Harry, she's a very big girl."

His eyes creased with a suppressed smile. "She gets that from her granddad. He was a big lad and amazingly fast. I'd love to see her. Just a pity Jerome won't be there."

There was a brief silence as Harry turned off the M25 to pick up the A3, and Martha came out with one last question. No frills or hesitations. "Did you send money to Julie?"

"The answer is yes and no. When my feelers went out, I let it get around there was cash available. I just didn't realise it would end up with Jerome's granddaughter."

He carried on before she could say anything, "I know you'll want to pay me back, but it's thanks to your dad I have some spare money. It's as if he invested in his daughter's well-being."

Martha scoffed.

"I'd do it again in a heartbeat — and it does Julie a favour, giving her a bit of cash without making a big fuss about it. So let's leave it there. I've got something else to tell you. Your invisible benefactor has put together a team of guards to watch Betty. They cover the school run, the school and the house." He saw she was alarmed. "They're very discreet. Even I can't tell they're around. I honestly think it's for the best — at least for now."

Martha gently pressed her face against the cool side window. "I wish all these people would come out and reveal who they are. I suppose that would be too easy."

They made good progress until they reached the Wandsworth one-way system, where the traffic ground to a halt. Even a traffic jam was better than being inside. Her brief but memorable stay in prison had brought home how important it was to have control over her life. She was certain that neither she nor Betty would be safe until she had rooted out the identities of those people connected to her father.

She leaned back in her seat. "You asked if I could recall any clue my dad might have left? I have remembered something, but it's a bit weird."

211

Harry remained quiet.

"A little while before he died, I had one of those conversations with him that didn't quite make sense. I'd asked him about the people he worked with and he said, 'Your cousin will know.' He wouldn't say any more — he had that infuriating way of talking in riddles, didn't he? So, I asked Mum and she was just as baffled. I don't have cousins. He didn't have a cousin, of any sort, and she'd had no contact with hers for over fifty years. I'd forgotten all about it until you told me about your theory that he might have left me a clue."

She twisted towards him, unable to keep the light of hopeful expectation out of her eyes. "So, there you have it. What do you think?"

Harry didn't immediately answer, but she could tell that he was thinking about it.

Finally, he spoke. "I can't quite pin it down but there's something . . ."

Martha nodded. She'd have to wait.

CHAPTER 43

The man known as the Fireman was gently rubbing his hands together as he waited in a car parked close to the hardware store. He liked to think warm, dry hands were essential for the work needed to be a top arsonist. There was no one better at delivering precise results, especially killing people, leaving no clues.

The Fireman liked to say that any fool with matches and petrol could set a blaze. But it took skill and experience to make the flames do your bidding. Sometimes hot and fierce was the way, reducing everything to a fine ash. Even bones would burn if the flames were hot enough. With other fires, it was low and slow. Gently flickering flames left to devour whatever was in their path.

He had orders for two fires tonight. This first one would require the gentle touch. His bosses didn't want it running out of control. He waited patiently while the "prep team" did their work.

Earlier in the evening, the woman who had given such damning evidence against Martha had gone out on a Tinder date. She'd thought she was going out a last-minute thing, after spotting someone she liked the look of and swiping right. She had no idea how much preparation had gone into that meeting. The prep team had analysed her data and discovered she had a thing for men with curly hair and dark soulful eyes who loved long-haired Norfolk Terriers which they would stroke while reading Shakespearean sonnets. Well, a girl can dream.

At lunchtime that day, a man named Mateo had popped up on her feed. He was perfect, fitting all the criteria — except the sonnets — and his South American background was the added bonus. They'd arranged to meet that night in a bar close to her flat, which was directly above the hardware store. She'd put her best underwear on, so convinced was she that he would come home with her.

But the meeting was a disaster. Mateo was about twice as old as his profile picture and had not aged well. She gulped down her glass of wine, gave him some money to pay the bill and legged it. He didn't pursue her. His job was done. The wine had enough ketamine in it to knock her sideways.

By the time she got back to the flat she was feeling dizzy, only just making it to the sofa before she passed out.

Helpfully, she had left the key in the front door, so the prep team were soon inside. They were after her tech, which they wanted to swap out with items they had brought with them. All the replacement items were then placed on the kitchen table. They needed to survive the fire as they were programmed with digital information the prep team wanted found. It would divert investigators from asking the right questions.

Ten minutes later, the preppers were on their way, leaving the Fireman to do his job. There were going to be a lot of fumes and a minor fire. His plan was to kill her through smoke inhalation, while the joint he had prepared would be what was seen as causing the fire. Given that the autopsy would show high doses of ketamine, it would look like dabbling in drugs had killed her.

A lot of effort went into getting this right. Any crime team could see the signs. The woman had planned a night in with some Special K and some hash. It had rendered her unconscious and then the smouldering joint had fallen on the floor, igniting the patch of carpet, which had generated the smoke which suffocated her. It was brilliant work, and only the most accomplished investigation would uncover the truth. The chances of that happening were slim to vanishing. A tragic accident. Move on. Nothing to see here.

After his work was finished, the Fireman was quickly on his way to the next appointment. This one was going to be the easiest he had ever carried out. His orders were to burn it, to burn it all . . . and to make it seem like arson. In many respects it was almost beneath him, but they had given him the job and he would do it.

He set off for the prosperous village of Westerham in Kent. On the edge of the village, in a large Edwardian house, lived the trial judge. She had lived there since divorcing twenty years ago and, despite her position, money troubles had built up. The problem was that she liked to bet on the financial markets. Unfortunately, her vanity impeded her sense of reality — and she was slowly drowning in debt.

Even then, she might have been OK. The house was worth more than she owed. Selling up would see her escape the crushing pile of debt.

The judge had been about to sign the papers when the offer had arrived: work for us and we take care of your money woes. Like greedy people everywhere, she said yes before thinking about it. And tonight, she would pay the price.

The prep team's task was to kill both the judge and the couple who lived in. Gunshots to the head would make it obvious it was murder, even on badly burnt bodies. But they weren't trying to hide anything about it being deliberate. The idea was to give it a frenzied feel. Judges send many people to prison, making enemies along the way. Eventually someone might put the two deaths together by making the connection with the Old Bailey case. But it was unlikely.

The witness was an accident . . . this was murder, and it was a murder with numerous suspects. Only recently the judge had handed out heavy sentences to members of a Dutch drug-smuggling gang. They were known for their brutality, and it wouldn't be a huge leap of imagination to see them as being behind the killings.

The judge would be an enormous story, the media full of lurid speculation about who had done it. It was the type of story that would generate all sorts of comments from politicians deploring an attack on the famed British judicial system. Elderly legal experts would be wheeled out, along with platoons of commentators on social media.

By contrast, the miserable, accidental death of a drug-taking young woman would be lucky if it were picked up by any journalist.

The judge's house was set behind tall hedging, which effectively hid it from view. The Fireman took his time; he'd brought eight gallons of petrol to make sure the house burned well. He poured the last of the fuel all over the hallway, stepped outside and threw in a small Molotov cocktail. There was a loud "whoosh" and the fire took hold.

Only at the end of the driveway did he turn round and study his work. Bright orange flames were dancing in the front windows. He smiled. Soon the house would be well alight. It was tempting to stay and watch. He loved big, roaring fires, especially ones that consumed entire houses. But self-discipline kicked in. He didn't want to be around when the local police turned up.

CHAPTER 44

Harry pulled up outside Martha's house to find Betty and Justin waiting. The little girl bounced into her mother's arms — and Martha forgot everything as she was caught up in the emotion. Justin had brought her home early for just this moment. It had only been two nights but felt like a lifetime.

Inside, Justin gently nudged everyone through to the kitchen, where a bottle of champagne was sitting proudly on the table.

"Could we save the fizz for later? I'm desperate for a cup of tea," said Martha, still holding Betty, who for once wasn't wriggling.

"They used to make a decent cup in Wandsworth," mused Harry to no one in particular.

"I can't speak for everyone here," said Justin, as he prepared the drinks, "but this is the first 'homecoming' party I've been to." He mimed air quotes around homecoming, glancing at Betty, who was oblivious. He wanted to be careful not to say prison in front of her.

Martha gratefully blew on her steaming mug before raising it to the two men. "To the best childminders anywhere."

She noticed Harry was staring into the middle distance. She wondered if he'd recalled something about the "cousin".

"Penny for your thoughts, Harry," said Martha, carefully putting Betty down, who was finally ready to let go of Mum and head off for her toys.

Harry made a seesawing gesture with his hand to indicate he might have something. But he was keeping the thought to himself.

Crossing the kitchen, Martha threw a playful punch at his shoulder, which reminded her she had sore knuckles. "You've got muscles as hard as rocks." She blew on her fingers in an attempt to reduce the sting.

He grinned. "This may be the one and only time I've been able to figure out one of your dad's riddles — that's got to be worth waiting for."

"Only because I did all the hard work," she grumbled.

Justin was puzzled. "What—"

"A new development," Harry interrupted him. "OK, I'm going to talk this through with both of you." He sipped his tea. "Your dad had all sorts of names he gave people. None of them made sense, except to him. Sometimes it was simple — so Harry might become George, or Justin get renamed Dan."

"He called me Dan?" said Justin.

Harry raised a hand in apology. "No, that was just an example. Actually, you were always referred to as 'Martha's bloke'. But that was the point. He came up with names that made sense to him. Someone else might be known as 'Uncle'. Maybe it was because they looked like an uncle."

He shook his head. "It sounds a bit mad when you say it out loud. The point is, it was all very personal to him, rarely making sense to anyone else. Well, there was one couple he called the 'kissing cousins'. They weren't cousins, not even close, just a couple who met each other while working for your dad and got married."

"When was all this?" asked Martha.

"I'm going back a long time. They were about my age, maybe a bit older, so that's going to put them in their late seventies now."

Martha was disappointed. "They could have died by now. Maybe this is all too late."

"Hang on a moment, hitting seventy is hardly old. And there's more. They had a kid, a son, and moved out to Epsom. I remember the location because of the racecourse, where they hold the Derby. Your dad stayed in touch. He even went to visit them a few times."

There was a long silence while Martha absorbed this information. She went to ask a question, clearly not totally convinced, but Harry had been saving one final snippet of information. "There's one other thing. Your dad used to call the son . . . the Bag Man. Maybe your dad called him that because he was storing something for him? In fact, I think the son, Ronnie his name was, ended up running all sorts of errands for your dad. This would have been when Ronnie grew up, obviously. I never knew that much about it. Once they moved to Epsom, it was sort of 'out of sight, out of mind'."

Martha let out a low whistle. "For a man who's dead, he certainly makes life interesting."

Harry sighed. "I can't remember the names of Ronnie's parents. Maybe it'll come back to me. There are still a few people around who might remember them."

"That reminds me, is the codebook safe?"

"I put the book in your 'bits and bobs' drawer. It was either that or start pulling up your floorboards. On balance I thought it was better to have it easy to get our hands on."

"A good a place as any, I guess." She took a deep breath. "There's something I'd like to run past you."

At that moment Betty reappeared, wanting Martha to come and play with her. Her words were left hanging while she went off with her daughter.

Justin and Harry had demolished most of a packet of biscuits by the time she returned.

"What did you want to say to me?" said Justin.

"My intention was to leave this for a little while, really give myself time to think this through, but being in prison

219

has changed my perspective. We need to act faster and I need to act like a proper detective." Martha threw her hands in the air, a picture of exasperation. "I've been letting my emotions get in the way. I need a proper plan, not just aimless running around. But . . ."

She gave Justin a meaningful look. "If we do go on the offensive, we're going to be mixing with some dangerous people. There are serious risks. So, if you want to back out, say so now. That way you won't know any detail of what we might need to do. And what you don't know, you can't tell."

Justin had held her gaze throughout, and now he smiled. "You know I'd do anything to keep Betty safe. I'd already worked out there was trouble ahead. Count me in and tell me what you want when you've worked things out."

"Have you still got Peter Shaw on your list of dangerous people?" Harry asked. "The more I think about what you said before, the more it strikes me that he was almost pleased when he turned up at that house where we found Betty."

"I was under the impression that he and my dad were thick as thieves, and that Dad was almost a mentor to him. I've been assuming you'd know all about that."

"Not really," said Harry. "You've got to remember that your dad liked to keep us all in separate boxes. He might have been your dad's best mate for all I knew. But he never, ever, talked about anyone else he worked with. I never asked because there was no point."

Martha nodded her understanding. "He really did seem to be trying to slow the investigation down — he was very keen to get after you, Justin, even though I told him that was ridiculous. And he asked if Dad had given me something the kidnappers would want — he's the only person who asked me that. I dismissed it at the time because I assumed he was a friend, and that he was asking questions any police would. But it was the *way* he asked. I couldn't imagine why he would want to chase after me, not if he was one of Dad's people. Now you've given me a fresh perspective. He's certainly powerful enough to cause no end of problems."

She stopped. "God, thinking about this makes you paranoid. Here I am coming up with theories against a man who worked alongside my father. We need more to go on than him being a bit tough on me."

"You aren't being paranoid," said Harry. "I've wondered a few times about how quickly he got on to where we were. Like he was following a trail. He claimed he got an anonymous tip about us going into the house with a Taser, but he could have got someone to do that."

"OK. He's our first name on the list — but we have to be super careful. What happens if it turns out he's actually on my side? He was a bit of a git about arresting me, but he didn't have much choice, not really. Maybe he needed to put on a good show, not make it look like he was trying to help me."

CHAPTER 45

The following morning, Betty was up at first light, raring to go as she jumped up and down on Martha's bed. Her mother groaned. "It's only a quarter to six in the morning! We've got ages before we go to school."

The little girl was pulled into a cuddle, then she was wriggling to be free. "I'm going to wake Daddy. He's always ready to do stuff."

A few moments later, a deep groan suggested that Justin was not quite as prepared as Betty had said. Martha trotted out of her room and went downstairs. Justin was lying on the settee, a blanket over his head. He was sticking around so that Martha could have the freedom to move at a moment's notice. "I'm more than happy to be a stay-at-home dad."

She laughed. "How about I deal with Miss Energy Bomb for the next hour, then you hang out with her while I have a bath?"

Deal done, Martha and daughter were in the kitchen, Betty tucking into a bowl of Coco Pops enhanced with slices of banana. Eating seemed to slow Betty down enough for the pair to curl up on the sofa and watch children's TV. Martha's jail visit may have been brief but she had learned one thing: take nothing for granted.

Having just handed Betty over to Justin, her mobile rang. It was Paul Avery.

Paul made no apology for the early hour. "Switch on the news," he said. It was an instruction, not a suggestion.

"I've been on childcare duties. What's going on to get you calling me so early?"

"It's the judge. She was killed last night. Cold-blooded murder. She and the live-in couple who worked for her were shot dead."

There was a moment of silence while Martha took it all in.

"We're hearing it was the work of serious professionals. They killed all three the same way — two shots to the head and another two in the heart. Somebody wanted to be very certain that she died. The house was set on fire by someone using an accelerant — someone who knew what they were doing. I don't want to worry you, but . . ."

"You think it's something to do with my trial? But she was one of theirs!"

Out of the corner of her eye, she saw Justin pop his head around the doorway, concerned.

"On that we're firmly agreed," said Paul. "But they could be covering their tracks, especially as you were released because of her actions — there would have been an investigation, surely. Can you be in my office at 10 a.m.? We're making phone calls — a lot of calls. So, hopefully, we can have something solid to tell you about the next legal steps."

"I'll be there," said Martha.

"Their own judge?" Justin said, when she told him. He threw his hands in the air. "I just don't understand what they want. Are they tying up loose ends? What about you and Betty?"

Martha went to make some reassuring remarks, but the words stuck in her throat. She was prepared for anything in relation to herself, but Betty was different. The thought of her little girl being hurt filled her with horror.

For a moment they fell silent until a sharp rap on the front door startled them both.

Before they could react, Betty raced to answer it, shouting, "Harry!"

Then she opened the door and they heard her say, "Who are you?"

Overcoming their paralysis, they ran to see who had been let into the house.

A man she'd never seen before looked up from smiling at Betty. "Sorry," he said to Justin, "is this inconvenient?"

Justin was leaning against the wall, breathing like he'd just done the 100 metres.

The man's grin broadened. "You might want to cut down on the doughnuts. Look, just a quick one—"

"Who are you?" Martha broke in.

"Eric," he said, holding out his hand. "Friend of Sally and Quentin's. Security detail."

Martha ignored the outstretched hand. So he carried on, unabashed. "My boss wants to see you, today, once you've had your meeting with Paul Avery and Charles Winter. She says you should go to the lobby of the Savoy Hotel at noon. Come alone — which means no Harry."

At the back of the house, a mobile pinged with an incoming message.

Eric looked smug. "That's a number we just sent to your phone. You should call it if you have a problem with the instructions." Then, after bending to pat Betty on the head, he left.

For a moment Martha almost followed Eric to finish the conversation. Instead, she closed the door and put the chain on. "Betty," she said, "what have I told you about opening the door before you know who's there?" It was senseless trying to reason with a four-year-old — Betty had already dashed off to look for her crayons.

"I assume he's the chief bodyguard," she said to Justin. "Is he always a total arsehole?"

Justin frowned. "You only just sorted the meeting with Paul. How do you suppose they knew about it?"

She picked up her phone and pointed it at him. "They must be bugging it somehow. Christ, with my luck they've probably got someone at GCHQ . . . I'm getting heartily sick of this. Everyone seems to know all about us, but we know nothing about them. It's long past time I did something about that."

CHAPTER 46

The offer was made, considered and rejected — in about the time it took to say no. Maybe a little faster. Legal briefings are most typically sedate affairs, where the issues are weighed and carefully analysed. It was a shame no one had told Martha.

She'd arrived for her discussion with Charles and Paul at the latter's office in Holborn. It was a spacious room with a desk and a large oval table big enough to seat a dozen people; for this meeting there were just four — Martha and Harry on one side, the two lawyers on the other.

It started amiably enough. Martha was keen to hear what her legal team had to say, and Charles indicated he had a plan. Paul served coffee and then sat back to watch Martha's reaction as the barrister explained his thinking.

He didn't need any expertise to see this was not going well. Martha was furious. She banged her fist on the table, shouting, "No!"

Martha's eyes blazed as she stared at Charles, who was suddenly glad there was an expanse of polished wood between them.

In case anyone was still wondering, she barked her final response: "That's not going to happen — never."

Paul Avery raised a sharp eyebrow, which Charles acknowledged. "I was warned you might not like the proposal. Forgive me, but it is my duty to you to inform you of what is on the table. Before you ended up in Bronzefield, I promised that I would only suggest a change of direction if circumstances changed. I think that has—"

He got no further as a still-enraged Martha jumped in. "Might not like the proposal? All this is something cobbled together by politicians eager to avoid a scandal! It isn't justice. It isn't truth."

In a rare show of solidarity, political special advisers and senior officials had found themselves in agreement. The optics on Martha Munro's case looked terrible, especially for a party about to announce a new law-and-order drive. The prime minister and his chief of staff were spitting feathers. Something had to be done. A meeting had begun at 6 a.m., starting with a discussion about the standard solution, one that would see a junior politician thrown under the nearest bus. But not this time. A murdered judge was gumming up the operation, making it difficult to anticipate the direction of travel — so a new scheme was discussed and passed to Charles at 9.30 a.m. It was relayed to Martha at 10.01 a.m.

The plan was for Martha to keep her head down for the next six months. Once the dust settled, ideally under the cover of a big story, Martha could be quietly cleared of all wrongdoing by special decree. To sweeten the pot, they'd even throw in an invitation to a Buckingham Palace garden party. Probably not with the Queen, but definitely one of the Royal Family.

At this moment, Martha stood up. "You tell them I will settle for nothing less than having my name cleared. Immediately."

Charles quickly apologised again. "I'll make sure that your feelings are relayed exactly as you've stated them. I shall not repeat the mistake of underestimating your determination.

"If I may beg your trust again, let me get back to you when I have a response. I shall make it clear that the murder of the judge only adds to the dangerous situation into which you've been dragged. It would be very helpful if you could also provide a full account of what happened to you in prison. I know you were at risk — and that is another stick to beat the system with."

Martha was sitting down again. "If it hadn't been for Harry, I don't know what might have happened. They could have killed me in there, and there's no doubt in my mind that some of the guards were in on it."

Sudden fury gripped her again and her lips compressed. "That judge almost gave me a death sentence."

"When we first talked about what might happen to you, it was in somewhat abstract terms," said Charles. "But hearing the reality is very disturbing. However, it strengthens our hand. Now, I need to raise compensation. Do you want to pursue that?"

"That's difficult," she said. "I'm fortunate that all your costs are being covered but I do have to think about the future. Why don't we put the ball in their court? If they come up with something sensible, we can all move on. The Met needs to pay for what they've done to me, and there's probably no way I'm going back — even though I'd only just made detective. Despite all this I'm still proud of that."

She was being pragmatic, but it was hard to say out loud. Even if she got a full pardon, she might end up walking away from a job she had dreamed of doing since she was a child.

For all that she was keeping up a rational front, Martha was sensible enough to recognise the pressure she was under. Having Harry close helped. His 'one step at a time' approach was ideally suited when the stakes could not be higher.

She decided to tell Paul and Charles about the Savoy. "My alleged benefactor is asking to meet up with me. Today, at the Savoy. I'm to go alone."

Charles looked at her carefully. "Did you get any idea of what the meeting is about or who it is you'll be meeting?"

She shook her head. "Not the faintest idea, I'm afraid."

"Are you happy to go it alone?"

"I don't really have a choice. I thought about insisting on Harry being with me, but that might scare them off. I need this information — it might be the only way I'll ever be sure that Betty is truly out of danger. I should be safe at the Savoy, and I need some clarity about who we're dealing with.

"This woman is acting the part of a friend; she's certainly putting her money where her mouth is. She may not be a real friend, but if she's my enemy's enemy, then I need to talk to her, try to get a sense of what she's like. She's already helping to keep an eye on Betty; maybe we can see what else is on offer — and why."

"What do you say, Harry? Is it too risky?"

"We're beyond risky now. I agree with you, let's see what happens next."

He flat-batted further questions in a way Martha understood to mean: let's keep a few things up our sleeves.

Suddenly, she wanted to be outside. "If you gentlemen are finished for now, I'd like to get down to the Savoy in plenty of time."

A few minutes later, they were on their way. Harry explained that he had been texted the names of the "kissing cousins" — Pat and Maurice Wyatt.

"While I'm waiting for you, I'll get some calls in. Do you fancy popping down there late this afternoon, if I can find an address? I took the liberty of talking to Justin and he's happy to keep an eye on Betty. If that's OK with you? We've been on the back foot till now, but if your dad left something with the Wyatts, that could change things."

She nodded. "I agree. We have to keep moving now — no more softly, softly. I'm concerned about Betty, but I'm hoping today will help with that. In another life I'd have got police protection, but how can I trust them now?"

Martha went to cross the road, when Harry suddenly pulled her back as a cyclist raced past. She was chagrined. "There I am — going on about being alert at all times."

Harry patted her arm. "No harm done. Let's stop for a bit. There's a small coffee shop. We've got plenty of time."

"Make mine a double espresso — and, if you have any cigarettes on you, I might be persuaded today is a good day for smoking."

"You're a bad influence on me. I was having a low-emissions day today."

"And you, Harry, are a terrible liar. I can spot the signs when you want a cigarette."

He looked puzzled.

"You roll your thumb and first two fingers together. I was about thirteen years old when I first spotted it. It's your tell."

Harry was staring at his hand as he made the precise gesture she described. "All these years and I never thought I had a tell about anything. People used to say I was very hard to read."

"Not to me, you're not. Don't get me wrong, I suspect that only someone who knows you so well could do it." Martha grinned. "Do you want to know what you do when you're hungry? Or when you fancy a beer?"

He grimaced. "Another time, maybe. What we need to do now is have a final talk about what you're going to say in there."

"I'm hoping that I'll mostly be listening — what can I tell her that she doesn't already know? She holds all the cards."

"Sure. I get that. But I can hear your father saying, 'There's no such thing as a free lunch.'" He tossed her the cigarette packet and lighter.

Standing side by side, they finished their coffee. Harry looked Martha in the eye. "There's still time to pull out of this meeting. You don't have to go."

"Oh yes I do." Her expression was fierce. "We go ahead and see where it takes us. I'm done with sitting around waiting for these bastards to make a move."

CHAPTER 47

Walking into the genteel bustle of the Savoy was like stepping inside a comfortable bubble. Glancing around, Martha was pleased that she'd selected the few clothes she had which stood up to this environment. Against her better judgement, she'd even applied a touch of lipstick, but had refused to go further. She shrugged. She wasn't here to win a grooming competition.

Her hackles went up as she scanned the lobby. This was enemy territory. She was sure she'd been under observation from the front entrance. Martha stopped near the check-in desk and waited. Her woman could come to her. She was assuming she would be in her late fifties, with an expensive suit and a perfect haircut.

Somebody tapped her on the shoulder before she even knew they were there. "Martha. I'm Carol."

Martha flushed. The woman had taken her by surprise. Carol was short, thin and elegant in a tailored black trouser suit, with high heels. She blended perfectly into the moneyed surroundings. Martha felt at a disadvantage but shrugged it off. Clothes had never been her thing. She did, however, need to raise her game.

Carol, meanwhile, was studying her closely. "I imagine the camera likes you, Martha. Good bone structure. Now, if you don't mind, follow me. I have a room for the next couple of hours."

They went up to the second floor without a word and entered a large room with a small working area.

"Sit down. Would you like some coffee, or is the one you just had with Harry enough to be going on with?"

Martha realised another error. She hadn't anticipated that she would be under surveillance, probably from the moment she left home. This woman was making her look like an amateur — which she supposed she was. She needed to show her she could be professional.

"OK, I admit, you've caught me with my pants down. I should have guessed that you would tail me. In your position, and with your resources, it's a sensible move. If I apologise for being a bit slow off the mark, can we start again?"

The woman surveyed her for a long minute, her face neutral. "You don't take yourself too seriously. Your dad was like that. Right, you go first."

It was disorientating to meet so many total strangers who seemed to know everything about her father. Carol's eyes were burning into her, weighing her up.

"It seems my dad was prepared to sit down with the devil if it got him what he needed."

The woman gave the faintest nod. "Go on."

"Dad was a pragmatic man. He knew he couldn't stop all crime. He couldn't even stop most crimes. But he found a way to stop some of the biggest.

"My guess is that, once he had people in custody, he made them an offer. Information for freedom. He wasn't too fussy about how official any deal might be. Somehow, and I can guess how, he had access to plenty of money. If someone had something he needed, he would pay. He didn't care what they'd done — so long as they helped him achieve his goals."

Martha paused, thinking. "It wasn't just the criminals. It was police officers too. His payroll wasn't exclusive, but it was secret — very secret. He was the only one who knew everything. Until recently, I was in a state of blissful ignorance, but now there's a big problem. He made enemies, some extremely dangerous enemies. People with long memories and major grudges. It turns out that those enemies are my enemies."

Carol had not so much as moved a muscle. She just sat there listening.

Martha spread her hands, palms out. "When I try to work it out, my head spins. Even my newfound friends are a puzzle." She inclined her head at Carol and then carried on. "I mean no offence, but for someone who says they're my friend, you're being very mysterious. At least I can tell who my enemies are because they want to hurt me."

"I was under the impression you hadn't identified your enemies," Carol replied. "And why do you think they want to hurt you?"

"Revenge?" Martha was beginning to doubt herself. "No, that seems crazy . . . I had nothing to do with my dad's work. Just to make matters worse, some of my enemies are powerful enough to corrupt a judge." Martha shrugged. "Maybe you can help? I don't know that yet. But I'm not running away anymore."

"It seems you need answers. I can provide them. But first I should explain why I've taken an interest — why your father left you my email address." Carol poured water into two glasses. She passed one to Martha and took a small sip from her own. "I knew your dad well. We were . . ." She paused, looking vulnerable, then pressed on. "Your dad and I were very close, but he wanted to keep it quiet." There was a glint in her eye. No hint of vulnerability now. "That's all you're going to get about our relationship, except this: it all happened after he'd been separated from your mum.

"Your dad was a complex and difficult man. Where he was concerned, you could never tell his friends from his enemies. John Munro was full of contradictions. A brilliant detective who let the guilty go free. An honest cop who was involved in corruption. A good father who abandoned his daughter."

"Not everyone can be neatly boxed up," said Martha, trying to keep the defensive tone out of her voice.

The woman shook her head in irritation. "I wasn't criticising him. He was what he was. I was there when he realised he had to step away from you. Even then, it wasn't just about keeping you safe. John Munro always liked a double payment if he could manage it."

She stopped. "You may not like this next bit. When he stepped away from you and your mother, it emboldened some of his enemies to come out of the shadows. They sensed a moment to attack. He deliberately put you at risk to find out who they were. It was a gamble — and he very nearly lost. But ask me if he lost any sleep over how close it came to disaster? I will always give you the same answer. Not at all. He was a ruthless bastard with ice in his veins."

A memory flickered within Martha — the sensation of being carried. *Her mother was holding her in her arms and there were men everywhere, their pale faces reflecting the light of a full moon. "Quickly," said her father. "Get in the car, we don't have much time."*

She did her best to hide her feelings as the memory retreated. She didn't doubt what this woman was saying. She also had the strongest sense that Carol was testing her.

"You say he used us as bait, and that may be right to a point. But maybe he felt there was no other choice. One way, he definitely lost us; the other . . . well, the other is why I'm here now."

Carol made no attempt to respond, so Martha changed tack. "Who is after me? And why?"

Carol weighed her response. "You're right to be concerned," she said. "Your father made some profoundly serious enemies. But he was ready for that. He made me promise I would be there for you, to watch your back. And I always keep my promises. Especially to John Munro. Plus, you have Harry, and he's a one-man wrecking crew."

Martha shook her head in irritation. "I'd worked most of this out — except your involvement — for myself. But who am I dealing with? Let me throw a name at you, one

Harry and I are both wondering about. Commander Peter Shaw of Scotland Yard."

Carol went very still, and Martha sensed she was right. "It is him, isn't it?"

The two women stared at each other, a silent battle of wills taking place. Then Carol surprised her with a brief smile.

"Just like your father. He could be as stubborn as a mule." The smile vanished. "Yes. Peter Shaw. I've only just confirmed his name. I also think there's someone else, someone in the shadows . . ." She held up a hand. "It's not a name for sharing. Not yet. But back to Peter Shaw — there aren't many people your dad was wary of, but he was one of them."

The news was a blow. "I was clinging to the hope it wasn't him. That he and Dad were friends. That my dad was virtually a mentor to him."

"All that is true," said Carol. "He got himself into your dad's orbit and at first they got on just fine. I think in some ways Peter Shaw was the son your dad never had. He loved you, don't get me wrong, but Shaw meant a lot to him.

"Then things started happening. Gangs were tipped off, arrests went wrong and, to cap it all, a young copper was killed in a shoot-out. Your dad couldn't prove it, but there was only one man, apart from himself, who had the information needed to sabotage operations so effectively."

"So why now? Why is Shaw coming for me when Dad died years ago?"

"It all comes back to the way your dad kept secrets. Only he had the full picture. Even I was kept at arm's length for a lot of stuff. But your dad weaved one heck of a web.

"He was smart, smarter than most of us, but even he needed to keep notes. The rumour was he kept a record of his key informants, and about a year ago people started saying you had got your hands on it. The secrets that John Munro never shared with anyone else." Carol took another sip of water. "Do you have it?"

Martha's father had once told her that a classic clue to spotting liars was when they stopped blinking. She made herself blink. Her training had taught her that to tell good lies you need a bit of the truth, combined with a plausible explanation. She put that practical experience to good use now.

"Like you say, I can work things out. If I was in his shoes, I would have kept a record. A very secret record. There must be something. But do I know where it is, or even have it? The answer is no."

Carol was too astute to be taken in. "That was very convincing. Let's say I believe you. Of course, it is possible that as John Munro's daughter you have a plan for this, some scheme to get back on the front foot? Maybe get revenge for what happened to your mother? I could quite understand that. But I would be failing in my promise to your father if I didn't tell you Peter Shaw is a very dangerous man. You should leave him to me." She briefly gazed out of the window. "As to the record of informants. My advice? If you find it — I strongly suggest you hand it to me. I can let it be known I have it, in fact had it all along, which takes the spotlight off you."

The meeting was over. As Martha stood, Carol held up a hand.

"I will contact you through Eric. Do not believe any messages from any other source, no matter how plausible they may be."

Martha marched to the stairs with renewed energy. She had the name of the enemy, fresh insights into her father and an understanding of why she was being targeted. The meeting had gone far better than she dared to hope.

Stopping herself from running down the stairs, she marched quickly through the lobby and was outside on the Strand, scanning the crowds towards Trafalgar Square, when Harry popped up behind her.

"We're being watched."

"She told me in the hotel. Good job we left you outside as requested."

"How'd it go?"

"Better than I expected. You were right to be worried about Peter Shaw, it seems. And everyone knows, or thinks they know, about my father's secret notebook. Apparently, there are many people who are very keen to get their hands on it. Oh, and the woman I went to see: she's called Carol and she was also Dad's girlfriend."

Harry's jaw dropped. He couldn't work out what to react to first. Eventually he said, "What girlfriend?"

Martha grinned. "Don't you want to know how I left things regarding Shaw and the notebook?"

A resigned expression crept over his face. "I'm guessing that you haven't done the sensible thing and left it all for this 'girlfriend' to sort out."

She prodded him in the chest. "What did Dad always say? If you want something done properly, do it yourself. Well, I want this doing properly."

"Before you get carried away with the master plan," said Harry, "do you want to hear my bit of news? I've tracked down the cousins. We can go there now if you're up to it. We can talk on the journey."

"Deal," said Martha. "I can tell you about Carol, if you like, and then we can think about what to do with Peter Shaw. I can tell you one thing, I won't sit back and take it anymore. Peter Shaw's about to discover what it means to tangle with me."

CHAPTER 48

Harry had thought of a way they might lose the people following them. "We'll head through the Savoy and pick up a cab at the back exit. Hopefully, they won't be expecting that." He set off at a brisk pace.

A black cab was dropping a fare off as they walked outside.

Harry trotted up and spoke to the driver. "Waterloo, please, mate." He flourished a twenty-pound note. "No need for change, we're in a bit of a rush."

It was generous for a short journey, and the now cheery driver needed no more encouragement. As they pulled away, it gratified Harry to notice a frantic couple running out and glaring at their departing cab. He'd noted the pair earlier and was confident they were part of the surveillance team. With no other cabs around, they were out of the running.

The cabbie manoeuvred his way along the Embankment before crossing the Thames at Lambeth Bridge. A few minutes later, they were dropped at the station. Harry inspected the information boards.

"We need the Dorking train so we can get off at Epsom. The 'kissing cousins' live a short distance from the station. We've just got time to get a sandwich. I don't know about you, but I'm starving."

They ate their lunch on the train as it passed through the London suburbs, Martha listening in as Harry phoned to say hello and get directions.

When he hung up, she mentioned the flashback she'd had at the Savoy. "It's something that happened when I was little. Mum and I were being moved in the night. It had something to do with Dad. Everyone was worried."

Harry lifted his head. "There was a real panic one night that some killer was coming for you and your mum. Luckily, it turned out to be a false alarm. Surprised you can remember it."

"I suppose it's not a million miles from what we're doing with Betty, so maybe that's what triggered it." She glanced out of the window. "That's my dad for you — still causing problems all these years later."

Arriving at Epsom forty minutes later, they hurried outside.

"Taxi or walk?" Harry asked.

Martha, as always, wanted to stretch her legs, so they turned away from the new-build flats outside the station and took a narrow footpath to the high street, enjoying the anonymity of the unfamiliar town. Soon the shops disappeared and were replaced with shabbily genteel terraces. It wasn't long before they were knocking on the door of a neat semi-detached house. A white-haired lady wearing a floral pinafore over her grey dress opened the front door.

"There's no doubt who you are," she said, looking closely at Martha. "John Munro's daughter." She switched her gaze to Harry. "And you can give me a hug, young Harry. It's been a long time."

Few people could call him "young Harry", Martha thought as they were shown into the living room, where a smiling man used his walking stick to haul himself to his feet. "I never expected you to show up with John's girl," he said.

Introductions over, Pat and Maurice Wyatt fussed over the pair of newcomers. It was obvious they enjoyed having company. Martha had been expecting a house full of chintz, but everything was pared back — no ornaments, just a few family photos, including one of a young man she assumed was Ronnie.

Pat spotted her looking around. "I can't stand clutter. This is much easier to keep clean."

Only after several cups of tea was it time to get down to business. Martha explained why they were there. "My dad played his cards close to his chest, that's a fact. Well, we have a feeling he may have left something with you. It might not be the biggest thing or look like very much. It might be a book, or a single piece of paper—"

Maurice held up a finger to interrupt her. "We have what you're after. Pat, you're the fittest. Do you mind?"

His wife walked over to a small cabinet. When she opened the door, Martha saw it was full of board games. Reaching confidently past the Monopoly box into the back of the cabinet, Pat pulled out a thick brown envelope, sealed with a metal clip. This she handed to Martha.

"We've never had even a peep inside. Not once in all these years. Your dad said it was something you would come for one day."

"How could he have known that?"

"He just did. Said you were a clever one and would work it out." Pat turned to Harry. "He said you might be with her too."

Now it was Harry's turn to look gobsmacked, although he quickly gathered himself. Pointing at the photos, he said, "How is Ronnie? He was working for John, wasn't he?"

The old man walked over to the photos. He patted the framed photo of the young man with the infectious smile.

"Ronnie did a lot for John Munro. It was all on the quiet, but Ronnie helped him. Remarkably close they were. Even after the accident he came to see him."

"Accident?" said Harry. "What accident?"

"Oh, it was a silly thing, really. Ronnie loved cycling. He fell off and hit his head. At first they said it was concussion but he kept getting worse. Eventually the doctors diagnosed vascular dementia. Your dad helped a lot. Got him into a brilliant clinic and made sure all the costs were covered. They hoped he'd get better. He never did. We see him once a month, but he doesn't know who we are anymore."

* * *

A couple of hours later, Martha and Harry were back in Dulwich, walking towards Idmiston Road. Martha, who was thinking there had been enough shocks for the day, still hadn't opened the envelope. Harry left her in peace. Perhaps she was being perverse, but she wanted the security of being home before finding out what was inside.

Martha's phone rang. It was Justin.

Martha's heart lurched as she answered. "Is there a problem?" she asked.

"Not as such. But there is an exceptionally large woman here who says she's come straight from prison to see you and Harry." Justin whispered conspiratorially, "If you want my advice, don't shake hands with her. She's got a helluva grip."

CHAPTER 49

The news that Julie had turned up was like an instant tonic to Martha, who felt a definite spring in her step. Even Harry seemed pleased, doubtless keen to meet his friend's granddaughter.

Martha's sense of eagerness increased the moment she walked through her door and made for the warm familiarity of the kitchen. She was nearly overcome with emotion as she caught sight of Julie, holding a laughing Betty upside down by one leg. Although hardly any time had elapsed since they'd said goodbye at the prison, it felt like a lifetime to Martha.

With surprising grace for such an enormous woman, Julie carefully placed Betty the right way up.

The two women hugged, then all round introductions were made.

Harry looked Julie up and down. "You've definitely got a bit of your grandad about you. He could have been a heavyweight boxer."

Julie flexed her biceps in response. "I like to keep myself in shape. I say make the most of what you've been given. Don't try to be something different."

Suddenly thirsty, Martha poured a large glass of tap water, before turning to her new friend. "Have you got any immediate plans for where you're going to stay? We'd love to have you here, especially my daughter — although I must warn you that you might be swapping one dangerous place for another."

"As it happens, I'm between digs right now," Julie joked. "If you feel a bit of muscle would help and you'll have me, I'd love to stay. Sounds like your house is one of the most interesting places to be right now. And you're definitely the most interesting woman I've met."

Feeling pleased with Julie's reply, Martha brought Julie up to speed, showing her the envelope they'd just retrieved from Epsom.

"It was really spooky. It was like my dad was there, but just out of sight. He actually told them that Harry and I would turn up one day."

She also took the chance to fill everybody in on what she'd discovered at the Savoy.

Julie leaned forward and poked the envelope. "When are you going to open that thing?"

Martha picked it up. It was time to find out what her father had left for her.

"It feels like Dad's reaching out. He would never have gone to so much trouble unless he thought it could help." The others were studying her with the same sort of nervous antici-pation that she was displaying. She waved the envelope. "I want a large glass of wine in my hand before I open this. And we'd better sort out sleeping arrangements." She smiled at Julie. "I'm glad you're staying here. You can have my mum's room. I've been putting it off, but it's time it was put back to use."

Julie started to protest but Martha was insistent. "You just volunteered to look after Betty, so wherever Mum's look-ing down from, she'd totally approve."

Justin agreed. "It's absolutely the right thing to do. Anyway, the alternative is the sofa, which I've been using, but it's a tad too small for you."

Julie rubbed her hands. "You've persuaded me. If I'm honest, anywhere will be great after being inside. Now, all we need to seal the deal is pizza, lots of pizza. I've been dreaming of pizza — and wine. Make my glass a bucket."

* * *

Once Betty was happily tucked up in bed, pizza delivered and drinks poured, Martha carefully opened the envelope.

With a wry smile, she glanced at her audience, then pulled out another envelope. A third envelope was inside that.

"It's like those Russian dolls," said Harry. "Your dad did like his little jokes."

Martha was holding the third envelope between her thumb and forefinger. "If this contains the answer to all our questions, it must be in tiny writing."

"Or yet another clue," said Harry, drawing groans from everyone.

Martha checked inside. This time there was something. Carefully, she pulled it out. This hadn't seen the light of day in a while. At first, she didn't immediately recognise what it was. Then she realised it was two newspaper cuttings, stapled at all four corners to another piece of paper.

She pulled out the cuttings. They were about the size of her hand and one had a thumbnail-sized picture in the top right. She peered closely at the image, then sat back, her eyes glued to the clipping.

"I think we all know who this is," she whispered.

She held it up for the others to see.

CHAPTER 50

Nervous energy made her hand tremble as she held up the cutting. The photograph wasn't the best quality, but you could see it was a headshot of a young man who was staring at the camera with the hint of a smile, as if he knew something of which the observer was unaware.

Julie and Justin leaned closer, but neither had any idea who it was. Harry clearly did. A small "Oh" formed on his lips.

"This," said Martha, "is the younger incarnation of Commander Peter Shaw."

"What are the stories about?" asked Justin.

"This one," said Martha, shaking the cutting with Shaw's picture on it, "is a description of a young Peter Shaw winning promotion to the National Crime Agency."

She quickly scanned the second cutting. "This one is about some krugerrands going missing from a police lock-up. The agency had salvaged them after they intercepted a team of bank robbers. My dad, in his usual obtuse way, seems to be leaving us a pretty big clue. He's obviously saying Shaw was involved in stealing the gold coins."

"So what's your plan? And don't tell me you haven't got one," Harry said to Martha.

Her eyes were glittering. "We need to follow the money."

She broke off as there was a knock at the door.

Harry went to answer, Martha on his heels.

It was Eric. "I have some news," he said, saying nothing else. Harry refused to respond to what was clearly an attempt to bait them about Eric's inside information. Instead, he looked back to Martha, who nodded.

Harry turned to Eric. "You'd better come in," he said, not bothering to keep the dislike off his face. He led Eric into the kitchen, pointedly refusing to offer him anything to drink.

Undeterred, Eric picked up a wine bottle, ostentatiously sniffing it. "I'd have to refuse the offer of a drink. Never touch it when I'm on duty, need to keep your wits about you."

He looked around. "Glad to meet you, Julie. I've heard a lot about you. I hear you're useful with your hands." Something about the way he spoke made her step towards him — not in a friendly way.

Martha wanted him out. "Just tell us what you need." She looked down at the table and her heart lurched. The cuttings were in view. She stepped over and covered them, unable to tell if Eric had seen. She wished she hadn't needed to draw attention to them.

Still displaying his infuriating sense of superiority, Eric took a breath. "My boss thinks you're at maximum danger, so she's asked me to tell you that we're making your security more obvious. From now on there will be at least two people outside the house, round the clock, and on the school run team."

Martha was worried that Justin still blamed her for putting Betty in danger. But when he lifted his chin, his expression showed he was on her side. "I've warned you, Eric, don't frighten the head teacher again," he said. "Keep your security lot out of her sight. She'll call the police if she sees you."

"She won't see my people."

Martha turned her attention to Eric. "What's happened to make your boss more concerned?"

He shrugged. "I just get told what to do."

Martha fought down her irritation with the man. "Tell your boss you delivered the message, and we thank her for her support. I want it clearly understood that you are here as a deterrent. I don't want your people getting involved unless there's an obvious threat to Betty, or one of us. Your boss gave me a number to reach her, so I will call and ask her directly."

Eric headed out of the front door without so much as a backward glance.

Martha stared angrily at the space where he had been standing. "What a bastard. Did he see those cuttings?"

"I was looking at him when you turned them over," Julie said. "He didn't so much as blink. But who can tell with a little weasel like that?"

"He's probably telling his boss all about it right now," said Harry. "It'll be interesting to see if she answers your call."

"No time like the present," said Martha. She made the call and Carol answered on the second ring.

"I gather you want to know what's behind me stepping up security."

"I do, and I have other people here who need to know," said Martha. "Any problem if I put you on speaker phone?"

"No problem, except this isn't going to be a question-and-answer session. I share my thoughts, then that's it."

"Understood. Do you want to start?"

Carol's voice filled the small kitchen. "What I will share with you is the edited version. My sources tell me that we are at the point where people are starting to feel the pressure to do something, especially now that you've emerged unscathed from prison. If it were me I would definitely be getting ready to move. So, this is partly about information and partly about instinct."

"Please allow me one question," said Martha. "Is it Peter Shaw? Is he the prime suspect?"

"I'll give you that one, and the answer is yes. What's unclear is the extent to which he has freedom to operate. I remain convinced there's another player pulling his strings. If he knew you were aware of him it might trigger a dangerous response. I'm sorry, but you'll have to make do with that."

"I guess I have no choice but accept your terms," said Martha. "Did Eric tell you that I have warned him there has to be maximum discretion?"

"I've told him to listen to your concerns." Then Carol was gone.

"At least you got the chance to tell her not to overdo it on the protection front," said Harry. "Having so many of his team there should be enough. It will certainly give us the chance to get Betty away from any problems."

"That's true. I want Betty to be the top priority. Much as I want to get at Shaw, I'm not putting her in danger."

CHAPTER 51

The plan came to her quite suddenly. Wanting to buy herself a little space to think about it, Martha told everyone she was going for a quick solo walk. A short timeout was what she needed. It was hard to shake the knowledge that Eric was probably watching her every move — he was good at not being seen, she'd give him that — but even a semblance of privacy was better than being in jail, she reminded herself.

By the time she got home she had decided to go ahead, but very cautiously. She outlined her plans to the other three. There were two parts. Justin would have a dual role. As their only computer expert, he would operate on the cyber front, trying to find if there was a history of unofficial payments going into Shaw's bank accounts. Meanwhile, he was also on the team which would put Shaw under surveillance. Or as much as they could, given they had few resources.

"This will have to be short and sharp because there will only be the three of you; you guys are going to get tired very quickly. I will not be part of the surveillance operation, which is unfair to you all, but I have to be there for Betty. From what Justin tells me, it'll do her good to have some proper time with me. I've been absent too much recently."

Justin, Julie and Harry all agreed with alacrity. She laid down key ground rules. "We can't pretend this is a top-level operation. There's just the three of you to cover each twenty-four hours, and we have to share cars.

"The best we can do is stay well back and avoid getting noticed. The last thing we need is for any of you to get into a confrontation with Shaw, or tip him off that he's being followed. Much better to lose him than get caught."

They discussed the plan until after midnight, when Martha called it a day. She needed her bed. They had agreed the surveillance could start the following day.

* * *

Martha woke up early to a cold, damp morning, with the sort of slate-grey sky that did nothing to improve the mood.

They fleshed out the details at the new Idmiston Road "HQ". Justin would take the morning shift, Julie next and Harry the night shift. He'd volunteered, claiming that "at my age you don't sleep that much".

Justin came up with a twist to the plan. "If we copy that krugerrand cutting, we can have it anonymously delivered to his house. That might just rattle his cage. If it was me, I'd need to go and check where I'd stashed them."

"Brilliant plan," said Martha, voicing the collective opinion.

Julie addressed the elephant in the room. "What about your dad's notebook? From what you say, there's no chance of peace while it's still up for grabs."

"It'll be a strong bargaining chip. If we can't nail Shaw ourselves, maybe I can go to Carol and offer her the notebook? In return, she uses her muscle to make sure we're left alone."

"Why not just do that anyway?" asked Harry. "Forget catching Shaw, leave everything to her."

"Because I'm not sure we can trust her. She insists it's all down to a promise she made to my dad, her secret lover. But we don't know that. I'd hate to give away the book and find out that once she has it, she loses all interest in us.

"One way, or another, I have to hand over that book. I just think I'd like to have a go at Shaw first, take him off the board, then give it to Carol. That way we do things on our terms, which has to be the best plan. Any news on the cyber front, Justin?"

Justin pulled a face. "I wish there was. But don't lose faith, I'll keep going."

CHAPTER 52

Day one of the surveillance had been an abject failure. It started well. Justin was first up, parking as close to Shaw's home in Beckenham as he dared. He had carefully followed his target but within a mile had lost him at a set of temporary traffic lights. Martha had known that her surveillance scheme would prove difficult, but this was hopeless.

Her friends' initial enthusiasm was quickly wearing thin. She needed to act. On day three, her team were at the limits of their patience. Much more and they'd start taking risks. It was time to change direction, and Martha told everyone that day four, tomorrow, would be the last. Once Justin finished his slot, that was it.

With this last throw of the dice, they finally got something.

For once Justin hadn't lost his target, who, instead of heading to Scotland Yard, deviated towards Knightsbridge. The policeman parked close to Harrods, then made his way on foot to a nearby office building, an undistinguished brick-clad box, where he went inside for about fifteen minutes.

When Justin reported in, Martha was thrilled that something had happened. "We need to find out what he was doing there," she said, eagerly. "Forget any more tailing, focus on that building. Could that be where he keeps his gold, or do you think he was meeting somebody, or maybe even a mistress? We hadn't thought of that."

"It's impossible to say from the outside," said Justin. "Although I would think this is office space, not residential. I'll see what I can find out and call you back."

Martha didn't have long to wait before Justin checked in.

"That building has a lot of security," said Justin, sounding breathless.

"After Shaw left, I tried to get in, but a security guard opened the door and said unless I had a special pass card, there was no chance. I counted four guards in the foyer, including the one I spoke to. The plaque on the door said Knightsbridge Investments. I'm just looking it up online." There was a pause. "It's a safe-deposit box company. Can't tell you what he's got in his box, but each one costs £4,000 a month to rent. Going by the publicity shots, it's aimed at Middle Eastern oil barons and their ilk."

"Wow," said Martha. "That's a big wedge of cash to pay out every month. Far too much for someone on a commander's salary. He must have something very precious stashed there — cash, bearer bonds, drugs . . . ?"

Justin was on a roll. Fifteen minutes later he made another call to Martha. "I've found an inside track to the company accounts department, so we have evidence."

"Fantastic. I knew that bastard was up to something dodgy. Let's meet up back here and talk about the next steps. I have a new plan."

CHAPTER 53

Everyone was pleased to be back in Dulwich. The surveillance had proved problematic for all of them, with their target frequently losing them within a short period. Julie was flexing her hands to ease out the aches and pains of "holding the steering wheel so tight I thought I might break it".

Even Harry had to admit it had been tough. "I followed Shaw for almost three hours on the second night. I got a headache from concentrating so hard. And the worry. He was so far ahead. Then just as I relaxed, I lost him."

Justin topped them all. "I was so busy watching his car I came inches from running over a group of school kids on a crossing. The world and his wife joined in to say what they thought of me. I learned some new swear words."

Martha let her team talk on for a moment and then said, "Justin's discovered that Shaw's keeping an awfully expensive safe-deposit box in Knightsbridge, not that far from Harrods. I'd really like to know what he's got in there."

Martha noted that Harry had a peculiar expression on his face. "Is everything OK?" she asked him.

"Is that Knightsbridge Investments?"

"It is," said Martha. "How—?"

"Some people I know run it. I've got some stuff there, just personal to me, but it's good that it's nice and secure. Mates' rates." He looked around, having now become the centre of attention. "Would you like me to talk to them?"

He didn't wait for an answer and stepped into the garden to make a call. Ten minutes later, he was back.

"They were horrified to learn that a copper's using the place. They've agreed that Martha and I can have a peek inside. Turns out they keep a backup set of keys. Usually it's for people who have lost theirs, but they're prepared to make an exception in his case. They really don't want to draw any attention to themselves."

"When this is all over, you must tell me about your safe-deposit box. But for now, when can we go?"

"First thing tomorrow, eight o'clock sharp."

* * *

The next morning was the sunniest and warmest in weeks, which Martha took as a positive sign. Both she and Harry had left at 6.30 a.m. Far too early, but they were happy to wait at the other end.

In the event, they were allowed in before 8 a.m. and met by a woman in a dark grey business suit with a white blouse. She didn't give her name but led them through to the secure room where the individual boxes were. The difference in sizes amazed Martha. Some had openings the size of a letter box, others were big enough to fit a one metre by one metre picture inside.

Noting her gaze, the woman said, "We have one client who requires a garage-sized box. Not in here, but elsewhere."

Even Harry was appreciative. "What do they keep in there, the Crown Jewels?"

The woman shrugged in a way that suggested all things were possible.

The atmosphere in the room felt slightly heavy, almost oppressive. When she mentioned it, the woman replied,

"That's because the walls are heavily reinforced. We don't want people thinking it's easy to get in here."

Their chaperone stopped by one of the smaller boxes, carefully tapped out a code on a keypad, had her retina scanned and only then inserted a key which opened the box.

She stood back. "We don't advertise it, but we keep an option to override the security. You never know what might happen."

She carefully slid out the box and carried it to a table in the centre of the room. Another key was needed to open the long lid. Martha's heart was pounding as she leaned forward to see inside.

"Krugerrands," said Martha.

She pulled on a pair of evidence gloves and picked one up. It had the image of the South African springbok on it. Turning the coin over, she noted the date. "It's from 1985. That's the right date for the stolen ones. I think we've got him."

She looked in the box again. Moving the coin had revealed something. She pulled it free. It was a sheet of paper with three random groups of numbers and letters.

"Just like Dad's notebook," said Martha. "I'm guessing here, but I reckon he somehow got hold of a few of the entries. I bet he couldn't work them out, so he stored them here."

She turned to the woman. "Can we take this bit of paper and these coins? There's quite a lot here."

"My instructions are to give you what you want. I can get a box for you to put the gold in."

When the woman returned, Martha had stacked the contents on the table, counting 281 coins. She asked the woman if she could put a value on them.

"It depends on the price of gold on the market. This morning krugerrands are trading remarkably high, at a bit short of £1,000 each."

Harry whistled. "By any standards, he's got more than a quarter of a million there. No wonder he likes to come and look at them."

Martha started stacking them in the box, along with the codes. "Let's take all this with us. If he wants these back, he can't go through official channels. A cop with that much stashed in a security box — that's going to make people ask questions."

Back in Dulwich, she unveiled her updated scheme. "I'm going to text him," she said. "I've got his number from my time as a cop. We grab his attention by telling him we have his gold. I doubt he knows that it's been taken, so hopefully that makes him worry about us."

Justin looked worried. "How will you explain that you have all his krugerrands? He's bound to be suspicious."

"I'll tell him I was approached by someone who knew about them and could take them. I'll explain that all I want to do is give them back to him — in return for him protecting me and Betty."

Julie was the next to react. "Won't he just call in the cavalry to descend on your house? We wouldn't stand a chance, especially if they turn up with weapons."

Even hardman Harry was nodding vigorously, and she could see the prospect worried him.

"If that happens, we don't fight back. You guys mean too much to me, and I can't have you taking crazy risks. If they do turn up in force, we just let them in, give them what they want — including the notebook — and watch them leave."

She looked around at each of them in turn. "But over the last few days, I've been able to think about the type of man Shaw is. He likes to play the big man, the type who sorts out his own problems. I'm confident he will try to do this himself because there's some sort of kudos to be had in getting the notebook. He obviously knows about it. Why else would he have that scrap of paper in a safe-deposit box?

"I'm hoping he'll be too full of his own self-importance to see through my scheme. And he may not want his operatives to find out how much money he has lying around. There's something about gold that makes even sensible people lose the plot."

"You're using yourself as bait," said Harry.

She sighed. "That was always going to be the case once these people worked out my dad had left a notebook. They won't rest until they get their hands on it."

"So, what are you going to say to the bastard?" asked Julie.

"I'll tell him I have his gold and something of my dad's he'll be interested in. He'll jump at the opportunity to get his money, and I'm willing to bet he'll think I'm also offering the notebook. He'll assume I'm crumbling under the pressure. He's the type of misogynist who probably can't imagine a 'girl' outsmarting him.

"He'll imagine I've spent the last few weeks scared out of my wits. He'll be so keen to get his hands on both the prizes he won't suspect he's being lured into a trap, and with a bit of luck he'll be so pleased he'll drop his guard and say something incriminating. Which we can record.

"I might need your help with that, Justin. Can you get your hands on high-tech recording gear? Something that won't get picked up by a standard electronic sweep using something like this?" She dug into a drawer to bring out the bug detector Paul Avery had given her.

Justin got on the phone. After a short conversation, he hung up and smiled nervously. "Something's on its way."

"When do you want to do this?" asked Harry.

Martha picked up her mobile. "I'll send the message now and ask for a meet tomorrow."

Seconds later, her text was on the way: *I have something of yours which needs to be returned to you. Also, something of my father's. In return, I need your help. You are the only one I can rely on.*

"Well, the cat's out of the bag now," said Harry. "If it was me, I'd just come straight round here. Get the money and notebook, by force, and have done with it."

"But you're not Shaw," said Martha. "My assessment of his character isn't just guesswork. While I was a copper, I heard he was a terrible boss. Always putting himself first and taking credit for other people's work.

"When he was dealing with me after they murdered Mum, he showed that same arrogance, as if I were beneath him. As I said, I'm hoping he still underestimates me now."

Martha's phone beeped. "It's Shaw. He wants to meet tomorrow night at seven. He'll text the venue closer to the time. It's good he responded so fast. If nothing else, it shows he's taken the bait."

CHAPTER 54

The recording tech turned up, as promised, contained in a small cardboard box. Martha opened the package and pulled out a pair of hooped earrings. "They look the part," she said, holding them up.

Justin scanned the instructions from the package. "This sounds easy. You just wear the earrings, turn them on with this—" he brandished a small controller — "and off you go. The earrings have enough power to record for fifteen minutes. It uploads straight to the cloud."

"I thought Martha would have to wear a wire," said Harry. "This is much better. Where did it come from?"

"I'm not sure," said Justin. "I thought it best not to ask."

"I know that song." Harry rolled his eyes. "Let's hope we can get them back before they're noticed as missing."

Martha shrugged. The device would help them; that was all she cared about.

* * *

Betty was home from school before Martha finally heard from Shaw. He'd set the 7 p.m. meeting place at the enormous car park attached to the IKEA store on the Purley Way, Croydon. Shaw said Martha must come alone.

Harry was ultra-cautious. "He might try something. He's a big man, and he's capable of anything. He might decide the game is better without you playing a part."

She nodded. "That occurred to me. That's why I'm only going to show him part of the notebook and take one of the krugerrands. But I am going."

Harry sighed heavily but she was past the point of being talked out of it. "I thought you'd say that, and to prove I can be just as stubborn, I'm going to be nearby. It's a massive area, so I'll be well away from you. You won't see me. But I have to be there."

Martha didn't want to waste any more time debating the rights and wrongs. It was time for action.

She told Harry, "Why don't you leave now and get a proper head start?"

Martha arrived at IKEA just before 6.30 p.m. She was meeting Shaw in the corner of the vast car park, furthest away from the store. She got out of the car she had borrowed from Lucy, who had just returned from seeing her mum, and sat on the bonnet. If Harry was nearby, she couldn't see him.

She waited. And waited. Just as she'd decided Shaw wasn't coming, a black BMW estate rolled up out of the gloom. It came to a halt next to her car. Shaw got out. He said nothing. Fearing this could go on all night, she talked first.

"I'm alone, I promise. I've got no one to talk to apart from you."

An unreadable expression flashed over his face. "Show me what you've got."

Martha produced an envelope from her bag. She handed it to him, along with one of the krugerrands.

He snatched them both, turning his attention to the gold first. "You'd better be able to produce the rest of these. I checked after you got in touch and I know they've been taken. I'll worry about how you did it later. And you'd better have a good explanation."

He was furious. She braced herself for an imminent attack. Instead, he switched his attention to the envelope. "What's this?"

She looked at him for a moment, trying to create the impression she was sizing him up. "It's a copy of the code in a notebook my dad left me. I've only just found it, and now I'm discovering some bad people want to get their hands on it. Someone who wanted this book sent the men who killed my mum. I need help and you can provide it. Dad always spoke highly of you. You were like a son to him."

She hated herself for the last comment, but it was worth it for the smug expression that briefly flashed across his face.

Gotcha, she thought.

Shaw stepped close to her. "I can understand how you got the codebook," he said. "Your father loved his secrets, and yes, he and I were close. But what about my gold?"

Martha took a breath. This was the hardest part of the story to pull off. "It was luck, really. Nothing else. I realised a couple of weeks ago that I needed help, and ideally it would be you. You're powerful enough to protect me. I was trying to work out the best way to approach you with the notebook — I just want to get rid of it. Trying to hold on to it could turn into a disaster.

"That's when I had a lucky break. A woman contacted me — I don't know who, she spoke to me over the phone. She claimed all sorts of things, including that you had cheated my father out of the krugerrands and she was going to get them to me.

"Sure enough, they turned up yesterday, dumped on my doorstep. That was when it hit me. If I could do you a favour by letting you have both, you would have a reason to be grateful to me."

He'd shown no emotion while she was talking.

"You say this woman told you I stole it from your dad. If you believe that, how can you trust me now?"

Martha sighed. "Because as much as I loved my dad, over the past few months I've discovered things about him that no daughter should hear. I don't know how you got your gold, and I don't want to know. As far as I'm concerned, it's yours and I'm hoping to get a reward by giving it back.

"As to the codebook. I can't understand it, and even if I did, what good would it do? It's the sort of knowledge that would probably get me killed."

She was putting on an award-winning performance, forcing herself to look meek and anxious, which was hard work. Shaw studied her in a calculating manner before he carefully opened the envelope, pulling out the two pages she had copied. He was wearing gloves. He spread the copies on her bonnet.

"Hold these. I need to shine a light on them." He ignited his phone torch and studied them carefully. "And you swear no one else has seen this?"

She shook her head. "My dad had it hidden away. I only just found it. It's obviously a code, but I have no way of interpreting it. I just want rid of the wretched thing."

Shaw paced off a few feet, doing his best to look thoughtful. "This may prove to be nothing of any interest. But it is intriguing."

Without warning, Shaw's hands whipped out and grabbed her shoulders. He was in her face, squeezing her hard.

"I want the book and I want my gold. How did you get your hands on it?"

She resisted the urge to lash out at him, confident she could easily take him down: she had a part to play tonight.

"Please, I don't want trouble. I just need help. That's why I turned to you, for protection. I'm sorry about the gold, I never wanted it."

Shaw had a deep frown on his face and Martha was wondering if she had laid it on a bit too thick. His next words seemed to support that.

"If I don't get that gold back, I will personally kill you and your daughter. The same goes for that book. I want that too, so you'd better not screw up. Have you got the money here?"

She shook her head. "Check my car if you like. Both the money and the book are somewhere safe and can be delivered to my house tomorrow, if we can agree a time. If anything happens to me, all bets are off, and the gold goes to your bosses with a detailed explanation of how it was found."

Martha hoped this little note of defiance would finally convince him of how desperate she was.

Shaw's fury was close to the surface — for a moment she thought he was going to hit her. "If you're trying to set me up, think again. I know all about you and your mates."

He pushed her hard, making her stumble and fall. She kept up her act.

"I'm sorry. I should have told you everything. The person who gave me the pages warned me I was in danger. What else could I do? Please," she added, "I need help." The wheedling tone she was using was sticking in her throat, but she sensed he was responding. "Tell me I'm right and you're a friend of my father's. You can help save me and my daughter."

He seemed to make up his mind at that. "Call me later tonight."

She watched him drive away, waited a moment, then walked up to her car and gave the front tyre a savage kick. Harry drove up as she landed a second kick.

"I nearly came over when I saw him grab you. But I could imagine you bollocking me if I gave myself away. That man doesn't know how lucky he is."

She glared into the darkness. "Next time I see that bastard . . . he's mine."

CHAPTER 55

Julie spotted the marks on her arms the moment she walked into the kitchen. "You said he got a bit rough, but bloody hell! I really hope he tries the same with me. I'll remove his nuts and hand them back to him on a plate."

Martha waved it aside. "No real harm done, although I might have come close to bursting a blood vessel in not punching his lights out. You can join the queue when it comes to settling this score."

Julie was still enraged. "Men who grab women like that need sorting out. One strike and they're out. Right out."

To underline her point, she chopped her hand down hard on the table, making everything bounce. Justin grabbed his glass of wine.

"The key thing is it went well. He was suspicious — but he was nearly falling over himself at the end. I think he had a pop at me because he wanted to keep me in my place. He's totally fallen for the helpless little lady act."

She paused. "I told him I haven't got the book and the money here — but I could get it. I have to ring him a bit later to say when it will be ready. I think I should say after five tomorrow, and he has to collect it from here. He'll be keen enough to risk it. I'm going to make the call soon. I want to look eager.

"I think you guys should call it a day. After tomorrow morning's school run, let's talk through what sort of plan we should have."

Second meeting fixed, Martha went for an early night and fell into a deep sleep. When she woke at dawn, she knew exactly what she needed to do. And no one was going to like it.

A few hours later, with her team assembled in the kitchen, Martha ran through the details. "I'm going to be the only one here," she said. "The rest of you are going to be next door with Lucy, and I want you out of here by four at the latest."

They all protested at once, with Julie and Harry the most vocal. "What happens if it gets rough?" said Julie. "That's when you'll want us here."

Even Justin put up a protest, but Martha silenced him. "If anything happens to me, you're Betty's only family. So, that's it. You cannot be in danger." As Julie and Harry piped up, she silenced them. "You need to be with Betty too. She's the one who needs protection, not me. There's less chance of it getting nasty if I'm here on my own. If Shaw sees you two, you'll intimidate him."

"That's the general idea," said Julie.

"No. It has to be my way," said Martha. "I keep saying, if it becomes difficult, he can have the bloody book. The fact that he's come here at all will be powerful evidence, and with luck I can record something incriminating. We don't need to risk a nasty fight to get him out of our lives. Even if he doesn't get done by the cops, he has to keep his head down or we turn over the safe-deposit box contents. That would be enough to put him inside, and he really doesn't want prison time."

"Have you thought about Eric and how he might react if Shaw turns up?" Harry asked.

"I have," said Martha. "I've spoken to Carol and she'll talk to him herself. Make sure he stays out of sight. I told her we're all just fed up and want our lives back. Hopefully, she won't work out we're handing something over until Shaw has been and gone."

"Tell me again why we don't just give it to Carol?" asked Harry.

"Like I said, I can't trust her. Not with our lives, especially with Shaw as the immediate danger," said Martha. "I really had to persuade her not to get involved though. I think she only agreed because I pointed out all the risk was mine. As to Shaw, he's already moved against me and tried to get me hurt. We need to deal with him first. Then, if Carol wants the book that badly, she can take it up with Shaw directly. With luck, we get Shaw off our backs and, in doing so, take the fight away from us."

Harry gave in with a wave of his hand. "I keep saying this, but you got your dad's brains and determination. Nothing could shift him once he'd made his mind up." He was looking at her with a mixture of exasperation and admiration.

By 4 p.m. Justin, Betty and Julie were at Lucy's place. Harry was upstairs, being as "quiet as a mouse", having proved quite implacable about leaving her on her own.

"What happened to your mum shows how dangerous Shaw is. If you won't let me stay in the house, then I'll just wait outside."

He seemed to think that Julie was enough protection for Betty and Justin. Martha hoped he was right.

Just before 5 p.m., Shaw messaged her: *I'm outside in the car. Open the door, I'll come straight in.*

Martha did as she was asked and waited in the hallway. She'd switched on her special earrings, hoping she had enough recording time — if she could get him talking. The next moment, Shaw was there, shutting the door behind him.

"Give it to me. Give it to me now." He wasn't here to chat. She'd have to hope she could drag some sort of conversation out of him.

"It's all in here," said Martha, leading him through to the kitchen. She turned and saw he had an electronic bug detector in his hand. He swept it round the room and inspected the small screen before putting it in his jacket pocket, apparently satisfied.

Fighting to keep her expression neutral, she asked, "What was that?"

"Just keeping me safe," said Shaw. "Now give me what I came for."

Martha pointed at the box and the notebook on the kitchen table. "All yours." Her voice squeaked with anxiety.

Shaw smirked at her weakness.

He grabbed the box and counted the gold coins. When he finished, he grunted, seemingly happy. Next, he turned his attention to the book. He spent several minutes flicking through it slowly and reading the entries. By the time he finished, Martha was longing to wipe the smugness off his face.

"I should thank you for this," he said. His tone was gloating. "A lot of people will pay big cash to guarantee this information never comes out."

He waved the book at her. "You don't know what you've given me, do you? Well, I do, and it's because I've proved cleverer than your father. It's true we used to be close, but that changed. He wanted to arrest me, but I threatened to expose his little scheme of informers. He couldn't risk that.

"He made a big mistake, though. There was one man he trusted. His name was Ronnie. Your dad used him as a sort of bagman who helped keep the secrets. Ronnie knew all about the code."

Shaw rubbed his hands in apparent glee. "You'll like this bit, it's where fate steps in. His man, Ronnie, developed dementia. Incredibly sad it was; he was only young. Had to live in a specialist care home.

"I found out and went to see him. I told the care home I was an old colleague and they lapped it up. Gave me loads of time with him. Sometimes he was OK, but other times he kept thinking I was your dad. It didn't take long for me to get what I needed to decode this. Then I just had to wait for you to dig out the actual notebook. Which I knew John would have given to you. He could never leave well alone."

Martha prayed the microphones had worked. His predatory stare chilled her to the bone. Then he pulled out a gun and brandished it at her. She had underestimated his capacity for violence.

He produced a pair of handcuffs. "Put these on. I was hoping your minder, Harry, would be here. I was looking forward to shooting him. And that dozy bitch with the red hair."

She thought about screaming for help but her intention must have been obvious. "I've got men outside with instructions to shoot on sight. Your team won't have a chance."

He grinned hatefully. "Your precious daughter might get hurt if you annoy my team. So, let's go quietly. I've got plans for you. You won't like it — but that's what happens when you lose against the A-team."

As he spoke, he was screwing a silencer onto the gun. With her legs turning to jelly, Martha moved slowly down the hallway. She'd been stupid to take him on like this. She passed the door of the living room, where her mother had been shot, and silently berated herself. If he shot her now, how would Betty ever recover?

As she approached the door, there was a commotion and Harry appeared at the top of the stairs. Without a moment's hesitation Shaw fired two shots, the silencer muffling the sound. At least one bullet made contact, throwing Harry back just as he was about to launch down the stairs.

Moving fast, Shaw grabbed Martha in one hand and opened the front door, pushing her quickly outside, where she saw two men standing by the open rear doors of a white van. Shaw marched her over and she was thrown inside, banging her head painfully. It all happened at a terrifying speed. All the control was with Shaw.

He leaned inside and said, "We're going for a little ride, then you and I can have a chat about all the other information you're hiding from me. My boys can have whatever's left of you."

As the doors slammed shut, she couldn't hold back her tears. She had never been so scared, not just for her, but for Betty. And what about Harry?

Martha heard the front doors slamming shut and the engine starting. The van moved, and she let out a low moan of fear. Then she was thrown forwards, jarring her knees painfully in the dark. Handcuffed as she was, she was struggling to get upright. Suddenly a man's voice screamed, "No!" This was followed by two ear-splitting bangs just a heartbeat apart.

Then there was silence. Martha lay on her front, totally helpless, as the rear doors opened. She was facing the wrong way and couldn't see who was there. She heard someone clamber in. Strong hands grabbed her and turned her over — Eric. He looked more self-satisfied than ever. She forced herself not to cry.

"You nearly got me killed," she snarled. "I thought I'd had it!" Martha flailed around for the right words. She could hardly have a go at the man who had just saved her life, but her emotions were running high. "You are one annoying bastard. Carol assured me you would stop this before it went too far. How much bloody further could you have gone?"

Her words had no impact. "You didn't get killed," said Eric. "None of your mates got killed. Betty didn't get killed. So, what's the problem?"

With a shock, she remembered Harry being shot. "Is Harry OK?"

"I've got someone checking him over. We'll know in a moment."

As good as his word, a young woman appeared. "Your Harry's a bright boy," she told Martha. "Turns out he was wearing a bulletproof vest. He'll have a nasty bruise on his ribs, but it saved his life."

Suddenly there was a commotion outside Lucy's house as Julie charged out, only to be confronted by a ring of armed men.

"Don't do anything silly," said Eric. "Everything's all right."

Turning, he helped Martha out of the van, and two men appeared with Shaw, holding him in a tight grip. They searched him for the key and freed Martha from her handcuffs just as Harry appeared with his hand holding a bandage on his side. He looked sheepish, but Martha didn't care. She rushed over and hugged him, careful not to press on his wound.

Eric was holding a memory stick. "I was ordered to give you this. Now, if you don't mind, we have some clearing up to do before the neighbours get interested. We're lucky this van masks the view, as it is. They're a dozy lot but even they'll have heard something."

He mock saluted her, then Harry.

Moments later, a freshly handcuffed Shaw was in the back of the van, alongside the bodies of his two men, who had been shot in the head. Thirty seconds later, all evidence of violence was gone.

Harry had worked it out. "You told Carol and used her for protection, didn't you? That could have gone so wrong . . ." He trailed off. "I'm lost for words."

"Good," said Martha. "I think I'd like to crack open that bottle of champagne now. Let's get inside and I'll tell you all about it."

It took two glasses before she was ready to talk.

"Of course you're all mad with me," said Martha. "But I couldn't think how else to keep you safe. One of you might have died for me, and I just couldn't risk that. As it was, Harry nearly ruined the plan by insisting on staying and getting shot. Even if you had been OK, what would've happened if one of you had hurt Shaw? I've already been sent to prison for doing my own thing. That could have been any of you."

"When did you decide this?" said Harry, disgruntled.

"Yesterday," said Martha. "I woke up and knew what had to happen to give us all a chance of getting out of this trap left by my father. I rang Carol, told her what was going on, and she agreed to step in and take Shaw out if things got rough. I told her she could have the book one way or the other — I just wanted to get Shaw's confession first.

"I must admit that, when they tossed me in the van, I thought I might have made a mistake. I promise to never muzzle you guys again."

Even Harry was mollified by her words. "I thought you were up to something. You have a tell too."

"What tell?" Martha demanded.

"Now that would be telling, if you pardon the pun," said Harry. He deftly opened a fresh bottle of champagne.

Martha remembered the memory stick. "This is from Carol. Shall we see what's on it?"

Justin fired up his laptop and soon had the details scrolling across the screen. He whistled, then turned the screen so they could see.

"Shaw was a complete psychopath. This is a list of emails between him and some other party. Shaw is telling this other person he wants all of us killed. Even Betty."

"But how—?"

Martha was interrupted by her mobile ringing. It was Carol. "This is not a long call, even though I'm sure you have many questions. You don't have to worry about Shaw's little clean-up crew. You can put all this behind you. I'll also make sure the right people know I now have your dad's notebook.

"One last thing. I've sent you some emails we pulled off Shaw's computer. We hacked him last night. You don't have to do anything with them, but we shall make sure they get to the new boss of Scotland Yard. If you're asked, express amazement."

She abruptly ended the call, leaving Martha staring at her handset. She passed the message on to her troops, which induced a fresh round of toasts.

CHAPTER 56

Three months later

The court hearing at the Old Bailey had been a long time in the planning, and less than fifteen minutes in execution. At its conclusion Martha was cleared of all charges, receiving a formal apology from the Home Office and a small cheque from Scotland Yard.

"You could get a lot more," Paul had told her more than once as they negotiated the compensation payout.

Martha had just shrugged. She wanted enough to demonstrate that she had been unfairly treated, not so much that she could be accused of money grabbing.

Outside court, Martha and her friends posed for selfies. Harry pointed out that the last time they'd been here had seen them fight their way through a small army of photographers, cameramen and reporters.

"I'm afraid journalists aren't so interested in happy news stories," said Charles.

Martha threw her arms around his neck. "Betty and I owe you a great deal. You not only got me out of prison but made sure I cleared my name. Words will never be enough.

You sure I can't persuade you to come back to Dulwich? I've even got champagne."

He smiled at her, looking a little like a proud father. "I'm flying home to Portugal shortly. But don't forget, anytime you need legal advice, call me. I'm supposed to be retired, but I suspect you'll continue to live an interesting life and I'd hate to miss out."

He waved at the rest of the team, winning handshakes from Paul, Harry and Justin, and a bone-crunching hug from Julie. Then he was off, quickly disappearing into the crowd.

Martha clapped her hands. "Come on, you lot, we need to get a shift on. Lucy is picking Betty up early and will have her home in an hour. We can't spend the rest of the day standing here talking. I don't know about you lot, but I'm thirsty."

Harry grinned at her and Martha couldn't resist wrapping him in a bear hug. She was just about to press harder when she stopped and let go. "I'm sorry, I forgot about your ribs. Did I hurt you?"

"All mended now."

Julie, who was listening in, held her arms wide. "You good for hugs again, Harry?"

Now the veteran hardman went pale. He backed away with his hands held out in a warding-off gesture.

Julie burst out laughing. "Don't worry, old-timer, you're safe with me." Martha couldn't help laughing at the little exchange. Julie had moved into Harry's spare room, and they got on like a house on fire. Harry had happily abandoned decades of living alone, while Julie had gained a friend, mentor and grandfather all in one. It had thrilled Martha that her new pal was so close and Betty was the outright winner, insisting "Auntie Julie" hold her upside down at every opportunity.

In Dulwich, they found that Lucy had set out a buffet for them before she'd left to collect Betty. There were plates of sandwiches, cooked sausages, sliced pork pie and crisps. It wasn't healthy, but it would soak up the alcohol. Taking centre stage was a pink-and-white cake with a real hacksaw and handcuffs on the top. They all agreed Lucy had surpassed herself. Justin took over as chief barman and, in short order, everyone had a drink in their hand. Martha tapped her glass with a spoon to attract attention.

"Before Betty gets home, I thought you all ought to hear the other news, the stuff we've been waiting for. I'll hand over to Paul Avery as he has the most up-to-date stuff."

All eyes turned to the lawyer and he took over with a confident air. "It's mixed news, at least from our point of view," Paul said. "Shaw folded straight away once he realised he might spend the rest of his life in a high-security prison. He's been singing like a canary, naming all sorts of people, including senior police officers.

"Of course, quite a few people have gone to ground, and the top brass at the Yard are having sleepless nights over what might happen once this gets out. It might become an issue for the intelligence services. It turns out Shaw had had dealings with top officials and seems to know rather a lot about national security. That might mean his crimes are dealt with under the Official Secrets Act. That would prevent any reporting on the matter."

"Is that a problem?" asked Julie. "I mean, so long as he gets taken care of, who cares?"

"It might be an issue," said Paul. "Shaw is bargaining hard and might get a lenient sentence, without us even hearing about it. It also means everything around Martha remains secret."

Martha interjected. "I'd been hoping that Shaw getting arrested would draw a line under all this. But I guess my dad's legacy of secrets and lies is just too big to go away. My supposed friend Carol's gone quiet, now she has what she wanted. Was she even on my side, or was she just after the profit she could turn from that notebook?"

"Well, she can't use it, can she?" Harry said. "That code's impossible to crack. Which is a good thing, for your dad's informants."

"Yes, without Ronnie, poor man, it's useless. I've been to see him in the care home — he's in a much worse state than when Shaw visited him, even. There's no way Carol's people could get anything out of him, if they find out his identity. And they gave Shaw up to the police sharpish. I bet they tried to get him to talk and he wouldn't play ball. But we held up our end of the bargain — she won't hold a grudge against us that it turned out to be useless."

The mood had become subdued. "I'm not trying to put a dampener on the party," she added. "In fact, I have an announcement to make which I hope you'll like. I just thought you needed some information first."

Now Martha really had their attention. "I've been wondering what to do next and I've finally realised something. I was born to be part of the Old Bill and I've negotiated to return to my detective duties with the commissioner's office."

This was greeted with warm applause, which Martha acknowledged with a quick bow. Julie held up her hands for attention. "I have a small announcement as well. In keeping with my new attempt to stay on the straight and narrow, I'm going into the security business. Guarding Betty made me understand how much I enjoy it. Harry here says he'll show me the ropes."

Martha drained her glass. She'd crouched on this very spot to say goodbye to her poor mother, while the man who'd caused her violent death stood over her. She hoped Shaw would be put away for a very long time. Looking up, she saw Betty and Lucy skipping up the road towards home. Nothing would ever be right again, but her little girl was home and safe — that was all that mattered.

"Watch out, world, is all I can say," she said, grinning at Julie. "Right, who's for a top-up?"

* * *

The following morning a bleary-eyed Martha took herself out for a "head-clearing" run. Julie had briefly offered to join her but instead settled for returning to bed. With Harry also opting out, she was on her own. As she ran into Dulwich Park she realised she hadn't been so alone for quite a while and wasn't entirely sure how she felt about it.

She was still making her mind up when her mobile rang. She didn't recognise the number and was about to let it go to voicemail when she wondered if it was someone from work ringing to give her a return date.

"It's Carol. Can anyone else hear this call?"

Martha glanced around. "No. It's fine to talk. What's the problem?"

"Peter Shaw. Someone got to him last night."

"When you say some one 'got' to him, you mean . . ."

"I mean he's dead. They were holding him in isolation at Belmarsh, which is meant to be secure. Clearly not secure enough."

"How did it happen?" said Martha.

"The official version will be he was found lifeless during a routine cell check at 4 a.m. The guidance will be that he took his own life having slashed his wrists with a home-made weapon."

Martha was amazed. "How is that remotely possible? How could he have got his hands on something sharp enough to do the damage? And you told me he was in negotiations, so he was in a strong position."

"That's because the official version is a lie. I'm hearing he was murdered. Basically a lot of money changed hands to make the guards look the other way, and then some sort of hit team got into his cell. He's a big bloke and there was an almighty struggle, but they got him in the end."

"Don't tell me, no one else on that wing heard anything and the guards reported a quiet night apart from a glitch in the surveillance system, which crashed in the early hours. I take it this mysterious man you won't identify is behind it?"

"That's what I know, more or less, and I'm not going to tell you how I know. But I will tell you who is behind this. Before I do you need to understand how dangerous this man

277

is. Just knowing his name can put you in danger, so be very, very careful."

Martha's hand was sweaty with tension. "Put me out of my misery."

"He's called Neil Thompson . . . and before you say you've never heard of him, he is THE man."

Martha took a step backwards. At last she had a name. "Is this the man my dad had at the top of his own most-wanted list?"

"That's exactly the man I'm telling you about. Your father viewed him as a fearsomely intelligent and ruthless criminal. You have to be careful — he's said to have a lot of policemen on his payroll. Not just the police, either — lawyers, accountants, private detectives. I could go on. He's currently based in Chile and always operates through third parties. You can be sure that now he's tidied up he'll be looking for the book again — if he ever stopped.

"I'm arranging to get a message to him that I have it, which will make him think, because I'm one of the few people he's wary of. It's in all our interests that he and I reach a deal, to avoid a sort of mutually assured destruction. If I'm wrong, it may come down to the last man — or woman — standing.

"There you have it, the name. Just don't make a move unless you hear that something has happened to me and you have no choice but go on the offensive."

"I hear you, loud and clear. I'll leave it to you," said Martha, crossing her fingers as she ended the call. She spent the next few moments trying to recall her father ever saying anything about this Neil Thompson. But she already knew her closed-mouthed father wouldn't have spilled any beans. She shook her head in exasperation. Her father operated on a need-to-know basis and had clearly decided she didn't need to know, which was so, so wrong. If this was the man in the shadows pulling the strings, she really did need to know. For a start, he had to have a coterie of trusted lieutenants who did his dirty work. Find one of them and maybe she could backtrack to the head honcho. She was grateful she had Harry. If Thompson really was her dad's bête noire, maybe he shared some of his knowledge with Harry. Maybe Harry could start to fill in some of the missing pieces of the puzzle, or at least know the right places to start asking questions.

She shuddered as she was assailed by a feeling of doom she had to work hard to shake off. Up to this moment she had been chased by ghosts, but now she had a name she knew, in her heart of hearts, that this wasn't over. Putting a name to her fear seemed to make it all more real. Carol might be confident she could cut a deal, but Martha doubted it would end there. If this was the man who had worried John Munro, then he sure worried his daughter.

At least this time she was ready and had a good team who would fight to the bitter end. She clenched her fists. This man had threatened her daughter . . . the most precious thing in her life. She would never allow him to do it again.

He might be clever, tough and ruthless. But so was she.

THE END

Thank you for reading this book.

If you enjoyed it please leave feedback on Amazon or Goodreads, and if there is anything we missed or you have a question about, then please get in touch. We appreciate you choosing our book.

Founded in 2014 in Shoreditch, London, we at Joffe Books pride ourselves on our history of innovative publishing. We were thrilled to be shortlisted for Independent Publisher of the Year at the British Book Awards.

www.joffebooks.com

We're very grateful to eagle-eyed readers who take the time to contact us. Please send any errors you find to corrections@joffebooks.com. We'll get them fixed ASAP.

Printed in Great Britain
by Amazon